Copyright © 2020 by Scott Moon

All rights reserved.

No part of this book may be reproduced in any form or by any electronic or mechanical means, including information storage and retrieval systems, without written permission from the author, except for the use of brief quotations in a book review.

www.scottmoonwriter.com

INVASION DAY

THEY CAME FOR BLOOD: BOOK ONE

SCOTT MOON

CONTENTS

Stay Up To Date	vii
Book Order	ix
Book Description	xiii
Chapter 1	1
Chapter 2	9
Chapter 3	15
Chapter 4	25
Chapter 5	35
Chapter 6	41
Chapter 7	51
Chapter 8	59
Chapter 9	69
Chapter 10	83
Chapter 11	91
Chapter 12	99
Chapter 13	107
Chapter 14	117
Chapter 15	127
Chapter 16	133
Chapter 17	145
Chapter 18	157
Chapter 19	171
Chapter 20	187
Chapter 21	199
Chapter 22	209
Chapter 23	219
Chapter 24	229
Chapter 25	239
Chapter 26	253
Chapter 27	267
Chapter 28	279
Chapter 29	295

Chapter 30	303
Chapter 31	309
Chapter 32	317
Chapter 33	323
Please leave a review!	329
What's Next	331
Also by Scott Moon	333
About the Author	337
Cool Stuff from the Moon	339

STAY UP TO DATE

Sign-up for my newsletter for notification of new releases and other stuff I'm doing.

Get Cool Stuff from the Moon by heading to *https://www.subscribepage.com/Fromthemoon*

BOOK ORDER

THEY CAME FOR BLOOD

Invasion Day

Resistance Day (coming soon)

Victory Day (coming soon)

Alien Apocalypse (coming soon)

A MECH WARRIOR'S TALE
(SHORTYVERSE)

Shorty

Kill Me Now

Ground Pounder

Shorty and the Brits

Fight for Doomsday (A Novel)… coming soon.

CHRONICLES OF KIN ROLAND

Enemy of Man: The Chronicles of Kin Roland: Book 1

Son of Orlan: The Chronicles of Kin Roland: Book 2

Weapons of Earth: The Chronicles of Kin Roland: Book 3

DARKLANDING

Assignment Darklanding Book 1

Ike Shot the Sheriff: Assignment Darklanding: Book 2

Outlaws: Assignment Darklanding Book 3

Runaway: Assignment Darklanding Book 4

An Unglok Murder: Assignment Darklanding Book 05

SAGCON: Assignment Darklanding Book 6

Race to the Finish: Assignment Darklanding Book 7

Boom Town: Assignment Darklanding Book 8

A Warrior's Home: Assignment Darklanding Book 9

Hunter: Assignment Darklanding Book 10

Diver Down: Assignment Darklanding Book 11

Empire: Assignment Darklanding Book 12

FALL OF PROMISEDALE

Death by Werewolf (The Fall of Promisedale Book 1)

GRENDEL UPRISING

Proof of Death: Grendel Uprising: Book 1

Blood Royal: Grendel Uprising: Book 2

Grendel: Grendel Uprising: Book 3

SMC MARAUDERS

Bayonet Dawn: SMC Marauders: Book 1

Burning Sun: SMC Marauders: Book 2

The Forever Siren: SMC Marauders: Book 3

SON OF A DRAGONSLAYER

Dragon Badge (Son of a Dragonslayer Book 1)

Dragon Attack (Son of a Dragonslayer Book 2)

Dragon Land (Son of a Dragonslayer Book 3)

TERRAN STRIKE MARINES

The Dotari Salvation: Terran Strike Marines: Book 1

Rage of Winter: Terran Strike Marines: Book 2

Valdar's Hammer: Terran Strike Marines: Book 3

The Beast of Eridu: Terran Strike Marines: Book 4

THE LAST REAPER

The Last Reaper

Fear the Reaper

Blade of the Reaper

Wings of the Reaper

Flight of the Reaper

Wrath of the Reaper

Will of the Reaper

Descent of the Reaper

Hunt of the Reaper

Bastion of the Reaper

SHORT STORIES

Boss

Fire Prince

Ice Field

Sgt. Orlan: Hero of Man

The Darklady

ASSASSIN PRIME

The Hand of Empyrean: Assassin Prime 1

Spiderfall: Assassin Prime 2

BOOK DESCRIPTION

David Osage is a dangerous man with a dangerous past, but these days he's just trying to keep his head down, driving big rigs. One night he saddles himself with a hitchhiker, a nuisance who's more than she seems. And that's when everything changes.

No one was ready for an alien invasion. Death is raining from the sky and the only question left is do you run, fight, or submit.

For David Osage and his family, answering is as easy as giving the alien invaders the finger.

CHAPTER ONE

"COPY THAT, Gummy Bear. I see Evel Knievel, one time on the overpass. Is he actually hanging paper this late?" David asked.

"Just looking pretty. Sittin' bike-to-car with Smokey." Gummy Bear's voice filled the CB radio with feminine richness. "I'll bet Smokey is behind on his quota. They've been lazy all day, like they're distracted. Gives me an unpleasant feeling. Watch your speed. Where you headed, Jackknife?"

"Motor City to Loveland, then all the way to Idiot Island," David said.

"What are you doing on I-70?"

"I like the Flint Hills. And Walrus says I-80 is a mess of construction. Four-ten?" David asked. He kept the mic near his mouth.

"Ten-four. Interstate 80 is a logjam," Gummy Bear said. "As long as you're heading west on I-70, keep your eye out for a sweet little thing with a guitar on her back looking for an education. Halfway to Salina, depending on how good she is at hitchin'. Talk some sense into the sweetie."

"Ten-four. Jackknife, out."

"One more thing, Jackknife."

"Go."

"Keep an eye on the sky."

David "Jackknife" Osage pondered the advice, holding the radio mic ready while his mind struggled for a response. "It's a little late to wish on a star."

"It's something I've been hearing on the radio freqs a lot. Weird shit. Meteor storms and stuff." Static and interference covered her words.

David racked the mic. He liked Gummy Bear. She was always happy but something about her tone tonight bothered him.

Thirty minutes later, he spotted the girl, guitar case slung over one shoulder, loitering under a tall highway lamp at the exit. *Stupid place to stand.*

With a high dollar backpack and two hundred–dollar boots to match, her wardrobe looked like she'd bought it on her father's credit card. She'd probably had it delivered by an Amazon drone.

He shook his head. Drones were for science fiction and about as real as his last five tax returns. Shiny gadgets couldn't whiz heavy freight coast to coast. That required trains and trucks. Which meant David "Jackknife" Osage would always have a job.

He drove past her, exhaust pipes booming like machine guns as the Jake Brake engaged. She had her hood down far enough to show a wisp of blonde hair and smooth skin.

If she were still there after he finished his dinner, he'd have a talk with her. But only because Gummy Bear asked him to.

He had two coffees and a grand slam breakfast at 11

o'clock at night. Kitchen noise and the agitated yammering of some good ole boys at the end of the counter prevented him from hearing the television. He watched anyway. Cops in Seattle wore riot gear for a protest. Made him worry about his little sister in the Chicago Police Department.

Cops looked after each other, he hoped. Laura had never been risk averse. Which reminded him of the runaway Gummy Bear had wanted him to check on.

The girl was still standing near the lamppost when he walked out, cleaning his teeth with a toothpick. He wondered how many rides she'd turned down. Her choosiness was a mark in her favor, but she was still an idiot. A sheep. Or maybe not. There was a better-than-average chance that if she was still hanging around like a lot lizard, she *was* a lot lizard, just a young one who was still cute.

He walked toward her—when he left, it would be in the other direction. Face-to-face contact was better for this kind of thing, anyway. He hated talking down at hitchhikers from his window. "What's your name, girl?"

"What's it to you?" she asked, stepping away from the pole—opening an avenue to run if he tried to grab her.

"You know Gummy Bear?"

"That scary old crone driving the pink big rig?" the girl asked.

"She's twenty-nine," David said.

The girl shrugged. "Looks forty-nine."

"How old are you?" he asked.

"Eighteen."

"How original. Eighteen and just barely legal." He was about done with this conversation. "You've got all your teeth and good skin. So if you're a meth head, you're new."

"That's bullshit," she said, huffing in disgust. "You take one look at me and assume I'm a drug addict."

He leaned closer, forcing her to look him in the eyes. "How many runaway girls working this interstate do you think have drug problems?"

"I'm not working the interstate, asshole." Her accent was hard and vaguely exotic.

David tried to place it but couldn't. He'd been all over the country, but her cadence didn't fit any particular region. "What will the sheriff say if I tell him there's a minor standing on the curb looking like she's gonna do some illegal hitchhiking? You realize it's illegal to walk on the interstate?"

She crossed her arms but otherwise ignored him.

"You're telling me he's not gonna come out here and run your name? Check NCIC and get you shipped back home to Mommy and Daddy?"

"You're not a cop. It doesn't matter how you talk. You know what's what. I bet you've got a criminal record," she said. "You been to prison?"

"I did time."

She laughed incredulously. "And I should take a ride with you? What'd you get locked up for?"

"Evade and Elude Police. Back in my street racing days. Gets addictive. Not a lot of consequences, until you kill somebody in a car wreck or fight with the cops."

"Which did you do?" she asked, facing him now—her attitude saying she could see through his bullshit.

He didn't have the time or energy to hassle with some tortured youth who thought she knew everything. "You want a ride or what?"

"Why should I trust you? What's in it for me?"

"My sister's a cop. I can have her run your name. See if anyone's looking for you," he said. "I'm safe. I didn't take this job to meet women."

"Does your sister have an opinion about your felonious past?"

"She's my *little* sister," David said. "I'm the reason she became a cop. Told her if she wants to drive fast, she should get a badge."

The hitchhiker's defenses melted and she laughed.

He waved her toward his truck. "Get in. This is no place to stand around. Local girls show up, they'll beat your ass and leave you behind a dumpster."

She followed him but waited while he climbed in and started the engine. *Smart.* What were the chances a strange man in a truck stop would push her in first, have his way with her, then push her out the other side?

He rolled down his window and leaned out. "You can come around on the passenger side and climb up. I'm going as far as California. Take it or leave it."

She hesitated, hefted her backpack and softshell guitar case, then ran around to the other side and climbed in.

"Are these audiobooks? You listen to romance novels? Maybe this isn't such a good idea," she said, one hand on the door handle.

"I've got a thing for Nora Roberts. Started listening to her books when two things happened: there was nothing left at the truck stop and I was feeling sorry for myself. Country and western music only takes a broken heart so far."

"You listen to country, and I'm out." She fastened her seatbelt.

"No promises."

She pushed earbuds into her ears and curled up facing the door.

"Hey," he said.

She pulled out an earbud. "What?"

"What's your name?"

"Call me Diamond Dust. Stage name," she said, tapping the guitar case she had positioned between them in the center console.

He laughed. "Can't call you Diamond. That's a stripper's name."

"Friends call me Dust." She put her earbuds back in and faced the door.

He concentrated on driving for a while, no audiobooks, no radio, no conversation with his guest. Traffic was heavy.

Three Kansas Highway Patrol troopers running radar on eastbound traffic seemed distracted and tense. He'd slipped through a lot of speed traps and this one didn't seem like it was for real. Which bothered him, because that didn't make sense. Why would they drive out here just to park along the highway? The girl uncurled from her power nap, and followed his gaze.

"What do you care?"

He picked up the mic. "Eastbound approaching Bob Dole's place, you got three full-grown bears with their hotshots out."

"We're westbound," she said.

"I'm talking to people going east. They're gonna reciprocate by telling me what's ahead of us."

"Westbound, be advised it's a turtle race up there, shoulder to shoulder. Thanks for the heads-up."

"Poker Face to westbound, what's your handle?"

"Jackknife. What's up, Poker Face?"

"Just watch the sky."

Other CB operators chimed in, promising he would recognize it when he saw it.

"I'm telling you, they're ships," a voice said.

Dozens of CB mic clicks and rude comments drowned the man out. "Shut up, Crazy Dude."

"That's not my handle."

"It is now."

"Hey, come on, clear the channel. The full-grown bears are directing everyone into way stations. Check your logs, people. You've been warned," a voice said.

"Do you need to check your log?" Dust asked.

David grunted. Eastbound traffic was slowing down to a crawl. "My logs are always up to date. Attention to detail is something I learned in prison. Because, rules."

He studied the sky with growing apprehension. Dust sat upright in her seat and leaned toward the window.

A meteor storm rained down near the horizon.

"Have you ever seen anything like that?" Dust asked.

"Nope. In this job, I see a lot of falling stars. But this is cataclysmic."

Traffic ground to a stop. Wave after wave lit up the sky. Dozens of people were standing on the road with binoculars, cameras, and cell phones taking pictures.

"Can't be sure, but it looks like there are Kansas State Troopers up there turning everybody around," he said.

"Can they do that?" she asked.

He shook his head. "The question is, why would they?"

CHAPTER TWO

OFFICER LAURA OSAGE rolled the police vehicle forward with the headlights off. Her backup wasn't close. "Unit 22, I'm not seeing forced entry from this distance. Do you have the caller on the line?"

The dispatcher followed protocol and procedures without enthusiasm. "Negative, 22. The call disconnected. Static interference broke up the call."

"Give me the description and narrative while I'm waiting for 12 and 29," Laura said, shivering despite her expensive gear. Staying warm on the street without sweating her ass off in the car or in a building wasn't something she'd mastered.

"The caller observed six large men with what looked like rifles but weren't. They smashed a breaker box on the outside of the Red Cross building."

"What do you mean they *weren't*? Are we talking shotguns? Airsoft carbines? Laser blasters?"

The dispatcher responded slowly, voice half asleep. "Unspecified. I'm just telling you what they told the call taker."

"Vehicle description?"

"The caller reported they were on foot."

"They had to come in a vehicle. There's not a lot of residential neighborhoods around here." Laura slipped out of her squad car and crept closer. She'd used the tactic before. Lookouts often spotted cars and fixated on them. At night, it was possible to get out of the car without being seen, depending on distance and other factors.

If whoever was breaking into the Red Cross building thought she was in the police car, she wanted to be someplace else—especially if they had weapons. The element of surprise saved lives.

There had been sniper attacks on uniformed police officers in recent months; two in Chicago. Why be a target?

Something moved around the corner of the building. "22 for 12 or 29, what's your ETA?"

Brock Green, Unit 12, answered. "Five minutes."

Justin Sans clicked his microphone without getting the words across. He was a jerk that way, pretending to respond when he probably hadn't even put his car in drive. Sans liked watching his dope houses. The guy made one killer arrest after another, but rarely helped with regular patrol calls.

"I have movement near the building. Park by my car and walk in. We need to wait for 29 for this," Laura said.

"29, it will take me at least fifteen minutes to get there. Is there anyone else close?"

Dispatch answered. "You're it, 29."

Laura listened to the radio without focusing on the subtle negotiations between Sans and the dispatcher. The scene required her full attention.

The Red Cross building was dark, completely without

electricity. At least part of the 9-1-1 caller's observations had been accurate. Someone had cut the power.

A figure stepped out of the shadows, looked right and left, then returned to the small group of burglars or terrorists or whatever they were. What stunned her, however, was the size of the figure.

Laura had only seen the suspect for a second—long enough to estimate his height at near eight feet and to see something in his hands that looked like a long gun. Was it a rifle, a shotgun, or something else? She didn't know, but shared the description as best she could with dispatch and the other officers.

"29, sounds like a hot call," Sans said. "I'll run code to it. I'm coming from a way off."

Laura locked her teeth together, not wanting to argue with the officer who had two years of seniority on her and never let anyone forget it. She just hoped the guy cut his lights and sirens before he arrived.

The exasperation in Green's voice crackled across the radio channel. "Unit 12, I've been flagged down on an active disturbance at First Street and Menlow. Looks domestic. Find me a backup. Start someone else for 22's burglary-in-progress."

"I'm almost out with her. We should be able to handle it," Sans, 29, said.

The sirens cut out a block away. Not great, but better than tearing into the scene and parking at the front door with a big target painted on the patrol car and the asshole driving it.

The suspects had been inside for a while now. Any minute they would wheel out computers and medical equipment for resale on the black market.

"Osage, I'm moving up behind you," whispered Sans.

"Glad you made it," Laura answered.

"This guy really seven feet tall with a fricking boomstick?"

"Eight," she said.

"Seven, eight—whatever," he said. "Are you sure?"

"I think they're all that big. Not sure if they're all armed."

Sans's gun belt creaked when he shifted his weight. "What are they, some kind of semi-pro basketball team gone rogue?"

Laura shook her head. "This guy was thick. Either a bodybuilder or wearing armor."

Sans laughed. "Okay. They're *wearing armor*," he said. She could hear the air quotes in his voice.

The burglars came out with the precision of a commando team—two scouting the way with weapons drawn, four pushing carts full of stolen goods, and one following as a rear guard. That's what it looked like to Laura. She'd never been in the military, but had attended several National Tactical Officers Association (NTOA) schools and had done a two-week rotation with the SWAT team.

"I don't like the look of that," Sans said. He whispered a call for additional units.

Three cars with two officers each arrived from Baker Sector. Green was still on the domestic disturbance he'd stumbled into.

"What do we have here?" the leader of the Baker Sector cops said. "We were on our way back from the jail when the call got updated. Sounded like fun, so here we are."

Laura pulled him forward and out of her way so he could see the suspects rolling out bags of blood. "This is the third trip they've made. I've got no idea what they're doing. And yes, they're wearing armor."

The seven perps gathered around a pile of plastic bags, eager anticipation apparent in their movements.

"Looks like cosplay gear. Is there a comic con in town?" the officer asked.

Five of the burglars jerked their faces toward Laura Osage and the other cops.

"Osage, we've been made," Sans said.

The burglars sprinted at Laura and the other cops, mouths stretched open to reveal rows of needle-sharp teeth. The freaks didn't scream so much as hiss in a frequency Laura couldn't hear well.

"What the hell do they think they're doing?" Sans said a second before the first giant reached him.

"Stop! Drop your weapons!" Laura shouted right before she opened fire.

It was too late for Sans. He went down like he'd been tackled by a velociraptor, blood arcing into the night.

The cops from Baker Sector yelled, fired, and screamed in terror.

Laura threw herself sideways but continued to pull the trigger. Time distorted. She didn't think she was breathing. Bullets left her gun with excruciating slowness—like small, gray Nerf darts. Combat veterans talked about apparent time dilation, auditory exclusion, and tunnel vision. These and other sensory distortions dominated her perception.

The next thing she knew, she was struggling to get up from the pavement. Scrambling backward with one hand and pointing her pistol with the other, she couldn't move her feet fast enough to create distance between herself and the nearest attacker.

Images of the scene polluted her vision right when she needed all her senses.

Sans was dead, his head twisted the wrong way and his arms protruding from his body at unnatural angles. Blood streaked the concrete. She glimpsed other bodies but didn't have much time to consider them. A giant in strange, ultra-modern armor loomed over her with his helmet visor up and blood smeared around his mouth.

Laura was certain it was the first suspect she'd seen. Maybe he was wearing a mask, or maybe the streetlights were giving his rough skin a gray-blue sheen of weirdness. Either way, Laura didn't enjoy looking at the freak.

"Go ahead and kill me, you son-of-a-bitch!" she shouted, knowing her life was over. They slaughtered Sans and the others in seconds. What chance did she have?

Something was wrong with her leg, something she didn't want to think about because it was just too terrifyingly strange.

A second suspect joined the first and spoke in a language Laura didn't recognize. It was full of sound gaps and dissonant harmonies that made her want to vomit. The first suspect pointed.

Laura followed his gesture to her left calf and saw something like a snake bite—right through her uniform pants and the top of her boot. A deep hole marked the center of the wound.

The funny thing was, it had already stopped hurting. In fact, she was feeling pretty good. Ice-cold euphoria wrapped her like a sleeve of new flesh.

CHAPTER THREE

FOR THE TENTH TIME, David wondered if it was possible to turn around before the designated area. The Kansas Highway Patrol troopers wouldn't be pleased if he attempted the maneuver, and he wasn't exactly in their good graces. He tapped his fingers on his left thigh as he weighed the pros and cons of taking the initiative.

Dust zipped up her expensive coat around her chin like a turtle. "Can't we run the heater?"

"We could, but I have no idea what we're getting into. A couple of guys up ahead are almost out of fuel." David was more worried about the unseasonable cold than fuel consumption. Winter was nearly over, but temperatures were ten degrees lower than they should be without wind chill. Northwestern Kansas could be miserable, almost always because of wind.

He didn't want to run the heater because it interfered with his hearing. He needed all of his senses operating at one hundred percent.

Away from the highway, there was no sign of frost on the

wild prairie grass stretching as far as the eye could see. The gently rolling flatlands looked cozy, just starting to get green. It had been unseasonably warm; now it was freezing.

Dust leaned over the center console to look at the fuel gauge. "You're basically full. Maybe your friends should have planned better."

"Do you have any idea how many gallons of diesel it takes to fill one of these trucks? Or what that costs? For most drivers, where and when to top off is a company decision. I do it my own way because I make my own rules."

"Fine. But even if you were low on fuel, which you aren't, how much does it take to run the heater? You have to leave your engine idling anyway. Why not be comfortable?"

He turned on the heat vents. "You weren't cold standing beside the road where I found you."

"This is different," she said, twisting away from him.

"Are you always this moody?"

"I'm a girl. What do you expect?"

Her answer didn't set right with him. She was holding back, playing a part even she didn't believe.

"I'm not cold," he said casually.

She spun on him. "Cold weather affects me differently, okay!"

She hugged herself and stared through the front window. "It's not as cold as you think, Dustvaria. It's not as cold as you think. It's not as cold as you think."

David tried to hear what she was muttering but couldn't catch all of it. "Note to self, don't ask the kid about being cold," he said.

"I'm not a kid."

"Exactly. Suck it up and stop acting like a baby."

The look she gave him was something out of a horror

movie. For about one heartbeat, he could've believed she wasn't human, but a demon-spawned harpy come to steal the souls of unwary truck drivers.

He turned on the radio, then did a few Google searches for news. His data plan wasn't great, and he'd already used most of it during a moment of weakness that had led to a Game of Thrones binge.

"It's an invasion," she said.

David looked up from the news feed. She stared straight forward, unblinking.

He shook his head at another round of *meteors*. Half-heartedly, he said, "There has to be a better explanation. I don't listen to conspiracy theorists or panic-mongers. And before you ask, I don't accept the Flat Earth theory either."

Dust covered her nose and mouth with her hands in a classic posture of horror and denial.

New objects streaked down from the night sky, filling the horizon like tears in reality. What was different was the size of these things.

"Yeah… those look like ships," David said. Then he tried to call Laura, Charles, and anyone else in his contact list. No one answered. When he tried again, he couldn't get a signal.

"Without shouting at me, explain what makes you sensitive to cold?" he asked, his useless phone taking up space in his right hand.

"I'm just not used to this weather. This cold front is focused on the highway. Doesn't that raise some red flags?"

"You can't prove that."

She snorted. "I saw you looking out there, all confused and worried. Don't bullshit me. The highway is frozen by whatever those things are."

He disagreed, but kept his mouth shut. She'd jumped to

a different conclusion than he had. It wasn't the highway that was affected differently, it was the unusual concentration of people. Drivers and vehicles moved sluggishly. This made him want to piss his pants, and he didn't understand why. He only knew it was bad. "They don't want us to escape."

Dust rocked in her seat, hugging herself and muttering under her breath.

"Stay here," he said.

"Where are you going?"

"Some of these vehicles have been abandoned. I have an idea—two ideas, actually."

"Tell me," she said, the fear in her voice making her seem vulnerable for the first time. It was obvious she didn't want to be alone in this caravan of human sheep.

"I want to move some vehicles out of my way so I'm not stuck here. The second thing, well, let's call it scavenging."

"Your cop sister won't like that."

"Nope, but she'd do the same thing if she had to," David said. "She's naïve and reckless, not stupid."

Moving cars and big rigs proved difficult. Many were still occupied. Deciding which needed to shift right or left or forward or back to allow him an escape route was like the world's biggest jigsaw puzzle. He did his best, smashing a few fenders in his haste.

Three were turned off and locked. "Nice. Wouldn't want anyone to steal your abandoned car as the world ends."

Looting proved simple, but only because he knew the guy driving the sporting goods truck. Ian Todd hadn't abandoned his rig. He'd armed himself and sent people he didn't like back the way they came.

"What's up, Jackknife?" Todd said, standing on the roof

of his trailer, rifle butt resting in the crook of his arm. "Heard you picked up a lot lizard."

"Man, news travels fast. But she's not a lot lizard. Probably a runaway or something, but I don't care right now."

"Nobody cares right now. I think that couple three cars ahead are getting one final romp in," Todd said, squinting to see better.

"This ain't good, Todd."

"Nope."

"My rig is full of canned goods. What do you have in yours?"

"Sporting goods. You need a gun? I promise not to tell your PO."

"I'm off parole."

"You're still a felon. Can't have a gun," Todd said.

"You're a felon."

"Not giving a shit right now."

"Me neither."

"What's up with this weather?" Todd asked. There was a parka lying at his feet like he might put it on, but only if it got really cold. Todd was the type of guy who didn't like to cover his tattooed biceps and shoulders unless he had to.

"I don't know. Something's happening back there. Let me gear up before you get overrun," David said, glancing nervously toward a group of people almost a mile up in the line. They seemed to be spreading out, hurrying between the parked vehicles like a routed army.

Snow and mist swirled in the air, stealing visibility and forcing him to hug himself to avoid shivering.

"Yeah, sure," Todd said distractedly. He stared at the same disturbance David had noticed, but from a much higher vantage point. "You better hurry."

David hesitated.

Todd raised the scoped hunting rifle to his shoulder and swept it across the unfolding scene to get a better look. "Shit."

David ran to the back of the truck and yanked it open, searching quickly and taking what he could carry. When he popped out with guns and camping gear, Todd had the coat on and looked ready for a forced road march.

"We're about to go off the rails on a crazy train, my friend," Todd said, his voice unusually subdued.

"Let's go, then. You can't keep all this stuff," David said.

Todd nodded. "Would have been worth more than gold in the end times." He woke from his standing reverie. "I'm right behind you."

Something like a fighter jet combined with an attack helicopter burst through the snow and fog above the panicked mob. Tracer rounds—or something like nearly colorless laser bolts—flashed from wing cannons. Vehicles exploded. Body parts flew into the air.

Todd aimed his rifle, pulled the trigger, and was blown apart by return fire. The translucent energy bolt splattered him across the top of his trailer.

David sprinted for his rig. "Dust! We're leaving!"

She opened the passenger door, transfixed on the top step, her face illuminated by flashing weapons and burning vehicles.

Explosions rocked the highway. Each blast sounded closer. David felt rhythmic shock waves behind him. He jumped halfway up the ladder steps, scrambled the rest of the way in, and slid behind the steering wheel.

"I'm sorry," Dust cried, one hand covering her mouth. "I'm sorry, I'm sorry, I'm sorry."

"Get in and close the door." He cranked the wheel and put the truck in gear.

A second ship, larger than the first, emerged from the mist. The closer it got, the more massive it appeared—like a freight train in the air. A side door opened. Dozens of large figures in ultramodern armor jumped to the ground.

"No!" Dust exclaimed.

They charged around cars in parallel squads, weapons searching for targets without firing. Each of them wore a red A with a circle around it—like the Anarchy symbol—but weird somehow, like it was dancing with red electricity.

Impressive discipline, David thought.

Human refugees swarmed past David's truck. The alien commandos ignored them.

"Why'd you say you're sorry?" he demanded.

"I don't know what you mean." She tugged on her seat belt.

He popped the clutch. The truck lurched forward, slamming a pair of the invaders back. Another went down under a wheel as David plowed into an abandoned Chevrolet Tahoe—which became intimate with a Honda sedan and a small SUV he had moved earlier.

"They're after you! Why are they after you, Dust?"

"No! They're not hunting me. They're just attacking the only moving vehicle on the highway. And your friend shot at them!"

David tried to weave between cars when he could but sent anything smaller than another big rig pinwheeling into the ditch on one side or across the median on the other.

He needed to get to the access turnaround. It wasn't meant for eighteen wheelers, but it was the best way across the median he would find. There was no way he could reach the official KHP sanctioned turnaround zone, which was hidden in clouds of snow and smoke anyway.

Huge alien commandos climbed both sides of his truck, breaking out the windows with their weapon barrels.

"Screw it." David cranked the wheel. Making a U-turn here was nearly impossible, but he was committed and out of options.

A gauntleted hand caught his wrist and frost spread across his skin. The humanoid's mouth opened—thin, nearly nonexistent lips parting to expose rows of needle-sharp teeth and a tongue that was a fleshy spike.

He slammed his left elbow into his attacker's throat and the creature fell backward, long tongue flailing grotesquely.

Dust was almost in David's lap, trying to avoid grasping hands from the other side.

"Don't you have that gun?" she screamed.

David twisted in his seat, then Sparta-kicked the creature attacking Dust. His boot struck the ugly freak in the face, launching him into the night.

"I'm a felon! Can't be caught with heat like that." Which was quicker than explaining he couldn't get the rifle he'd stolen out from behind the seat, load it, aim, and fire it right now.

A ridiculous part of his mind was excited he'd finally benefited from hours of alternating, max effort single leg presses in the gym. Unlike his previous life-and-death encounters, sensations and memories flooded through his brain like intentional distractions.

The truck bounced across the median. He fought to control the bucking wheel, swerving onto the pavement with enough momentum that his trailer nearly twisted onto its side. Cold flowed into his hands, arms, and torso until he wanted to cry and beg for it to stop.

There were fewer cars in the eastbound lanes. He rammed anything that got in his way.

"Check the mirrors," he said. "Are there any holding on?"

"No. They fell off or jumped down," she said.

"You're bleeding."

She pulled her sleeve over the wound. "It's nothing. I think we got away."

"I can't outrun those ships," he said, checking his rearview mirrors. "But hot damn, it looks like you're right. They're not chasing me."

She stared into the night.

"Why were they after you?" He wanted to interrogate her, but his truck was having problems—either from getting shot by ray guns or whatever, or from smashing cars and jumping the thirty-meter-wide median.

"They're not. I told you, they were just trying to stop the only vehicle trying to get away," she said. "And it looks like they have needs."

"Prove it."

"If they were after us, they'd still be chasing us," she said. "And they would catch us. They know we can't escape without a translation starship."

He realized he should be paying more attention to what she was saying but couldn't look away from the strangers herding people from their cars into tightly packed clusters of humanity. "You might be right."

Warmth flooded his body and he realized he had nearly been paralyzed by the agony of the sensation. He wanted to go back and help the people he'd seen, but that was worse than hopeless. This was a job for the Army or the Marines.

"Start looking for a truck or car we can steal. My baby is struggling," he said, thumping one hand on the dash. Then, like the part of a nightmare that was better forgotten, he saw why their attackers were no longer pursuing. They'd been distracted by a packed cattle car.

"What are they doing?"

Dust's voice was thick with horror. "You know what they're doing."

CHAPTER FOUR

THE NIGHT DARKENED when the meteor storms ended. *Those weren't meteors, dumbass.* Enemy attack ships, maybe. Dropships or something. Pod creature distribution bundles. Whatever.

His truck groaned, dragging something he couldn't see but didn't dare stop to check. The encumbrance would come off, or his axle would tear away. As long as it wasn't the corpse of an alien super commando, he didn't care. Smashed side windows, bumpers filled with dirt plowed up from crossing the median, and blood smears did nothing to lessen the drunken limp his truck had acquired since the world went crazy.

"Where are we going?" Dust asked.

"There's a Kansas National Guard base not far from here," he said. "I think it's linked with the Kansas Division of Emergency Management."

"How do you know all this stuff?" she asked sleepily.

The encounter at the turnaround point seemed to have drained her of energy. She was injured, but she refused to let him look at her. With his luck, she would bleed out and he'd have to explain why he had a dead girl in his cab.

He shook his head. "You talk to a lot of people on the road, usually at a late-night diner eating bad food and drinking worse coffee."

She listened with interest, more like the young woman he'd first met than the emotional wreck she'd become during the attack.

She's a survivor, David. She knows how to act.

"Didn't your parents teach you stuff like that?"

"My parents died getting me here. It's complicated and tragic," she said. "If you'd never bring it up again, that'd be great."

David held up one hand defensively.

"None of my guardians talked about things like that. Education wasn't their priority. Rules, constant interrogations, containment," she said, smiling to take the edge off her words.

"I'm sure your flair for dramatic language wasn't part of the problem."

"You wouldn't do any better." Her face regained its youthful vitality.

"I'm a grown ass man," he said.

"Lucky you. Listen, if you're expecting to hear a bunch of sob stories, forget about it. It's nothing exciting. Foster parents don't often show the same level of commitment as biological parents. The circumstances of my… placement are complicated."

He laughed grimly, steering around a stalled vehicle without slowing. "Don't go assuming birth parents are all they're cracked up to be. Plenty of them get it wrong too."

She gave him a look he couldn't read.

They were silent for a while—radio off and one headlight pointing forward. The Milky Way filled the sky above them, with no moon, city lights, or explosions to compete with the brilliance of the stars.

"We're almost there. Looks like we're not exactly first in line."

David downshifted, cringing at his transmission grinding itself into nothing. He was surprised the truck made it this far. In a few hundred miles, the rig would be a total loss. If he found a repair shop, he'd probably have to do the work himself. Huge pain in the ass. Not something he had time for. *Because... killer aliens. Welcome to the end of humanity, bro.*

His truck sounded slightly less horrible when he parked in line to wait his turn. Without windows, it was a bit chilly but nothing like during the attack. But the crowds of people and abandoned vehicles at the turnaround point was nothing compared to what they faced here. I-70 was a busy highway, a major east-west transportation route across the country. Kansas wasn't an overly populated state, and this region was even more rural. He'd guess Salina had a population of fifty or sixty thousand.

The numbers were deceiving, however. Crowds of people with their vehicles demanded entry to the base. National Guard troops who looked about two days out of high school directed traffic. There were checkpoints on the highway every quarter mile, with squads of soldiers in Humvees.

The problem with Kansas, he'd always thought, was the disproportionate number of four-wheel drive vehicles. Many of the citizens making their way to the National Guard base had decided roads were unnecessary and they could make better time by cutting straight through fields, ditches, and over back roads.

A soldier directed him into a special lane that moved him ahead of much of the traffic. The reason was obvious. After about an hour, he reached the checkpoint and his theory was confirmed.

A pair of young soldiers motioned for him to stop. One climbed up to his window while his squad mate stood ready with an M16.

"Good evening, sir, I'm Corporal Travis Young. I need to ask what you're carrying and if it could be useful to relief efforts," the soldier said.

David handed over his log. "That shows what I'm carrying and where I'm going. Got a lot of canned goods and other discount store items. A bunch of useless junk from China as well. I'll need something official if I'm going to surrender it to the government."

The soldier looked over the unfamiliar document. He wasn't a state trooper who inspected civilian vehicles regularly, and this probably wasn't in his job description. He seemed to adapt quickly.

"Thank you, sir. The log makes it easier. I'm not sure what will happen to your load from here. I was just told to find out what people had, then report it."

"Fair enough." David gestured at all the vehicles waiting in front of him. "I could use some information. What's happening? What's the government doing about it?"

"You came from the west, so you know better than I do. My orders are to gather information and keep the peace, not disseminate information." Corporal Young spoke at his own pace, neither fast nor slow. "I wouldn't worry just yet. This line is long. They may not even need your truck."

"That's reassuring, Corporal. Tell me, just between you and me. What's the situation?"

From the height of his rig, David could see most of the burgeoning refugee camp. Few people were ready for this. He assumed that all the half-crazy end-preppers were safely tucked away in their bunkers as far from this circus as possible. One family, from grandchildren to grandparents all dressed in pajamas, struggled to make a tent out of bedsheets. What scared him was they had left home that way and gotten this far. Pajamas and flip-flops and didn't seem to have a tool between them. He wanted to explain to the bedsheet family what would happen to their new home as soon as it rained or snowed.

The post apocalypse was gonna be hard on these people.

"Your guess is as good as mine, sir." He looked past David. "Nice truck. Who's your passenger?"

"She's my niece. Don't get any ideas."

"No, sir. Sorry, sir. I was just wondering what kind of guitar that is? Care to open it up so I can have a look?"

"What if it's not a guitar?" Dust asked.

"That might be a problem, but you're messing with me, right?" Corporal Young asked.

Dust smiled. "You're cute."

"Thank you." He waited a moment. "So what kind is it?"

Dust opened the case. "It's a Taylor. Nothing special."

He raised an eyebrow. "Looks pretty nice to me. I'd like to hear you play sometime." He glanced at his partner and nodded once. "Don't let anyone without authorization in your truck. We already had a mini-riot over a grocery truck up ahead. If people think they can get supplies, they'll get unruly."

"What kind of authorization?" David asked.

Corporal Young patted the M16 hanging from the front of

his load-bearing gear. "Stay safe. Stay in your truck as much as you can."

He lowered himself to the pavement and went on to the next vehicle with his partner.

"There are too many people here," Dust said. Her voice was low, lending gravity to the mood in the cab.

David didn't disagree. He kept a watchful eye on the crowd and listened to three chapters of his Nora Roberts audiobook. Dust slept in the passenger seat, injured arm curled beneath her. The more he thought about the incident at the turnaround, the more certain he was she had been wounded.

His big brother instincts urged him to drag her arm out where he could check for lacerations or bruising. He had a comprehensive first aid kit behind the seat. He'd used it more than once on traffic accidents he'd rolled up on. There was no way she was strong enough to resist his ministrations.

His prisoner instinct told him to just let it be. If she was hurt badly enough, she'd ask for help. Better if it was her idea rather than him being pushy. He was just starting to relax when he saw the crowd gathering.

Another group joined the first. The leader of the original mob pointed at David's truck.

He looked for a way to clear the traffic jam and bypass the growing refugee camp altogether. It was a pointless mental exercise. He'd already performed it a dozen times without finding a solution.

Ramming occupied vehicles out of his way would surely earn the M16 powered wrath of many young National Guardsmen.

Dust woke up. "What are those people doing?"

"I imagine they're coming to steal my load," David said. "Normally I wouldn't care, but Corporal Young told me not to let anybody take my stuff. Rules are rules."

"Seriously?"

David snorted a laugh. "Gotcha. I don't take orders from kids your age, but he knows what's what. I can't allow a bunch of half-assed panic mongers anywhere near my truck. It'll be a feeding frenzy with you and me as the side dishes."

Sarcasm bubbled through her worry. "You know a lot about riots?"

He pulled the Ruger 10/22 carbine from the sleeping compartment and made sure it was loaded. "I survived a prison riot once."

The weapon was only a .22 caliber with a small boxlike magazine holding ten rounds. Two or three of the distinctive bullet carriers could fit in the palm of his hand. His father, uncles, and grandfather had considered .22 rifles to be kiddie guns, something to learn with and hunt rabbits.

The ammunition was small, cheap, and easy to carry in bulk. It also left the muzzle of the lightweight gun at 1,100 feet per second, more than sufficient to punch into flesh. What made the round deadlier than it should be was its inability to punch back out again. The small slug often lacked the kinetic momentum to exit a human body, causing it to bounce around inside the skull or chest cavity looking for a way out.

All good reasons to select the Ruger 10/22 as his end of the world survival gun. Not that he'd say no to an assault rifle with a half-dozen extra magazines and thousands of dollars of aftermarket optics. Until then, he'd make do with what was either an assassin's weapon or a Boy Scout's varmint gun.

It wasn't great for self-defense. It would kill a man but wouldn't knock him off the front of a Peterbilt, for instance.

He opened the door. Briefly, he considered climbing down. Instead, he hopped onto the expansive hood. Standing there scratched the paint but made him feel like a king looking over his realm.

His truck, once his prize possession and largest asset—the financial equivalent of a middle-class house—looked like it belonged in a road warrior movie. He kind of liked it.

"That's close enough. None of you are hungry enough to die for my cargo," David said.

"You're bluffing," the leader said.

David aimed the Ruger 10/22, stock pulled tight to his shoulder, hands gripping the fore stock and trigger housing, cheek pressed against the wood as he aimed the weapon. "Try me."

The leader stopped, holding up a hand to halt his followers. Several latecomers ignored him and hurried closer to the truck.

David fired one round in front of each looter, kicking up dust and bits of pavement.

"That corporal and his friends are coming," Dust warned.

"Good. I hope they hurry." David swept the carbine barrel over the crowd.

"Get back, you assholes!" the mob leader shouted. "This guy's crazy."

"He can't use everything on that truck. Everyone has to share. We need that stuff to survive!" a man yelled.

"You don't even know what this stuff is, jerk off. Come closer and I'll shank you to save a bullet," David said.

Dust retreated into the sleeping compartment.

"You people stand down!" Corporal Young shouted as he arrived with four other soldiers. "David Osage, surrender your weapon."

David lowered the barrel. "Not going to happen. Sorry, Young. Not today."

The crowd surged.

David aimed the Ruger at the mob. The National Guardsman formed a circle to protect themselves.

"I said stand down, people. Go back to your assigned areas or you'll lose any aid the Kansas Department of Emergency Management can provide to you!" Young shouted. He pointed at David. "We're going to talk about that rifle, Osage."

"I don't mind talking. You know where to find me when you get all these people the hell away," David said.

CHAPTER FIVE

LAURA CONTROLLED HER BREATHING. The two aliens—that's all she could call them right now because they were so outside anything she understood—ignored her as they argued.

"In with the good air, hold it, out with the bad air..." Laura murmured, then laughed maniacally. Her leg was messed up, barely under her control. Her arms worked fine, however, so she clawed backward.

"Stop!" the strange giant growled.

Laura barely recognized the word as English, but she got the point. "You stop yourself, freak!"

She twisted onto her stomach and low-crawled like her life depended on it. Each grab and pull of the pavement tore skin from her hands. The asphalt carved huge grooves in her patent leather gun belt.

The second giant—every bit of eight feet tall in his armor—stomped around the first to the patrol car and blocked Laura's progress.

Desperate, unable to think of anything but escape, Laura

dragged herself to the opening of an alley and forced herself to stand. The concrete had that behind-a-restaurant greasy feel and smelled like piss, body odor, and old beer cans.

The euphoria she'd felt shortly after being bitten was gone, or more accurately, it receded whenever she moved. As long as she waited for her killers, everything about her world was cold and blissful.

She didn't want an ice palace of serenity. She wanted the burning fire of murderous revenge.

She took a step and pain exploded through her leg. Grinding her teeth, she took three more steps. What she accomplished next wasn't exactly running, but herky-jerky ambulation in the right direction. Hellish pain pushed coherent thought from her mind and opened the door for hallucinations. The world was ice. Her brain was cold, her soul frozen like it had never known heat.

Words she couldn't understand whispered harshly in her brain. Someone or something was telling her to stop, surrender to the cold, and embrace the warmth of obedience.

"Screw that," she sob-cursed. Every muscle in her body cramped, nearly undoing her resolve.

She put one palm on the wall for balance, breathing shallowly and forcing herself to relax.

There was no way she could get up if she fell. Her fingers dragged across chips in the paint as she slid her way forward.

"No! Human! I said stop," the first giant shouted, chasing Laura into the shadows between buildings.

"Not today, champ. You want some of this, you come and get it." Pain distorted her words.

Silhouetted by light at the mouth of the alley, one of the armored giants pulled a pack from his back and opened it.

She didn't see what happened next but didn't like what her gut was telling her. The figure had the manner of a K-9 handler about to release a dog.

"Shuak! Shuak!" he shouted.

If she had time to think—and maybe she understood this subconsciously—she would've figured out it was a drone operator unpacking a remote-controlled flying machine.

Hating the way her pain-filled voice sounded, she keyed her portable radio mic and shouted for help. "Put us out in trouble. We're under attack! Multiple suspects, armed and dangerous!"

That was when she reached the dead end—a ten-foot chain-link fence about a foot away from an even higher brick wall. On a good day, she could have parkour'd her way up it, maybe grabbed the bottom of the boarded-up window ledge.

She put her back to the chain link, then checked the magazine in her pistol. Two rounds left. These needed to count. The nine-millimeter rounds had to hit some part of her attacker that dropped him instantly.

Three winged creatures, fleshy cyborgs trailing ominous tendrils, arched forward, sweeping into the alley. Shooting at the small flying things seemed pointless, so she aimed at the man launching them and fired twice.

Both rounds struck. The giant staggered.

Others rushed past the alien she'd injured. Holstering her weapon, she considered fighting hand to hand. As desperate measures went, it was lame. The fence and the window were a better option. Reaching safety in that direction seemed as likely as flying to the moon but failing to take action was unacceptable.

She dug her fingers into the chain link, stabbed the toes

of her boots into the diamond shaped gaps that were slightly too small to stand in. Up and up she went.

The aliens shouted strange words that hurt her head and made her bones cold. A waffling non-sound battered her ears. It was like driving with one window rolled down, annoying but nowhere near disabling.

One hand found the windowsill. She grabbed with the other, knowing two things: she wasn't strong enough right now to pull herself up with all her gear on, and if she missed the second grab, she would fall fifteen feet onto her back.

And then be murdered by giant blood-smeared alien commandos.

"Shit and double shit." She looked toward the street below and saw the freak shaking a fist at her.

"Come down, human. You survived the bite; you may bite others and live."

Weeping with desperation, anger, and frustration she found herself two-thirds of the way through the window. Her face hit the floor of the dark room when she tumbled inside.

"Do not forsake the Gift. The strongest among you may serve us for a thousand years!"

Knowing it was a mistake but too tired to care, Chicago Police Officer Laura Osage looked down on her pursuers.

"Come to me, human," the alien shock trooper said. Blood smeared his face. "I will show you how to feed on the blood power of this planet."

"Why don't you climb up here and I'll show you how to go to hell?" she asked, then presented both of her middle fingers.

The alien commando leader smiled.

She realized her mistake a second too late.

The flying bio-drones slammed into her, launching her back into the abandoned apartment. Darkness swallowed her. Winged techno-serpents held her to the ground.

Heavy footsteps shook the stairs. The door flew in and she was surrounded by the armored giants.

One who was less bloody than the others dragged her away from the airborne drone creatures that had been holding her. He cursed in his strange, painful language. Others argued with him.

She didn't see what happened as rough hands dragged her this way and that in the semi-darkness. All she wanted was to make it to the window and see the lights of her city one last time.

The commotion stopped.

The leader of the alien shock troopers squatted over her. "I have decided. You will feed. You will serve us. Maybe I spare more of your race if you comply. If you do my bidding. If you help me secure this city and make the occupation peaceful."

"No," she groaned.

He tilted his head. "Do you not love your people? Do you not wish to protect them?"

"Why don't you ask a fair question, asshole?" she grumbled.

"You are more interesting than the others. But do not question too many things. The virus will keep all good servants alive even if it must change you inside and out."

CHAPTER SIX

CHARLES OSAGE REVIEWED the information like a scientist, or least a code writer. He was thorough, testing the facts and making lists of questions that needed answered. *If the invaders are aliens, what do they want? What could sentient beings capable of intergalactic travel need from Earth? What is the government doing to control the chaos?*

Why was the Warfighter Games Company fully prepared for Armageddon?

For the first time in his life, he was glad his office was underground. The ultramodern, bunkerlike facility had been a huge inconvenience and the source of many complaints since the software development company moved in. No one was complaining now. They had power and other amenities many people lacked as the global crisis unfolded.

Thank God for small favors.

Facts were facts. Aliens were invading. There had been live video streams of the planetary assault for about five terrifying minutes.

News was still available through the HardNet. Unfortunately, the government and military personnel working to resist the invasion controlled access to that resource. The internet was unreliable at best.

He stood and paced his small office, sweat dampening the back of his shirt. Time passed with agonizing slowness. When he was about to lose his mind, the intercom buzzed. His family had arrived at the front gate and were being admitted to the facility.

When the crisis began, his supervisors had mandated strict regulations. Employees weren't allowed to roam the halls. Now that his family was here, he had authorization to go upstairs to collect them.

Running to the escalator, he looked to see if anyone was going his way. Some were. Others had already taken their loved ones down into the depths of the Warfighter Games Company.

Facts were facts, and he accepted them. Yet it was surreal.

I make video games, for Christ's sake.

Emily released the girls the moment he appeared. Little Cara and Debbie sprinted at him and jumped into his arms. He held them, looking through the jumble of arms to see his wife.

"I thought I'd go crazy waiting, but you got here pretty fast," he said.

"We were in the area when the first attack hit. The girls were playing with Henry and Caroline's kids," Emily said.

Guilt washed over him. He hadn't gotten around to telling Emily that Henry and Caroline were having trouble and were practically separated at this point. They were pretending to be the perfect family, afraid that if someone at the software company detected the drama, they'd both be fired.

"We would have been here an hour ago if not for all the security checkpoints. Charles, they took blood samples before letting us inside," Emily said.

"I'm just glad you're here. We have to go down to the cafeteria for in-processing," he said, feeling like he was sending his wife and kids to boot camp.

Emily was the most gorgeous woman he'd ever dated. He still couldn't believe she'd agreed to marry him. Two kids later, he wondered why she hadn't left him. She was smart, funny, with looks that made other women envious and men chase after her.

He knew he should be jealous of the attention she received from men at the real estate firm she worked for, but he wasn't. He trusted her. That's what people who loved each other did.

"Daddy, Daddy... we saw ships in the sky!" Cara said.

"You cried!" Debbie said.

"You cried too!"

Charles bounced them in his arms as he walked toward the escalator. "It's okay, girls. Do you want to ride the elevator or the escalator today?"

"Don't coddle them, Charles," Emily said. She brushed some of her auburn hair behind one ear.

"Trying to nip their bickering at the bud," he said, shifting the two girls higher to get his shoulders under them. He wasn't built like his brother David, who could undoubtedly hold both girls with one arm.

His big brother had bulked up in prison—claiming it kept people from jumping him. Everyone in the family was more athletic than Charles. His sister, Laura, the middle child, was a beat cop in Chicago. She'd developed a lean athletic physique few people could ever achieve, no matter how many trainers they hired or gyms they belonged to. She was both stronger than she looked and faster than she needed to be—always challenging David to a wrestling match or foot race on the rare occasions the Osage family gathered.

"I'm exhausted," Emily said. "It's late. I need to get the girls to bed. Can we get checked in and find our quarters?"

"Sure, honey. I'm glad we're all here now."

"Did Henry and Caroline and their kids make it?" she asked.

The easy answer was yes, but he didn't want to break the news about Henry and Caroline to his wife. If not for this crisis, they would be in divorce court right now. "They made it."

She was facing away from him when she nodded, and crying he thought.

———

THE OSAGE FAMILY morale improved dramatically when they arrived at the cafeteria. Warfighter Games had a play area for younger kids filled with activities and three young women who were probably certified kindergarten teachers and school nurses. They had a way with children. All the parents in the room seemed ecstatic at this sliver of good fortune.

Everyone was issued a meal card when they signed in, along with a printed form that assigned housing and set basic rules to be followed during the emergency.

"I'm still amazed we're this well prepared," he said, not realizing what he was doing until it was too late.

"Honey, you're thinking out loud again," Emily said, not

seeming to care. Normally this was a pet peeve of hers. The mood in the cafeteria was overwhelmingly of relief. Everyone felt it, including his wife. Which made him glad.

She knew him better than he knew himself. It wasn't that he lacked focus, it was that he focused intently on more than one thing at a time. Joy at his family's arrival mixed with the sour feeling the bunker had evoked in him since they moved the company here two years ago. This place wasn't right. WFG was too well prepared.

An epiphany about the games he'd been working on eluded him by a single data point. Everyone else in his group wanted to cash out their stocks because the games were too hard. No one could beat them for long. That level of impossible didn't sell.

Charles had been the only one who enjoyed making them harder than real life... like training modules for pilots or spec ops commandos. Sometimes he got email from real life SOCOM or MARSOC operators complimenting him on the gameplay and asking where he served. To his surprise, every one of them had been cool when he told them he'd never spent a day in the military but was a big fan of people who did it for real.

"What's on your mind, Charles?" Emily asked. "You seem distracted."

"Sorry." A chill shivered up his spine. He didn't trust obvious connections, not when he was exhausted and confused and prone to mental weakness. The entire world was confused right now. No one could blame him.

Why would anyone blame me? And for what? It's not like we... I... knew there was an alien invasion about to happen. His mind worried the inner dialogue, far faster than he could articulate it. *You knew, Charles. You followed the clues a long time ago but was afraid to be labeled a crazy man. All these people are dying because you were afraid of what people would think of you.*

"I'm going to my office for a minute. I need to see if I can contact my siblings," he said.

And figure out who put all these provisions in place.

Emily looked worried. "You haven't done that already?"

"David is hard to get ahold of. Always on the road." The idea of confronting the mastermind behind the plot he believed existed (without a shred of actual proof) sickened him. He wasn't as physically robust as his big brother.

"I hope he's okay. It seems like the worst place to be right now," Emily said.

He loved her for that. She barely knew David, but was concerned for any member of his family. Concerned and protective, that was his wife.

"Maybe Laura knows a good way to get ahold of him. I'll look into that. Will you be okay up here?"

"I'll be fine," she said.

He powered up his office as quickly as possible. If not for his family, he could probably live through the crisis in the small room. He had a cot for naps between late-night coding sessions, a coffeemaker, a small dorm fridge containing enough food to survive several days—so long as he had power to both the fridge and the small microwave on top of it.

His computer, a state-of-the-art machine, struggled to life. He started coffee and wondered which would finish first, the log-in process or the Columbian roast. By the time he had access to the HardNet, ten minutes had passed—a process that normally required only seconds.

Email alerts popped up. He ignored them. The last time that happened in such volume it had been a Trojan Horse drill mandating every machine to initiate quarantine and immediate shutdown procedures. He didn't have long to locate his siblings. The IT people were about to suspend everyone's online privileges whether they be internet or HardNet.

He located Laura almost immediately. Apparently, his sister was last seen during a disturbance just prior to the invasion. What was less clear was her current status. He'd never seen the term *missing in action* used in a police report.

Charles had read every public record of every officer-involved shooting Laura had been a part of. Such incidents were always a mess of excessive documentation, hard to follow even after they'd been sorted through by district attorneys and federal investigators.

He wouldn't get any clarification until he spoke to someone directly.

Next he searched the HardNet for David. To his surprise, his brother was off parole—he hadn't had a speeding ticket or been in a fight for three years. Charles knew he could find his location with enough time, but that was one resource he didn't have.

A warning chimed on his computer—an immediate shutdown order. The message arrived just before the power cut off. What surprised him more was the banging on the door, followed by the armed guards entering his office.

"Step away from the computer, sir," a man dressed like a soldier said.

"I have work to do. Our planet is being invaded, in case you didn't notice." Charles avoided eye contact, stalling for every second he could get.

"You're Charles Osage, aren't you? I'm a big fan. Loved

Warfighter 5: The Red Massacre. Bitchin' scenario. Took me three weeks to survive the attack and five more to win."

"Few people ever win without hacks," Charles said, off-balance at the sudden change in the conversation. The guard still had a hand on his Colt M4 that was slung across the front of his load-bearing vest.

"I wasn't given a choice."

"What do you mean?"

The man smiled, then offered his right hand for a firm handshake. "Chris Halloran. Security, Level 1 Supervisor. It's equivalent to being a sergeant. Think of me as your friendly neighborhood team leader."

"What do you mean you weren't given a choice?" Charles asked. He wasn't sure why this was important, but it obviously had something to do with how prepared Warfighter Games Inc. was for the current global crisis.

"Beat the game or get fired. We all had to run five miles at a seven-minute mile pace, deadlift twice our weight for ten reps, bench one hundred and fifty percent of our weight for ten, and squat clean our weight for… you guessed it… ten reps," Halloran said, "just to start the training."

"I'm not sure how that gives you the authority to shut down my workstation," Charles said.

Halloran shook his head sadly. "Come on, Mr. Osage. I know you saw the shutdown order. I'm here to make sure you don't hack around it. That's a pretty common problem in a facility full of computer programmers."

Chris Halloran reminded Charles of his big brother, but not as thick and without prison tattoos. His buzz-cut hair was probably brown but might as well be blond. He radiated confidence.

"Just let me make a quick call, then I'll head up to be with my family for the duration."

The security officer laughed.

"What's so funny?"

"You said 'for the duration' like this will be over in a few days," Halloran said.

"Just a quick call."

Halloran grabbed the phone from his hand. "Nope. Rules are rules. No contact with the outside world."

"This is ridiculous. Why not?"

"You could be working for them, and by them, I mean the alien invaders," Halloran said, serious as a man with a machine gun could be.

CHAPTER SEVEN

DAVID PULLED INTO THE LOT, following directions from the National Guardsman until the last moment, then blasting the Peterbilt horn, bullying his way to a parking stall near the exit.

"You're not very good at following directions," Dust said.

"They told me to park, so I'm parking." David wasn't in the mood. "Why don't you let me look at that bite wound?"

Her eyes darkened with fury. "What are you talking about?"

"You should probably be in quarantine or something. I bet your boyfriend Corporal Young could arrange it."

"I'll run. No one is going to lock me in a cage. Never again." Her hand was on the door handle, her body twisting to make good on her words before she finished speaking.

He grabbed the collar of her jacket and pulled her back. "Stop! Listen to me. I won't say anything, but I need to look. I have a first aid kit."

The truce didn't come easily. Eventually he was cleaning the nasty, freakishly symmetrical bite wound on her right forearm without saying a word or passing judgment. In the center of the punctured flesh was a neat hole.

"I've never seen anything like this," he said, examining every detail of the damage but also thinking about the electric *A* on her attackers' helmets.

"What are you, a paramedic now? I suppose you picked up a medical degree at some truck stop when you weren't learning about disaster management," Dust said.

"I was in prison. I've seen people get shanked."

"What the hell is shanked?"

"You've never heard of getting prison shanked? Don't you watch TV?" He felt like a jerk for snapping at her. "Inmates make weapons out of whatever they can get their hands on, usually cardboard or *safety* toothbrushes."

She flinched as he cleaned the wound with hand sanitizer.

"Where do they get the cardboard?" she asked.

"Toilet paper rolls. Milk cartons. A dude has got to be creative to murder someone in prison," David said. "I've seen some weird injuries. Never anything like this. All done. How does it feel?"

"Like I was bitten by an alien. Or maybe getting stung describes it better."

He was about to respond when she tensed.

He turned to see what she was looking at, expecting an alien commando attack or the military police on their way to put her in quarantine.

What he saw was a serious-looking man moving through the crowd like the alien apocalypse hadn't just begun. He was dressed like a civilian which probably made him a federal agent.

David scanned the rest of the nervous crowd and saw

two more men following the first, several meters back and to each side like they were part of a tactical squad.

"That's my handler," Dust muttered resentfully. "Foster father, technically."

"Are you going to introduce me?" David said, wanting nothing less than a confrontation with someone he recognized as more than a run-of-the-mill cop or regular field agent. *And who calls their stepdad, or whatever, a handler?*

Dust put her back to the door, facing him across the cabin interior.

"I'll take that as a no," he said. "You can't stay in here forever. I don't know what history you have with your foster family, but it's time to make peace."

"He's not my foster dad. And I'm still not sure if the family I was placed with was even a real family. He sure didn't treat them like he cared two shits for them."

David crossed his arms. "Most people would be calling you a dramatic, overlyimaginative teenager right now."

"It's complicated and you don't want to be involved."

"I'll give you that, but it's kind of too late. You're in my truck, so I need to know what's going on. There's a difference between abusive parents and foster parents and pimps and CIA agents." He tossed in the last detail to lighten his tone but felt the weight of it immediately.

Dust tensed. Her eyes dilated. Cornered animals, trapped runaways, and prison inmates shared the same look in moments like these.

There was something else in her posture, a murderous intensity he'd only seen one other time.

"What did this guy do to you?" David felt tense, his entire body getting ready for a life-and-death struggle, even more than when the alien airships had raced down the highway blowing people to hell. He was scared and ready to fight because there was no more time to think about this.

Dust moved. David shifted to block her escape. "He's afraid to do anything to me except keep me locked down. That's the term his bosses use. *Keep her locked down,* they say it all the time. They forget I speak their language better than they do."

"It's not just you. Adults talk like kids aren't in the room half the time," David said, tracking the movements of the three men—watching them scan the crowd in search of their quarry.

"Are your problems with this guy worse than an alien death bite?" he asked, hoping she wasn't about to tell him she'd been trafficked.

"I tried to kill him."

"Because you don't want to be locked down?" David probed.

"Do you want to be locked in a box and watched twenty-four hours a day?" she snapped, eyes wet with angry tears ready to fall. "I thought I'd gotten away this time."

"All three of them are headed our way."

"There will be seven of them. They don't normally split up," Dust said, calming herself breath by breath. She cradled her injured arm but seemed resolved to make a run for it.

"Don't go anywhere." David held her eyes until he believed she understood this was the best he could do for her, then he climbed down from the cab and stood with his thumbs hooked in his belt as the top-tier federal operative reached the truck.

You're going to regret this, Osage, he thought, with a long, slow exhale to prepare himself for the confrontation.

The fed was bigger than David, maybe six foot five with

the frame of someone who played football years ago. His hair was thinning and he was well-dressed for the apocalypse. His khaki pants had been pressed when the day started. World-ending invasions had a rumpling effect on clothing, but the man looked professional. Slightly scuffed shoes that were sturdier than normal dress shoes and slacks with concealed tactical pockets. His golf shirt had a logo David immediately recognized—a cleaner version of the electric *A* inside a circle. Like a good poker player, he allowed his eyes to slide over the clue without reacting to it.

Coincidence, has to be.

"What's up, Chief?"

"Do you want to explain why you have my daughter?" The agent pointed a thick finger.

"She's eighteen." David lost sight of the other men and worried they were going to flank him or try to grab Dust while he dealt with this Jason Bourne wannabe.

The man laughed bitterly. "Is that what she told you or just what you tell yourself? You're harboring a runaway under the protection of the federal government."

He tried to push past David to the truck.

David took a firm hold of him and guided him back a step. "Chill-lax, dude. What's your name? And when did the feds take over child protective services? That's normally a state function."

"None of your business." He pushed forward again.

David shoved him with one hand, sending him back several steps. It was a testament to the man's athletic ability that he caught himself before he fell on his ass. His eyes widened in shock as he flailed his arms for balance. Apparently, he wasn't used to being pushed around, especially not by someone smaller than he was. And not by a civilian.

"I said chill out, dude. Maybe that wasn't clear enough for you. Around here, you don't go up on a man's truck without permission. I don't care if you saw the Virgin Mary up there holding baby Jesus and a fistful of Powerball winners."

"She sure as hell isn't the Virgin Mary." The man smirked. "And you definitely didn't win the lottery."

"I still don't know your name."

"You don't need to know anything about me. She's a minor. She's in federal custody."

"Doesn't look like it to me. If that's your job, you suck at it," David said, glancing back casually. He couldn't see Dust or the other two men he was still worried were trying to pull a fast one.

"She told me she's eighteen and you abused her when she was in foster care," David embellished.

The agent's tan face flushed red. "I'm going up there to get her and you can't stop me," he barked and started toward the door, but David didn't step aside.

He readied himself, shifting his weight. Sill appearing casual, David was ready to tackle or punch, depending on what the situation called for. "I'm not warning you again."

Posturing, Agent Buzz-Cut puffed out his chest and raised his voice. "What are you going to do, push me some more? I was an offensive lineman at OSU. That won't work a second time."

"How about I beat you to death?"

"Did she tell you what I do for a living, or why the government dumped her on me?"

"Nope. I didn't ask and don't care, bud. You're one step away from getting knocked out. If you're a government agent, you should have already identified yourself. So I'll tell the judge I thought you were some pervert, and all I was doing was protecting an innocent girl."

"You have no idea what you're fucking dealing with!" the man shouted, then looked around to see if anyone in the crowd was paying attention to the confrontation.

David hated how stupid the entire situation was. Tangling with feds was never a good idea. And he didn't like that *A* symbol. He barely knew Dust. This guy was right; he didn't know what the hell he was dealing with.

But a line had been drawn, and he was going to hold it—out of pure stubborn meanness if nothing else.

The agent assessed him, perhaps really looking at him for the first time. "I'll be back with the police or a state trooper or whatever legal authority I can find."

"Or the rest of your team," David suggested.

A familiar voice joined the conversation. "What problems are you causing me now, Mr. Osage?" Corporal Young said. The three National Guardsmen behind him looked tired and pissed off. Probably sleep deprived and done with the unreasonable crowds they were babysitting.

"Sorry, Young. This guy was trying to take stuff from my truck."

The agent pointed at Young then at David. "I want you to take this man into custody immediately."

Young, a soldier in his early to mid-twenties and probably already a veteran of at least one tour overseas, regarded the agent coldly. "You're not my boss, sir. Cause problems and I will deal with you."

The other guardsmen moved into position, ready for trouble.

"Listen, Corporal. I have the authority." He flipped open

his wallet, displaying something to Young. "Do what I say, and I'll be out of your hair."

The flankers David was worried about joined the party, standing silently to his right and left.

"I've never seen credentials like that. Let's go back to headquarters. If my chain of command verifies that thing is real, then I'll do what you say as long as it doesn't endanger the people under my protection," Young said.

"You'll do whatever I say no matter what," Dust's foster-father-federal-agent barked. His goons gave the guardsmen hard looks.

"We'll see. Now let's move. All three of you," Young said, raising his M16 a half inch to indicate the direction he wanted them to go.

"You're going to regret this," the agent said.

"I regret a lot of things, sir," Young said, voice dry as a desert in Afghanistan.

CHAPTER EIGHT

WHILE THE FEDS and the guardsmen faced off, David retreated.

"Are you okay?" Dust asked after he climbed into the truck and was squeezing the steering wheel hard enough to make the veins stand up on his forearms.

"Yep," he said, not looking at her.

"Was it your temper that got you locked up?"

"I wasn't angry. When I'm mad, I lose control," he admitted. "This is something else. Walking away from a fight has never been easy for me."

"Good thing that soldier came and stopped it."

"Yeah, good thing." He reviewed the incident, looking for any details he missed. In prison, breaking down every near-death encounter taught him which mistakes would get him shanked or thrown in isolation.

He needed more information. "Who is that man? What's his name, what does he do?"

"His name is William Boyne. He works for the government," Dust said.

"Really? I thought maybe he worked for the Make a Wish Foundation," David said.

"Don't be a jerk," she said, but her rejoinder was tired and sounded defeated. "They assigned him to me the last time I escaped. He caught me easily and probably got a promotion or something. The first time, he was working with a partner. Now he has a team."

David studied her body language, comparing what she said to how she acted.

"You shouldn't have picked me up," she said quietly. "I shouldn't have run."

"Why did you run?"

"They hurt me, David. And I'm not going back," she said. "But that doesn't mean you need to be involved. This isn't your problem."

"It is now, and fuck that guy," David said, turning his attention back to the still growing camp. "I meant what I told him. No one walks up on my truck and tells me what to do."

New arrivals were directed to a grassy field turned into a parking lot with orange road cones to designate lanes. Cars, trucks, campers, and a group of motorcycles arrived and did as they were told. David didn't see Young in the group of soldiers directing the newcomers and wondered if he was off-duty or was getting his ass chewed by a superior for shutting down the federal agents.

"I need to pee," Dust said.

"It's not a good time," David said. "You told me there would be seven agents. I only saw three. Leaving the truck is risky."

"We can't stay in here forever," she replied, setting aside

her guitar case and climbing into the front passenger's seat. "I wish we'd never stopped here."

"You and me both," David agreed, watching an argument between refugees over their 'property line.'

"I've been holding it for an hour. Don't you have a bladder?"

He handed her an empty bottle. "Here's your new bladder."

"That's gross! Do you really pee in bottles? How do you do that while driving?" she asked with morbid fascination.

"Very carefully," he said, and they both laughed.

Tears ran down her cheeks as she fought her mirth. "Now I really have an emergency. I'm going right now."

"Okay, okay," David said.

Dust bailed from the truck and hurried toward the row of porta-potties at the edge of the parking lot.

David locked up his truck and followed her. Leaving everything he owned behind, even briefly, worried him in this environment, but he was still in a decent mood from the laugh fest. He knew he shouldn't be cracking jokes because alien invasions were serious as fuck, but he didn't care. It was good to let go.

No one realized it yet, but law and order were a thing of the past. He hadn't needed to shoot anyone at the turnaround spot, but he would have. That brought him back to reality. He scanned the crowd, sweeping his eyes left to right and then back to center, careful to check Dust's location often. She was too far ahead of him for comfort but he didn't want to start pushing people around.

The camp was getting crowded. From his truck, the growing number of stranded travelers had seemed academic. On the ground it was frightening. There were thousands of people here, each of them reacting differently to the crisis.

Violence wasn't really his thing anymore. He put on a good show, which prevented him from having to get dirty. But he'd been ready to kill people to keep them away from his rig. What worried him was the sudden return of his anger. He'd gone through a lot of counseling to get it under control. He still didn't know where it came from.

Charles and his parents had told him he had a hero complex and just couldn't accept defeat. To them, he was the ultimate type A personality.

But Laura had it right. Or at least that's what he hoped. She said he didn't have a hero complex, he had a guardian complex. His parents and his brother didn't get the difference even when Laura explained it. Basically, David couldn't tolerate bullies, abusers, or predators. The federal agent, William Boyne, was probably all three—or that's what his instincts were telling him.

For one moment, he worried Boyne wouldn't file a complaint to have Young chastised or demoted, but would just pull him into the shadows and murder him.

If David had had any feel-good juice running through his veins, it was gone now. The end of the world sucked. People were desperate and the predator personalities were going to run amok.

There were a lot of men and women on the road who didn't share his sense of right and wrong.

Dust reminded him of his little sister. She even looked a bit like her. But that wasn't the only reason he wanted to protect her. Of all the people he'd seen in the last few hours, she seemed like she had the best head on her shoulders. If this was Armageddon, it was time to surround himself with survivors. She'd given the finger to the federal government after all, and that wasn't easy for a girl on her own.

Dust wove through the growing crowd of refugees, keeping her eyes on the ground. She pulled up the hood of the shirt she was wearing, not a sweatshirt but some lighter fabric. She had probably been around enough to know that a cute young thing like her attracted the wrong kind of attention anyway, much less in a world about to go lawless. Even if Boyne and his team weren't looking for her, she'd be smart to keep a low profile.

Dust got in line and waited quietly. Corporal Young and his friends were back and were also keeping an eye on her. They seemed like a good group. In their current roles, David trusted them to do the right thing. It helped him relax—and he needed to, because now that the anger had returned, he needed to be in control. Going into a rage now would only get him killed.

He ducked behind the plastic outhouses and relieved himself. Waiting in lines wasn't really his thing, either. And he wasn't staying here. The decision was abrupt and easy. Nothing good was going to come of this refugee camp.

In front of the porta-potties, Dust was still in line but getting closer. She shifted her weight from foot to foot, almost dancing.

David stepped onto the bumper of the waste removal truck to get a better view of the crowd. William Boyne was out there somewhere with six agents. He wondered if Dust was telling the truth about trying to kill him.

What the hell have I gotten myself into? Reality pressed on him. The cycle was familiar—conflict, followed by rage, followed by self-doubt and regret.

Dust finally got her turn, slamming the plastic door behind her. David breathed a sigh of relief. She was out of sight for a few moments at least. He looked back toward his rig. It was still there, in all of its battered glory. The problem now was that other truckers were blocking him in. There was no way he could get out with the trailer hooked up.

Fewer and fewer vehicles were pulling into the lot. A shambling crowd of pedestrians arrived with nothing to eat or drink. Tired, hungry, and windblown, they looked ready to give up.

David approached Corporal Young on the perimeter. "How are you doing, Corporal?"

"Five by five, Mr. Osage."

"Sorry about that guy," David said. "I think he beat on Dust before she ran away."

"Is she a juvenile?" Young asked, as though one answer would allow him to play dumb and another would require him to take official action.

"She told me she's eighteen and that the guy isn't her dad," David said. "Foster dad, the bad kind."

Young nodded like that was good enough for him—for now. His expression suggested he was also having regrets about the confrontation.

David desperately wanted to know what happened to Agent William Boyne. Seconds passed. Neither spoke. He knew better than to pursue the question.

Corporal Young broke the silence. "So what can I do for you? Or did you decide to surrender your firearm?"

"I think I'd better keep it." David jerked his chin toward

the sad road march of refugees. "Why are there so many and why are they all coming here?"

Young, his expression grim, replied, "All the population centers are in chaos, even small towns like Salina. The emergency broadcast system listed our base as a shelter right before it went off the air. Everyone in the area is coming here. There were a lot of people on the road as well."

"Why aren't the invaders hitting this camp? I bet they were monitoring that channel," David said. "These people wouldn't stand a chance."

"That would be a good question if I were allowed to acknowledge the existence of invaders." Young looked like he was tired of the game. "Official word is that whoever these... aggressors... are, they want as many of us alive as possible. We have no offensive capabilities."

David didn't like the sound of that, not after what he had seen. "Thanks. I'm ready to move on but a couple of fuel trucks blocked me in."

"Can't help you," Young said. "Sorry."

"Is there any news about the invasion? Are we winning or losing?"

Young's face reddened, irritated that David kept throwing the truth in his face. "Didn't you hear me? We're not supposed to call it an invasion."

"Have you seen them up close?"

"Have you?"

David stalled. "Define up close."

"I was just wondering, because there are claw marks on both your doors."

"Weird, huh?"

Young didn't laugh. Hard experience showed through the veil of his youthful appearance. He'd probably been deployed at least once and stayed in the Guard to pay for college or something.

"Things are going to get strange. Keep your head on a swivel, Corporal Young."

"Are you going somewhere?" the soldier asked.

"Away from here, first chance I get."

"This is a good place to be now that the incident is over," Young said.

"Invasion," David corrected. "And I doubt it's over. I need to round up the kid and get her out of this crowd."

"Probably a good idea. Good luck to both of you. I mean that. Tell her to hang onto the guitar if she can. I've seen a lot of people ditching too much of their lives already."

"We'll do our best. Thanks, Corporal." David waited for Dust to emerge from the porta-potty until he was sure he'd missed her, which caused a knot of nervous panic in his belly.

He approached one of the disaster management volunteers. "Did you see a young woman, blonde hair, new clothing, hiking boots come out in the last five minutes?"

"Be patient, sir, it's not like she can fall in one of these," the woman said. "Give her some space."

"I saw her," said another volunteer. "She headed toward the Red Cross truck, maybe to get some food."

"Thanks," David said, then hurried toward the food line.

Checking himself, he stopped short of the crowd and looked around. This wasn't like him. He knew better than to rush to failure. How many times had he avoided getting shanked in prison or caught by police during his hardcore street racing days?

The only way to win was to be smart, and to do that, he needed good information. Studying the crowd methodically he spotted one of Boyne's goons. The man's clothing was logoed with the *A*, but this time it was athletic gear—running pants and a waterproof jacket with reflective striping on the sleeves and the collar. It was one of those brands that had both casual and athletic wear options. *And it definitely has the symbol.*

And he moved like Boyne had. Fit and aggressive, he also appeared smart enough not to tip his hand early.

David didn't like this at all. He had dealt with authority figures all his life, mostly because of his bad decisions. But he'd had positive interactions from time to time and didn't fight authority just for shits and grins—not anymore. Boyne and his men gave him a very bad feeling.

A group of bikers were hanging out, as relaxed as though this wasn't the end of the world, and drinking beer. Some of them whistled at girls but they weren't really bothering anyone. David didn't join their party but edged close enough that a casual observer would assume he was with them. Because, tattoos.

The ruse worked flawlessly. Two of Boynes's men went past, not recognizing him. He watched them gather intelligence, then meet Boyne to report.

Unable to find Dust among the thousands of refugees, he followed the agents instead. They searched in vain and eventually went into a temporary shelter where they did secret agent shit or whatever.

David let out a breath he'd been holding too long. Confident they didn't have Dust, he went back to his truck, but watched it for a time before approaching.

Before long, he saw two men in blue jeans and expensive flannel shirts—the kind that off-duty cops liked to wear to conceal sidearms—drinking coffee. They were near the truck but not close enough to make their presence obvious.

He backed away and set up his own stakeout for Dust. He could get into the truck without being seen, but wasn't sure if she would spot these guys.

Still, something told him she was even better at this game than he was, and that made him nervous.

CHAPTER NINE

WHEN SHE RETURNED, Dust looked like she'd taken a shower and had a good night's sleep. She'd also picked up a new jacket somewhere, one that lacked bite marks. If her arm hurt, she hid it well.

"Dust," he said, and guided her away from the agents.

"There you are." She glanced in the general direction of the feds. "I wasn't sure if they'd already picked you up."

"I don't think I'm gonna let anybody pick me up, not with the way the world is headed." David couldn't stop marveling over how all the rules had changed. He wasn't sure if it was terrifying or liberating. "If you ask me, anyone who stops moving is going to have problems. Getting jammed up by the feds will definitely slow us down."

"Us?" she asked.

David didn't respond. Instead, he led her around to the other side of the truck and held a finger to his lips. Carefully opening the door, he motioned for her to climb in and keep her head down.

"Won't they see us?" she asked when they were inside.

"The angle is bad. Just stay in the sleeper and don't move around a lot until we figure out what to do."

David wondered what it was like in Chicago where his sister the cop worked, or Seattle, where his brother was a software engineer—game designer or something.

Very little of what he'd seen here bolstered his confidence in humanity. The volunteers were quickly overwhelmed by people who weren't equipped to survive without climate control and fast food.

The soldiers and civilian cops became less patient with each incident. He looked for—and saw—a few examples of small groups pulling together and helping each other, but it wasn't enough.

Everyone had a look of tired expectation, like was going to be over in a few days. Some of them probably knew better, but hope was all they had.

"You did pretty well for yourself. Maybe you want to stay," David said.

Dust smiled tiredly. "I'm going with you."

"I thought you'd say that. There's no time like the present. Buckle up," he said. "Boyne will be back with reinforcements and a National Guard officer. I won't be able to tell them no a second time."

Dust looked grim. "No, you won't."

"Glad we're on the same page, because we're leaving," he said.

"I saw those trucks pulling in," she said, skepticism in her voice. "You think you can drive around them?"

"I took some things from the trailer, then dropped it. I've never failed to deliver a load but there's a first time for everything. Without that thing behind us, I should be able to pick my way back to the highway. I don't think the

National Guard will stop me. We're leaving the good stuff and we're two fewer mouths to feed. But staying isn't an option. If Boyne has any real power, or if he has superiors who can give orders to the National Guard, we'll be in big trouble."

A few people looked around when he started the engine. No one tried to block him. He pulled the chain on his air horn to get some civilians out of his way and was soon clear of what was becoming a city.

"We're going to take southbound I-135, then US 254 to avoid Wichita if we can—if my rig holds up. Not sure good things will be happening in the cities," he said, thinking out loud. "We'll avoid them as long as the truck holds up and we have fuel. If not, we'll make a quick stop to grab my car, get in and get out."

Dust patted him on the arm. "Okay, wake me up when we get someplace."

Bringing her with him had been a risk. He wasn't sure why he'd done it but was strangely at ease with the situation.

"Do you have anything besides Nora Roberts and country music?" Dust asked.

"How about AC/DC?"

"Ugh."

"Check the center console. It's deep. I rent most of the audiobooks from truck stops, but I own a few. I download the newer ones when I can." David said, watching her dive into his collection. He drove with half of his attention on the empty road and half on her. He appreciated how carefully she handled his property.

"This truck is literally everything I have," he said to test her reaction. She had far less going for her and no prospects.

Most girls her age, especially if she was as young as she looked, would jump to compare miseries.

Dust had only what she could carry. Her only real asset was youth. In his experience, youth was a cruel gift because it was nearly impossible to appreciate until it was too late.

"You didn't own the trailer?" she asked.

He smiled.

"What?"

"That was a test. I was wondering if you would start crying about how much harder your life is than mine. I didn't own the trailer, just the rig. Works like this: get a contract, move the load, pick up a new load, and head back the other way. Easy."

"Would your sister think it's easy?"

"She'd think it's boring. My brother—he's a software designer with a family in Washington State—would think it's easy. But he'd never risk proving himself wrong by trying it out. Smart kid. A little soft around the edges."

"Your brother's a kid with a family?"

David laughed. "No, he's a grown man."

"But still your little brother."

"Exactly. What are we listening to?"

She held up *The Eye of the World* by Robert Jordan. "This looks interesting. I like the people riding horses. They're on a journey, I think, just like us."

"Put it in. Tell me what you think."

The characters in the book were about to be attacked by Fades and Trollocs when David pulled into a rest stop north of Wichita.

"Why stop here?" Dust asked, pausing the story.

"I need to think this through, see if anyone has information on the road ahead. We haven't seen one vehicle. I thought there would be people camping here. There's water, toilets, and some vending machines. It looks like everyone pressed on or never made it this far."

"I'm not a fan of dark rest stops," she said. "Yes, Mr. Osage, I have hitchhiked a lot more than you assumed."

"Maybe on the next stretch of road we'll talk more and listen to audiobooks less. If we're going to travel through the end of the world together, we should trust each other."

"I was just getting into the book."

He parked the rig and faced her.

"Why are you letting me stay with you? Should I be worried?"

"Maybe you should. What exactly do you have to offer a guy like me? You can't fight, you don't know anything, you're in trouble with the law—Boyne will be asking some hard questions of anyone harboring you."

"I know things."

David nodded. "Don't take this the wrong way, but you're not old enough to know much I haven't already done ten times. I've been around."

"I know how to survive. And you have no idea how old I am."

He winked and pointed a finger at her like a pistol. "That's why I let you back in my truck."

"You don't think those people back there will survive, not even Corporal Young?"

"He might. I misjudged him at first."

"What about the rest?" she asked with genuine interest.

"Only by accident."

That made her think. He almost regretted the harsh words.

"And Boyne? How will he do in this nightmare?" Dust asked.

"He might be the real nightmare."

Silence.

The sky above them looked like it was the entire universe. He breathed it in and suddenly had the feeling it was all gone, or would be soon.

"You said we needed to trust each other, so I guess that means being totally freaking honest even when it sucks," she said. "Does that include omissions?"

"What are you talking about?"

The girl didn't reply but curled up with her earbuds in. David slammed the door shut.

"*THIS IS the Emergency Broadcast Network. If you have found shelter, remain in place and wait for contact by government officials. The United States and her allies have engaged the invaders on all fronts. The alien threat is a clear and present danger. All is not lost. Battles have been won. Remain where you are and be prepared to act when called upon to do so.*"

David sat up, rubbing his eyes and wondering how long he'd been out. Saying he slept well would have been a straight lie. In his nightmares, space vampires fed on the refugees—stabbing men, women, children through their throats with spike-like tongues. Corporal Young and his friends stood by, watching, directing traffic—smiling because their leaders finally allowed them to call an invasion an invasion. One of them carried a huge guidon on a pole. In the center of fabric that twinkled like the night sky was a crackling letter *A* stretched across the moon—or something that looked like the moon.

Alien feeding zone, this way. Please show your intergalactic identification papers before entering the kill zone...

He relived the attack at the turnaround point over and over. It was like his mind worried he might forget how real the danger was. Razor-sharp teeth, hate-filled eyes, and the feeder appendage he'd thought was a tongue or a mouth stinger... The world was going to hell and he couldn't get to his sister or his brother.

"This is the Emergency Broadcast Network. If you have found shelter, remain in place and wait for contact by government officials. The United States and her allies have engaged..."

David sat up straighter than he had since the crisis began. He hadn't expected the military to last this long. Any species able to travel en masse to another star system had to be more advanced in every way. Still, Earth had the home court advantage.

He turned off the radio on the third repetition of the message.

Dust came from one of the vending machines with cold, disgusting coffee. He climbed down from the truck and took a cup.

Dust smiled. "Good morning."

"Hell yeah, it's a good morning. Did you hear the broadcast?"

She shook her head. He turned on the radio long enough for her to hear it start to finish. Her reaction was hopeful but guarded, probably because she wasn't an idiot.

Dew sparkled in the grass all the way to a windbreak of trees that would never have grown here if someone hadn't planted them. Orange-gold sunlight gleamed off everything.

Blue skies and white streaks of cloud stretched over the prairie.

He sipped the bitter drink someone claimed was coffee. A guy he met at a diner a couple of weeks ago had explained to him that some coffee could be stored in warehouses for ten years before being used, and that most of that ended up in vending machines or hospitals.

The thought faded when the contrails appeared. Dread battered against hope. "Looks like round two is about to begin."

She turned to see, giving him the impression she understood this time would be worse. He didn't know where his belief came from—gut instinct, maybe—but it was real.

A hundred contrails became thousands of ships. Before long the blue horizon was blotted out by vapor trails. He couldn't see the ships landing but he did see the response from NORAD.

A wing of jet fighters streaked across the sky, missiles racing ahead of them.

David climbed into his truck and started it. The engine shook the cab as it roared to life.

"They don't stand a chance," Dust said, climbing into her seat.

"Nope. But I think they're just a tactic—an attempt to pin the new aliens in one place while we do something stupid," he said, bile burning in his throat.

"Like what?" she asked.

He pointed at the mushroom cloud on the horizon. "Like that."

He waited for an electromagnetic pulse to shut down his truck. He wondered if he was doomed to live with cancerous sores all over his body and flesh rotting off his bones.

Three large alien ships veered away from the others at near the same moment the nuke detonated, firing energy beams that converged to form a bubble around the explosion. The effect might have taken seconds or minutes, but felt like hours to David.

The mushroom cloud turned into a roiling tempest inside the bubble, then shrank to nothing. It was like the explosion had been forced through a window into nowhere.

Or that's what it looked like.

"I can't believe that just happened," David muttered.

Dust didn't say a word.

"I should be relieved, I guess, but I'm really not. We're FUBAR'd."

She regarded the growing number of airships in the distance and said nothing.

"If they can neutralize nuclear warheads, including the fallout that should be hitting in about thirty minutes, then we are way outclassed," David said.

"Was there any doubt?" Dust said, so quietly that he wasn't sure she'd meant him to hear it.

"Keep your eyes open for mushroom clouds," he said, then dialed through the radio until he'd checked every possible news service on the AM and FM bands.

"Jackknife southbound for anyone," he said into the mic. "Who's on the road with me?"

"Beanbox reads you, Jackknife. Did you see the light show?"

"I did, Beanbox. What's your 20?"

"Southbound at Moundridge. I don't think there's fallout." The man had a smoker's voice and sounded drunker than David normally heard on the road. "How's that possible? What the hell is going on?"

Static garbled the transmission. David could hear other people talking and he wanted to be part of the conversation. That was normal. That was the sort of thing he understood.

"Jackknife southbound, does anyone copy?"

Dust looked at him sadly, and for one crazy instant, she wasn't a kid but an old soul—still young on the outside, but someone who had been around and learned the hardest lessons life had to teach.

David drove past a truck stop without slowing.

Dust looked at him questioningly. "Aren't you going to get gas and beef jerky?"

"I'm betting the fuel pumps are already dry, and there could be trouble," he said. "It might be too soon for people to go Mad Max, but I worry about the forward thinkers who understand supply and demand and the principle of taking what you want by force."

She thought about that, absentmindedly rubbing her injured arm.

"Beef jerky." He shook his head in mock digest.

"So we're going to drive around the country until you run out of fuel?"

"No. There's a pretty big ranch up here, a small privately owned feedlot. They have diesel fuel for their tractors and a small fleet of trucks. Guy named Bob Jackson runs it. We might be able to help each other out."

She raised an eyebrow. "Really? What do you have that he would want?"

"News. It's not much, but it might be worth something," he said, not meeting her eyes.

"Whatever. You're not telling me all of it. Who is this guy to you?"

He forced down a sudden wave of anger. This girl he

barely knew could push his buttons like no one he'd ever met. "You're a nosy little…"

"Nosy little what?" she demanded.

David used the progressive relaxation technique he'd learned in court-ordered anger management class. Inhale, hold his breath, release slowly.

Dust waited.

"His son was in El Dorado Prison when I got there. Some gangs were giving him a hard time. I helped him out. Herb, his boy, never thanked me for saving his life but when I got out, Bob Jackson made sure I had a job. Paid my tuition and testing fees to get my CDL. Sent the word around to some trucking companies basically telling them to give me a job," he said. The words sounded strange because he'd never spoken them aloud before.

"How did you save his son's life?" Dust asked.

"I shanked a couple of people."

She snorted. "I'm surprised you're not still in prison."

"I did a little extra time, but the crew I went up against was out of control. They'd attacked some guards. My self-defense plea got more weight than maybe it should have."

"Wow, you're a regular hero."

David squeezed the steering wheel so forcefully his knuckles hurt. What pissed him off was that she was right. "I'm not proud of the shit I did."

When he looked at her, her eyes held more understanding and compassion than a girl her age should have.

"Was it a milk carton or a toilet paper roll?" she asked.

"What?"

"The shank, what'd you make it out of?"

"I used my early release paperwork. Rolled it up so tight it was like stabbing the guy with a pencil."

"You were going to get out early but went after this gang boss instead? How long did it add to your sentence?"

"Two years," he said.

"Was it worth it?"

He hesitated, looking for his turn. "We'll find out. If Mr. Jackson can help us with fuel and shelter, I'll probably feel like it was time well spent."

"I'm glad you helped Jackson," she said. "And not just because he might give us stuff."

"You're assuming his son was a good man who deserved saving."

"Was he?"

David wasn't sure how to express himself. "He was a decent guy, but flawed. His addiction took him down about a month after he was released."

His truck rattled down the off-ramp and onto a small country highway, a two-lane affair with no shoulder between the asphalt and a deep ditch on each side.

Kansas was a flat state with few exceptions in the rolling plains. It seemed flatter when driving on the interstate because engineers had leveled parts of the terrain and cut through what passed for hills in this region. Away from major highways, the roads went up and down like a roller coaster. His truck struggled on the inclines and raced down the declines.

He saw signs of trouble long before they reached the feedlot. Some of the pastureland was scorched. One field held slaughtered cows near a water trough.

Dust sat up straight and peered out the window. "Don't stop."

"I wasn't going to, but now I have to look."

"They're only animals." Moisture in her eyes revealed suppressed emotions that conflicted with her hard words.

He parked the truck and walked into the field. The world seemed quiet. His actions felt portentous, and he sensed he wouldn't like what he was about to learn.

The cows had in fact been slaughtered but they'd been stampeded in a circle first. He looked at the intentional chaos and destruction. The animal corpses had been sucked dry then smashed apart. He felt rage building inside.

Dust touched his shoulder, then stood beside him with her arms crossed. Tears ran down her cheeks. "That's the most horrible thing I've ever seen."

"Who the fuck are these assholes?" he asked, examining a cluster of holes in one of the cows. "Whoever... whatever did this was out of control. This was about violence. A feeding frenzy or something."

"Can we go back to your truck?"

"That's a good idea. I'd hate to be here if the freaks who did this came back," he said, then glanced toward the glow of the feedlot lights over the next hill. "I not sure Mr. Jackson will be able to help us."

"So what do we do now?"

"I need to check on him and his people," David said.

"Does he have a family?"

"No. Not anymore. But he employs a lot of people around here," David said, striding toward his Peterbilt. She ran to catch up.

Before long, he was nursing the big vehicle forward. They crested the hill and looked across to the sweeping panorama of gently rolling grasslands. The feedlot was intact. David had expected there to be bloodied carnage after seeing the slaughtered animals. Instead, he found the organization of a professional army.

Spaceships were parked at each corner of the facility. Bob and his workers moved cattle from one pen to another. Armed guards loomed over them.

"What are they doing?" Dust asked.

David considered the scene for several moments. "I think they're counting the livestock. What we have here, are a bunch of intergalactic cattle rustlers."

Dust stared at him, wide-eyed and incredulous. A heartbeat passed, and they began to laugh hysterically.

They sobered as a few dozen of the cows were led toward aliens. Half of them took off their helmets and bent to feed on the livestock. David couldn't see the details, only shapes and movement.

He didn't look away. Expecting savagery was one thing, but this was organized like a military chow hall. It didn't match up to what he had witnessed in the field when they turned off the highway.

Tears filled Dust's eyes. "I wish we hadn't come here."

"We need fuel," David said as he looked in his rearview mirror. Leaving the truck in neutral, he disengaged the brake and allowed it to roll backward. Getting to the bottom of the hill was easy. Making the seventeen point turn it took to get moving the other direction was difficult and slow.

"I shouldn't have thought big," David said. "All the farms in this area keep diesel for their tractors and grain trucks. Hopefully we'll find some fuel we can use before I run out."

"What if it's the same everywhere?"

He shrugged. "I'm betting the invaders are focusing on the big fish before mopping up us little people."

CHAPTER TEN

LAURA STARED at her feet as she walked. Light hurt her eyes. Sounds boomed through her head. All she wanted was to get away from the monsters guarding her. A tendril of alien flesh bound her wrists. Light pulsed in rhythm with the hot, throbbing vein that fed her blood into the tendril that nourished itself as it restrained her.

"There are easier ways to handcuff a prisoner," she muttered. She hated the feel of the restraints. Feeling the pulse of an animal who not only wanted to feed on her, but hated her.

The alien walking behind her hissed angry laughter. "You know how to capture people. For this reason, you will be useful to the Fosk-ha."

"Not on your life, freak," Laura said. "Get this fucking parasite off me."

"Those are not polite words in your language," one of her captors said, almost laughing at her.

"Eat shit, space jerk!"

The guard on her left slammed the butt of his rifle into

her side. She fell to her knees, thrusting her bound hands forward. Asphalt scraped flesh from her palms. The alien guard kicked her in the ribs, smashing her sideways.

The leader who had taken such a liking to her cursed at the guards but did not make them stop. Their language was painful to hear. Some syllables felt like holes in her awareness—objects she couldn't hear or comprehend.

Curling into a ball, she wiggled closer to a nearby sewer. If someone had asked her a week ago whether she could fit into a drainage opening, she would've said no way. Now she was ready to try anything.

Images of drowning after she plummeted face-first daunted her only slightly. She had to try something. The one who had been abusing her realized what she was attempting and grabbed for her belt. She couldn't see what he was doing but thought he had one long finger through her empty holster where they had taken her sidearm.

Down she went, headfirst into the murky gloom, while her captors screamed and hissed. She splashed into stagnant water, clipping the edge of the walkway with one shoulder on the way in.

She floundered. Kicking with her feet, grabbing with her bound hands, and twisting onto her back she was able to keep her head above the surface of the shallow water. Twenty feet above her, back lit by streetlamps, were three alien faces slashing the air with overlong tongues.

Painful ranting turned into a sonic attack. She heard the first few seconds of their screams before the volume overwhelmed her senses, or perhaps her mind's willingness to interpret the audio input. She felt distortion in the airwaves all around her. Screaming like she never had before, she couldn't compete with the barbershop quartet from hell.

Air seemed to freeze in her lungs. She shivered uncontrollably as she fought the urge to seek warmth. Her arms and legs felt cold, heavy, and weak the farther she fled her captors.

Time lost meaning. She traveled a long distance through a concrete tube not much bigger than she was. Where was the old brick labyrinth every monster movie showed under the city? All she had was darkness leading her nowhere.

Dank air, slime, bugs—this was her world now. Pain raged through the bite wound on her leg and she was cold. Her nerves felt like they were on fire sheathed in the absolute icy blackness of deep space.

"I should have done what they said, then looked for a chance to escape."

Several minutes of crawling forward on her belly passed.

They killed Sans and the guys from Baker Sector.

She stopped, crying into her hands, fiercely glad she was in the one place absolutely no one would see her.

When she could move, cold hatred gave her strength. "I'll never submit."

The restraints around her wrists bulged. That was when she realized what her guards had been doing each time they checked the bonds. They'd been sipping away some of the blood the parasite collected from her. Now it was too full for its own good.

She wasn't sure, but thought it wanted to be done with her. Reaching toward the ground, she placed the toe of her boot on the parasitic restraint and pried the creature free. It hit the concrete and wiggled away.

"Bye," she spat sarcastically, wishing she had the strength to kill it or the wits left to say something clever.

Time passed, and she began the cycle of arguments again.

"I won't submit. They lie. All they do is lie. They won't let me help my people; they are here to enslave them."

But what if I can keep humans from needless death and suffering?

Each time she worked through the dilemma, her conviction weakened. She moved slower and trembled more violently.

What had the alien meant about the blood power of this planet? Had something been lost in translation? She understood they were a bunch of blood-drinking freaks, from somewhere… *else*, but the leader had meant something specific. Like she was going to thank him later.

Light shone from behind her. Something metal made rhythmic crawling sounds. Another cyborg-drone was after her. This one had spider legs by the sound of it. It killed something that shrieked mournfully, probably the parasite that had been used to bind her hands.

What the hell am I doing here?

Scraping the final section of undamaged flesh from her elbows, she sprinted forward—except that she was nearly prone, barely moving, and trembling uncontrollably instead of performing any maneuver that could be described as sprint-like.

She wished David was here. He had always been the one she ran to when she hurt herself on the playground, not her parents and definitely not Charles.

Tears streamed down her face to mix with the snot running from her nose. "Get away, David! Save yourself!"

Nothing she said or did made sense. This was what it was like to be a blindly fleeing animal.

Her alien hunters hissed in their inhuman language, then repeated the horrible English they used to demand she stop.

The cyborg spiders clattered after her, every click and scrape of their pointed legs sounding like fingernails on a chalkboard.

"Goddamn it! I can't do this," she gasped, but struggled toward a pinprick of moonlight.

The drain opened into a concrete ditch she recognized. More than a few times, she'd been sent down here to roust camps of homeless people, men mostly but also women. None of the dregs were here now. They'd been smart enough to move on or had been run off.

She ducked into a structure made from cardboard and army surplus blankets. A shopping cart without wheels anchored the shelter on one end and an old wide-screen television on the other in. She remembered it from her first week of field training. It hadn't worked then but each new group of homeless people kept it. Maybe it had sentimental value to the area.

Putting her back to the old TV, she shivered uncontrollably. Her hair was loose and filthy, hanging down around her dirty face.

I'm in hell.

She sat that way for a long time, only rousing herself when she heard a man running from one of the aliens, except this alien was different from the soldiers.

It looked almost as ragged and crazy as the homeless men she'd often encountered here. The creature made no attempt to hide its feeder tongue as it tackled a human male. Horrible hissing sounds filled the night air. The alien squealed in its terrible language, sounding rushed and insane. There wasn't a way to know if this one was different, but she thought it was more savage and crazy than the others.

What it did to the homeless man… she didn't want to see.

More aliens shambled along the spillway, each as shabby as the asshole still feeding on the hapless victim that could have been Laura if she'd shown herself. She watched in horror as the man's body crumpled inward from the force of the alien's sucking.

Laura fell to one side and dry heaved.

A dozen disheveled aliens spotted her.

She levered herself into a standing position and floundered away from the growing horde. Her muscles ached. She felt like she was freezing and burning at the same time. Nothing mattered but getting away from these things.

Climbing the side of the slanted spillway tore up her already damaged hands. She left bloody prints and drag marks in her wake. Getting to the street above felt like it took a lifetime, but eventually she made it and found herself staggering toward a squad of alien soldiers.

The one that had bitten her and seemed so keen to keep her in captivity came to the front of the squad as others drove away the crazy looking feeder aliens who had savaged the homeless camp.

She faced down the tall alien. Images of her being bitten polluted her vision, then mingled with the memory of the homeless man being sucked dry…

She heaved on the street, muscles spasming hard enough to make her cry in misery.

The alien boss watched, waited, and refused to let any of the others near her.

On her hands and knees now, she looked—tears in her eyes and drool mixing with the blood on her chin. "Who the hell are you?"

"We are the Fosk-ha and you will serve us," the squad leader said, standing over her, staring down with grim conviction. "I thought you might escape—truly escape. It would have been impressive, but terribly bad for you and all of your tribe-family."

Laura didn't even have the energy to curse. She wanted to die.

"Carry her," the Fosk-ha leader said. "There are too many over-feeders in this neighborhood. She doesn't understand our ways or the favor we are doing for her."

Other aliens rasped in their own language.

God, she hated that sound, loathed their words, dreaded the sight of them. Euphoria returned the moment she quit attempting to escape. The cool bliss washed over her, and she hated herself for her weakness.

Gazing across the plaza near the bus station on Baker Sector, she saw other aliens without armor swarming through a traffic jam to rip men, women, and children from cars. The wild, undisciplined Fosk-ha sank their faces into throats and armpits and groins. Blood spurted into the air, spraying their strange faces and bodies.

What revolted her was the thrashing spike-like tongues they used to drain victims.

"Why didn't that happen to me?" she asked. "Why am I still alive?"

"Because I am Hahn-Foek-hon, highborn of the star tribe-clan-family. Not all Fosk-ha have the discipline to rule. They cannot control themselves, so they cannot control lesser creatures. You were foolish to run from my warriors." He pointed at her and one of the guards attached a new parasite restraint to her wrists.

"You think you're one of the good guys?" Laura said, incredulously.

"We care not for good or bad as you understand it. To survive the void, all races must bind with the cryo-virus."

Laura felt stronger already. She strained against the living handcuffs sipping her life blood. "Let me go!"

"Do not ask this of me again. You may save many of your people, or you may proudly resist and cause them all to die. Badly. At the mercy of the over-feeders. Or in the chambers of the Ysik."

Laura quit moving. Her skin was on fire. She understood it was the burning pain of extreme cold. She also knew that the next time she tried to escape, they would kill her. And maybe that would be for the best.

CHAPTER ELEVEN

THE TRUCK WAS PARKED a quarter mile behind them when David's phone rang, illuminating the plowed field with the shockingly bright screen. His ringtone blared Metallica.

"Shhhh!" Dust hissed as she crouched low to the ground.

"The dirt clods and corn husks don't care how loud we are," David grumbled. "Hello, Charles? I can barely hear you, brother. Are you okay? Where's your family?"

Dust moved away, losing herself in the shadows. He felt her watching him. "Speak up, Charles. I can't hear you. We've got a bad connection."

The conversation went where all their conversations had gone over the last ten years, nowhere. He hung up, frustrated.

"What did he say?" Dust asked.

"Said he had to go, or they'd kick his family out of the bunker. Wasn't making a lot of sense. Something about video games being too hard and asked me if I ever beat one of his story lines," David said, putting the phone in vibrate mode and slipping it into his pocket.

"Have you?"

He looked at her incredulously. "I don't play video games."

"Right. Too busy driving."

He shrugged. "My prison guards talked about their games all the time, never stopping to think I had no idea what they were raving about. Got on my nerves. But, you know, you try to be nice. Smile and nod and all that. Since then, I've become anti video games, social media, fake news, real news…"

"Basically anti everything."

"You make it sound ugly." He looked at the silhouette of his truck, then toward the dark farmhouse. "We should've walked up the road. I've got a feeling the family here will shoot us or turn loose their dogs."

"How do you know there will be a family?"

"Farms are labor intensive," he said. "Everyone over age five works."

"That's not an answer."

David didn't want to explain everything and his tone revealed some of his annoyance. "I've never been to a farm that wasn't run by a family. Sometimes there are three generations living on the property. It's just the way it is around here."

He walked toward the long gravel driveway, making no attempt to hide his approach. If the place were abandoned, he'd stock up, refuel, and move on. If there were people, things would be more complicated. Dust fell in beside him and remained watchful.

"We need to get from here to Seattle. My brother said

something about a bunker. He'll have the best information." David sensed movement on the front porch of the house. "We'll pay for what we take here and share news. Once we make it to my brother's company bunker, I'll find someplace safe for you."

"No, let's go anywhere but there."

David waved away her words. "I know what I'm doing. Been thinking the entire time you were sleeping."

"If we're going to Seattle, why have you been driving south all night?" Dust asked.

He shrugged, most of his attention on the direction they were moving. "I've got a place to park my rig there. And a car. Might make better time in the Hellcat."

Her eyes widened. "Hellcat?"

"Seven hundred horsepower of awesome," he said. "It guzzles gas, but I can find more."

"We should go someplace else. I don't want to put your brother's family in more danger."

Movement at the front door of the farmhouse dragged David's attention away from Dust. "There's a man on the porch with a shotgun."

Dust moved closer. "I see him. There are also people watching from the windows."

He thought about telling her they should spread out but didn't. "Hello?" he called out. "We don't want any trouble. I'm looking for fuel. My truck is parked a mile or so back."

"I heard it," a man's voice said. "What are you doing out here? Why did you go toward the feedlot?"

"I'd hoped to find fuel. Trying to get across country. I have family in the northwest."

"Lot of problems in the northwest, from what I hear," the voice said.

David took a step forward.

"That's close enough, friend. You're not one of them, but that don't mean I trust you."

"No problem. We're stopped. Have you seen them up close?"

"Have you?" The man wore blue jeans and a button-down shirt. His boots and belt buckle marked him as a rancher and a farmer; his hard eyes marked him as a force to be reckoned with.

"A little closer than I'd have liked, but I was still in my truck." David took his time and spoke clearly. "I managed to drive away before they could stop me."

"You're one of the lucky ones, then. But not that lucky. When the Feeders want you, they'll come and take you," the man said, tucking his thumbs into his belt.

David studied the farmstead. The driveway came through a windbreak of trees and circled a large yard of short buffalo grass. There were two houses, one old and one newly constructed. He saw two barns, a grain bin, and fuel pumps connected to large aboveground tanks, just like a hundred other farms he'd seen over the years.

"Do you have weapons?" the man asked.

"I have a Ruger 10/22."

The man laughed. "So you're not exactly loaded for bear, is what I'm thinking. Better than nothing, and it tells me you're not with them. They don't let their servants carry firearms."

"Can we come in?"

A pause.

"Sure. But I'll hold on to that cannon you're toting," he joked without humor.

David shrugged. "Works for me. Maybe you have something bigger I could buy from you."

The man held a hand to stop them at the bottom of the steps. "I've got some guns. Might even give them to you if you can do something for me."

"You have my attention."

The man nodded. "I'm sure I do. Name's Travis Brighten. Those two strapping lads behind you are Dutch and Jacob. My nephews."

David looked at the tree line and saw two men step into view wearing hunting camouflage and carrying scoped hunting rifles.

"We should leave," Dust whispered. "I don't want to get these people hurt."

"They can handle themselves." David turned the rifle upside down to hand to Travis Brighten. "They're better set up than we are."

"That's the truth. Don't worry, miss. We'll let you know when you're not welcome. Until then, you're guests and will be treated as such. It's late for dinner, and we already ate, but you both look like you could use a meal. Come into the kitchen. We'll fix you up."

"Thank you," Dust said, keeping her eyes down.

David was careful not to look aggressive. He'd been told he had "a presence" that unnerved people. Travis sat across from them at the kitchen table.

Dutch and Jacob stood near the doorways, one to the back porch and one to the living room they had come through. He was certain there were other people in the house. Dutch and Jacob had the look of fathers to him. He imagined the entire Brighten clan had rallied at their patriarch's farm as soon as the crisis began. He suspected they might have a few farm hands and their families as well.

Mrs. Brighten brought out cold cuts, warmed-up corn on the cob, and mashed potatoes. She met his eyes unflinchingly. None of the Brightens had slept recently. They looked determined and worried.

"This is good," David said between mouthfuls of food.

"Tell me everything you know," Travis said. "I'm not wanting to be rude, but I think we're way past small talk."

"My niece and I were traveling west on I-70 when they came."

Mrs. Brighten snorted. "She's not your niece."

"He was trying to be polite, ma'am," Dust said. "I was hitchhiking back to Fort Collins. I'm going to school there. Majoring in music and theater. Everyone we meet thinks I'm a runaway or a stripper."

"The thought crossed my mind. What's your name?" the farm wife asked.

"Dustvaria. My parents were hippies."

"Right. I'm Beth Brighten. Can I get you anything from the kitchen?"

Dust shook her head.

"You were saying," Travis prompted.

David told them everything but went light on the details of the attack.

"You get stabbed or bitten?" Travis asked.

"No."

"What about her?"

David locked eyes with Dust for a moment, then nodded for her to show them her wound. She complied, clearly upset with his presumption.

She took off her jacket.

David was surprised at how lean and athletic she appeared. Her physique was different somehow—like something out of a movie. It lacked the youthful softness he expected.

She rolled up her sleeves. Everyone leaned closer.

Travis cursed.

Beth threw a hand over her mouth and left the room crying.

"How long ago did this happen? She should be dead or turned," Travis said.

"I told you when it happened. Almost two days ago," David said, staring at the single hole in her forearm. A thick scab had grown over the damage. He blinked, thinking it looked silvery, like liquid mercury.

Travis leaned back in his chair. "Maybe we don't know as much about them as we think we do. Beth," he called to the next room, "this could be good news. My cousin, Jed, lives out near Jetmore. The descriptions he radioed me don't match what I've seen around here."

"He isn't exactly reliable, unless you need some cold-cooked meth," Jacob said.

"Shut your mouth with that." Travis locked eyes with his nephew and it looked like the argument might get physical.

"Just saying," Jacob insisted.

Travis snorted. "And I'm just saying we don't know nothing about aliens. Could be we're dealing with more than one kind."

David heard the argument but didn't care. His attention was on Dust. She rolled down her sleeve and held his gaze, remaining as unreadable as she was calm.

Beth came back with tears in her eyes, and Travis got up to put an arm around her. "They took our daughter. If you can bring her back, I'll give you anything you need to get to your family in the northwest."

David shot Dutch and Jacob a look. "Why not send them?"

Travis glanced at his wife before answering. "We can't afford the repercussions."

"You figure I'm expendable, and Dust too."

The man sighed. "I can't make you do it. I only said I'd reward you if you could bring back my daughter."

Dust touched David's arm and spoke softly. "Let's go. I don't want to stay here. I'd rather sneak into that place and rescue their daughter than stay here and put them in even more danger."

Decision made, David said, "I need to see everything you know about the feedlot. If there's been failed rescue attempts, I need the details of those screwups as well."

CHAPTER TWELVE

TRAVIS PROVIDED DETAILED maps of the area including a schematic of the feedlot. He had been a farmer and rancher in this area for a long time and knew everyone who worked at the place.

"We take about a hundred head of cattle there each year," Travis said as they parted ways. "The access road takes you around back. It's not paved. Wouldn't be surprised if it's full of weeds. But watch out. Those alien bloodsuckers are part of an army, disciplined shock troops I wouldn't underestimate."

"Thanks for the pep talk." David hefted his backpack and nodded for Dust to get started. "We'll bring your daughter back if we can."

Travis hesitated, then motioned to the dining room table. "Spread those maps out some. Just humor me. I feel like I should be doing this, not you."

David didn't argue. Travis seemed like a good man at odds with himself.

"There are five silos full of animal feed. Paddocks are

here. Weigh stations here. That small building is the large animal vet. This is the main building, full of offices and a cafeteria," Travis said, reviewing much of what they had already talked about.

David didn't like the man's hesitation. He was working up to something, building his courage for a big reveal under the guise of providing useful information. The layout the man was explaining wasn't complicated. Everything was constructed on a grid, very utilitarian and functional. Feedlots weren't made to impress visitors.

"What's on your mind, Travis?" David asked.

"Nothing. Just, be careful not to lead them back here. I've already pushed my luck with the bastards."

"You've talked with them?" David asked.

The rest of the man's family looked stunned at this information.

"I tried to buy her back. Negotiate. It didn't work," Travis admitted.

"How'd that meeting go?" David asked, aware that to press the man here was going to put the rancher on the spot. "What exactly did you use to bribe blood-sucking aliens?"

"I'd rather not talk about it," Travis said.

David crossed his arms. Tension built in the room.

"They offered him a job," Dust guessed.

Travis snapped his gaze toward her, jaw set angrily. "You should mind your age, child. Respect your elders and speak when spoken to."

Dust didn't flinch. She seemed older and more mature than the very angry and very uncomfortable man.

"Is that true?" his wife asked. "Did they offer you a job? And what kind of job?"

"Goddamn it," Travis swore. "I was just trying to get our daughter back."

"What would they want you for?" his wife asked, alarm growing in her tone.

"He knows how to raise cattle," Dust said. "And other livestock."

David waited until it was clear the conversation was going nowhere good, then stepped between Travis and Dust, facing the rancher. "We'd better get going."

They walked out to the porch.

Travis followed, then gripped his arm, squeezing with strength born of manual labor. "Bring her back or don't come back. We can't stay much longer."

"Fill my rig while I'm gone."

"I can do that," Travis said. "Consider it done."

"Why didn't you take the job?" David asked in a low voice.

"They didn't want me to raise cows," Travis said.

"People?" David asked.

Travis held his gaze a second, then nodded.

They parted without any more words. Jacob and Dutch followed David and Dust for a while, holding their rifles like hunters. At the edge of the property, Travis's nephews stopped and faded into a line of trees that had been planted ninety years ago as a windbreak.

David looked for Dust but couldn't see her. She moved with less noise than a shadow. Rural darkness made them invisible as they made their way to the feedlot.

The odor of manure competed with the damp smell of fermented fodder. Mounds of musty silage made shadows along the north end of the facility. Fences corralled animals into half a dozen sections.

"Dust? Where are you?"

"I'm here."

David squatted down beside her dark form. "Their ships are parked on the west side. Why haven't we seen spotlights or patrols? This feels like a trap."

"Maybe it is."

David wished his little sister were here. In high school, she'd helped him sneak out of the house several times and eventually blackmailed him into bringing her to parties she had no business attending. Looking back, his favorite part of those days was just sneaking around the neighborhood. She probably had her hands full in Chicago.

He was about to confront Dust about her mysterious past—the girl seemed entirely too skilled at stealth—when it hit him. His little brother Charles was the person he needed right now. This scenario felt like one of his games.

"Feels like a trap. I need to make a call," he said.

Dust's eyes reflected starlight. "Really? Can't it wait?"

"Just keep your eyes open. I'll be quiet." He felt the weight of her dismay, a blend of disappointment and impatience.

"Your phone will be visible a mile away in the dark," she said.

"That's a risk I have to take."

"Why do you need to talk to your brother?"

"He designs war games. I want his assessment of this scenario."

"What games?" she asked.

"The Warfighter franchise."

She raised an eyebrow, her expression barely seen in the shifting shadows of the low Kansas clouds.

"I guess I'm the only person who hasn't played the

games," David muttered.

"Don't call him. This is a trap, but not for us. There's no way they would come across the galaxy and fail to post a guard."

David shielded the phone screen and made the call. Whoever answered didn't speak.

"Charles, it's David."

No response.

"Listen, little Chuck, I need your brains for a minute. I'm trying to sneak into an alien feedlot—"

"You can't do that!" Charles whispered harshly. "Are you trying to get killed?"

"You know me. Would I do something reckless? Are you okay? Is your family okay? Why'd you hang up on me before?"

"Listen, David, the rules are really strict here. If it were just me, it wouldn't be a big deal. But if they kick my family out…"

"Can you help me?"

"What do you need?" Charles asked, quiet but no longer whispering.

"I'm trying to sneak into a feedlot that has been captured by the aliens. There's someone in there I need to rescue. I don't see guards or security measures. I think it might be a trap."

"Of course it's a trap." Something rustled on the phone, like Charles was hiding in a closet or crouching behind his desk. "Rescue missions are a terrible idea. Almost impossible in any real-world scenario. If you had a commando team and two weeks to plan, maybe it could be done."

"I have one person to help me. She's a quick thinker."

"Jesus wept, David. Take my advice and get the hell out

of there. I'm sorry about whoever you were trying to rescue, but you're only going to wind up in the cage next to them or worse."

"Never mind, Charles, I have an idea."

"Wait!" Charles said too loudly, then immediately lowered his voice. "You've always got an idea. Listen to me. This is way beyond anything you can do. Leave it to the professionals."

"There are no professionals coming to help these people," David said, and ended the call.

"What's the plan?" Dust asked.

"We're going about this the wrong way. Of course we can't sneak past alien commandos with advanced technology and who knows what else. Forget that. What do they need to make that feedlot run?"

"Are you asking me what the aliens eat?" she asked uncomfortably.

He hesitated. "You know the answer to that question? I mean, besides blood and people's faces?"

She frowned, ignoring his comment. "I think I know what you're planning. You want to drive your truck in there, deliver food or something for the cows."

He pointed at her. "Now you're thinking. We need to work smarter, not harder."

They went back to the farm, explained the plan to Travis and his family, and were soon hooking up a load of feed to his semi. He forged a delivery document, and started toward the feedlot around dawn, the normal time for a delivery.

The two burly alien guards at the gate were the biggest yet, ten feet tall and four feet across the shoulders. Their armor looked bulletproof… and rocket proof… and anything proof. A bright blue light glowed from the eye sockets.

"Am I seeing their eyes, or is that a function of their helmets?" David asked.

"Why would you ask me something like that?" Dust demanded.

David got the impression she would jump out of the truck and flee if he answered incorrectly. He minimized his inquiry with sarcasm. "Don't girls your age know everything?"

She studied the gate and the two alien soldiers, a grim determination on her face. "We told those people we would rescue their daughter. We can't turn back now."

One of the guards went to the control booth and shouted something through the window. Moments later a man came out. He was young but looked more like an administrator than someone who would work at a feedlot in the middle of nowhere.

"Human or alien?" David asked.

"I think he's working for them." Dust's voice was dry and emotionless. "Sometimes people have to do things they don't want to. Like Travis and his family."

"You've got that right," David said. "Duck into the sleeper and stay out of sight. I know you can handle yourself, but the driver wouldn't bring a hitchhiker to a job site."

She complied, but he felt her watching him.

The delivery supervisor approached the truck and waited for David to get out.

Forged delivery order in hand, David climbed down and met him well in front of the truck, hoping he wouldn't notice the claw marks on his door.

The guards were already regarding him and his vehicle with suspicion. They growled something at the human in a mishmash of English and some other language.

"Okay, okay," the man said, waving him back. "I don't have a delivery scheduled for today. Your truck is beat to shit. If you came here to rob us, you really picked the wrong feedlot."

David shrugged. "I got this order. Seems dumb to keep going, but I don't know what else to do. It's bad everywhere. But maybe after I deliver this load, you'll let me stay."

The man took the documents and scanned them. "Looks like a normal bill of lading. What happened to your truck?"

"It's crazy out there. Everywhere I stopped, people tried to mob me. Until they realized I was just carrying grain. Before that, I got caught in some sort of crazy riot and some of your friends there ripped up my door."

If looks could kill, David would be dead. "You better watch that talk, asshole. They're not my friends."

"Is Bob Jackson still running this place?" David asked.

"You know Mr. Jackson?" the man asked suspiciously.

"I looked after his son in El Dorado."

"Shame what happened to him when he got out."

David nodded, feeling bad. "I was still locked up when he OD'd."

"Get back in your truck and make your delivery to silo C. Don't talk to anyone and don't make any of the guards angry. You won't get a second chance with them."

David climbed back behind the wheel. The guy was clearly under duress, but David doubted they would've been friendly in the pre-alien invasion world. Something about the guy rubbed him the wrong way. It might have been his perfect hair, or that he wasn't fighting back when he was clearly fit and able, but something about the dude made his skin crawl.

CHAPTER THIRTEEN

THE TRUCK ROARED TO LIFE. He inched forward.

Dust peeked out of the sleeper. "Why are you driving so slow?"

"I'm looking around. Taking it all in. So far, I don't like what I see." He turned the wheel toward silo C, a large structure already half full of grain and silage to fatten up the animals before slaughter.

A group of young men, practically kids, mucked out a stall. One bad-tempered teenager sprayed a ramp spotted with mud and manure. Adults in blue jeans, Timberland boots, and Carhart jackets manhandled cattle from one section to another, counting, weighing, and checking them for illness. There were a lot of people working, but not as many as were needed to run the place well. He'd never delivered cattle, not because he had a problem with eating them, it just wasn't his specialty.

"What's taking them so long?"

"Hell if I know. I eat hamburgers and I drive through Kansas on a regular basis, but that's the extent of my knowledge about cows. Stay in the truck. Don't let anybody in, and be ready. We may have to leave in a hurry."

"What exactly do you want me to do if someone tries to get in the truck?" she asked.

"Use the rifle." He opened the door and got out before she could argue.

It wasn't long before one of the big guards blocked his path. It spoke through a voice box that translated his words to English. David struggled to understand what it was saying.

"Where go?" the guard asked, standing between David and the main building.

"Ugh. Me Tarzan. You dumb spaceman," David said.

The giant, heavily armored alien leaned down to examine him more closely. "What is Tarzan?" he asked the other massive guard, the barrel of his weapon drifting off target. David made a mental note. These soldiers weren't perfect, despite the deadly appearance of their armor and weapons.

"My word box isn't working," the guard said.

His partner answered, sounding sleepy. "Just put him in the prey zone. We can eat him and say we didn't know what he wanted."

"No need for that. I've been on the road all night. I just wanted to go to the cafeteria," David said.

Both alien guards stared at him. "You understand my words," the first guard growled. "The word box is functioning. Do not play the fool."

David raised his hands submissively. "Hey man, I just want a cheeseburger."

In the seconds that followed, David wondered if he'd overplayed his hand. Then the leader waggled his weapon toward the building. "Go eat something. Talk to no one. Do not to cook the food. It is disgusting and makes us see you as animals."

"Thanks," David said. Unable to let that go, he added on, "That makes absolutely no sense, by the way. Animals eat raw meat. We invented the hamburgers and pizza."

He was almost three steps away before the guard yelled, "Stop! I do not like the way you talk. What do you mean by that? Are you calling us lower life forms?" There were gaps between some of the words as though the translation box couldn't handle the words.

"It's been a long night. I really need to eat. If I said something wrong, I'm sorry," David said.

He felt their eyes all the way to the door. The layout was simple, offices on one side and a giant workshop on the other. On the office side, there was a cafeteria-style lounge with a lot of people looking scared. It wasn't really the way he had pictured the cafeteria.

He passed another guard and noticed this one seemed distracted, asleep standing up, or blind by the way he stared straight ahead without moving. There was no way to tell what its problem was; maybe his helmet was malfunctioning or maybe the translation box was turned off, effectively muting the scene.

That's a lot of wild-ass speculation, David. The surreal scene pressed in on him like the walls of a prison. *What the hell am I doing here? I'm acting like these are normal guards. Just some big, serious sons-of-bitches with no sense of humor. Wake the fuck up, David.*

In the lounge, a couple of people had plates of food but most were just sitting around, defeat written on their faces. He spotted Brighten's granddaughter, recognizing her from the picture he'd been shown. Taller than many teenagers, and blonde as a Viking, she would probably stand out anywhere.

"Are you Abigail?" he asked.

She nodded vigorously. "Did my family send you?"

A hard-faced young man cursed. "It doesn't matter who sent him. Where the hell do you think you're going? No one who runs ever comes back."

"Maybe that's because they escaped," Abigail snapped.

The corn-fed farm boy's nostrils flared and his eyes narrowed. David understood what was happening. This guy wasn't accustomed to back talk. He'd reached some internal threshold and his base behaviors were coming out.

David stared straight into his eyes, into his soul, into that place where alpha males challenged each other for dominance.

Mr. Cornfed took a step back, muttering something David couldn't quite make out.

"You got a problem, Cornfed?"

The man shook his head.

"Did you come to get us out of here?" Abigail asked.

A middle-aged woman in the back of the room gasped. Several people started trembling. David felt cold seeping into his hands and flexed to keep them warm.

"You heard the screams. They didn't get away," Cornfed spat. "Can't you feel the escape blocker? And we haven't even tried to escape. You take one step, Abby, and you're gonna lock up like a popsicle."

"No I won't," she said sounding more like a petulant child than the half-grown woman she was. "I've got bigger balls than you do. And I'm not afraid of shivering."

Cornfed shook his head in disgust, then sneered at David, "Can you believe that kid? Someone ought to tell her mother what kind of girl she is. I don't know you, mister, but if you go out there, you won't get five steps before your blood turns to ice."

His words confirmed some of David's theories he hadn't been able to articulate, or had been unwilling to accept. The invaders used some sort of field to immobilize people. He needed to know if it was real or in his head.

I can beat the demons in my head. Every damn time.

Just keep telling yourself that, dude, his inner voice taunted him back. *Just keep driving on. The road always goes somewhere.*

But he wasn't going to leave Abigail. It wasn't just the promise he made to Travis Brighten. She didn't belong with these people. She was a fighter and her family needed her.

"I'm here for her," David said. "But I'll do what I can to help the rest of you get out if you want. I'm not staying, so it's time to shit or get off the pot."

Hushed conversations punctuated by whispered protests indicated some of them were closer to making a break for it than others. A man ducked through a door like he was looking for a place to vomit.

Most of the feedlot employees wanted to leave, he thought. Cornfed looked tough as nails and probably had a mean streak a mile wide but he was totally whipped by these alien invaders. That was worth remembering. Even a big man with a bad attitude could be cowed into submission.

It was time. "Come on, Abigail. Let's go. I'm not waiting for people to make up their minds."

She got up to join him, shoving past a man who tried to stop her. "Get your hands off me, Billy."

David's knife was suddenly in his hand. "You better listen to her."

Billy backed away, hands up in surrender. David led

Abigail into the hallway. They hadn't gone three steps before an alarm blared across the feedlot. It didn't sound like any fire alarm he'd ever heard.

"That's not for us," Abigail said, but peered nervously out the window all the same. "That's something else. When someone tries to escape, there's always an alarm and then an announcement or something in their language. This sounds more like a warning."

"You're sure?" David asked.

She nodded. "My granddad taught us all to be ready for something like this," she said, behind him down the hallway.

"For an alien invasion?"

"Don't be a jerk," she said. "Granddad's not crazy."

"Hold up," he said, stopping her before they crossed in front of an open bathroom door. He didn't want to be seen if one of the freaks was in there taking a crap with the door open. When he was sure it was clear, they continued.

"Where's Mr. Jackson?" he asked.

"They took him away first thing," she said. She looked like she might cry. "They beat him pretty badly and hissed at us to do what we were told. I didn't see it. Billy told me they put him in one of the bigger ships and took him away."

The sirens died, then started again. Several ships could be heard launching through the walls of the building.

David picked up the pace, practically dragging her behind him. He found a side door and looked out. Squads of the big aliens assembled in the courtyard, getting orders from one of their leaders.

He tried a second hallway. The building wasn't huge and there were only so many exits. If he didn't find a way back to his truck soon, they'd be in big trouble.

He pulled her arm harder, and Abigail gave him a resentful glare. "Who the hell *are* you, anyway?" she asked.

David ignored her, keeping his eyes on the next hallway intersection. His heart pounded like a drum solo. He couldn't remember the last time adrenaline had hit him this hard.

"Jacob and Dutch are with you, aren't they? I told those stupid jerk offs not to try something like this," Abigail said.

"Questions later. I don't plan on getting stuck here, so I hope you're ready to run," David said. He was starting to feel claustrophobic, his days in prison coming back with surprising force. He thought he had put those years behind him. He didn't think about it, didn't dwell on it, and never let it affect his day-to-day life. But now it felt like he was running toward the door that was closing and was already too small to escape through.

"It's all in my head. I can do this," he muttered to himself.

Abigail wasn't sure what to make of his words.

Some strange and horrible language announced something over the speakers, and was repeated in hissing English. "Human servants of the Fosk-ha, defend the Fosk. Remember, it is better to die than to resist."

David looked at Abigail. "Better to die than resist?"

"That's what they tell us, over and over," Abigail said. "Something really bad is about to happen. We wouldn't have made it this far if the guards weren't busy. It—do you smell that?"

David felt a draft but couldn't identify the smell. Glass shattered and he understood the new breeze. Something came through a window. More glass getting smashed warned him of new danger.

"Oh shit! Some of the wild ones are in the building. Fuck, mister! They're worse than the soldier aliens," Abigail warned, searching frantically for somewhere to run or hide.

David grabbed her hand and pulled her down the hallway. "Don't quit on me now. I don't want to carry you."

He turned a corner, pulling her like he was a speedboat and she was a reluctant water skier.

"Not that way! I can hear them," she said.

David heard it too, but the sound came from everywhere. This hall was as good as any other. When he turned the next corner his understanding of the alien invaders changed.

Two guards stomped on an unarmored alien with matted hair and tattered clothing. It looked bestial and crazed. Dried blood caked around its mouth. The guards ranted in their own language.

David used their preoccupation with stomping their victim to death to slip into an intersecting hallway.

Abigail shook her head in denial, babbling, "Not happening! Not happening! This isn't real. Aliens aren't real. Stop playing around. This isn't funny. None of this is real." She dug in her heels, refusing to move.

"If we can get to my truck, we can get out of here," David said.

"Out of here?" Abigail repeated, her eyes wild.

"Shut up. We're going. It would be easier to carry you than drag you. But if you just get a grip and start moving, we might actually make it."

The girl sized him up and apparently realized he could carry out his threat. She traded her mania for outrage. "Why do you have so many tattoos? What are you, an escaped convict?"

"Something like that," he said dryly.

She had the decency to look embarrassed.

Moments later, they were running across the courtyard to his Peterbilt. Abigail was fast. David could imagine her running bases in a varsity softball game and realized he was getting out of shape.

She stopped when she reached his truck, staring up at it like it was a sleeping dragon. From the ground, it was impossible to see into the cab. David slowed to a jog, then a walk, and then passed her to climb up. He opened the door. "Come on."

Abigail looked back at the building still holding her friends and coworkers.

"They've made their choices," David said. He should be starting the truck, not coaxing the farm girl.

Abigail climbed up. She didn't look at him. He thought she regretted leaving the others behind.

He pushed in the clutch and cranked the key, and the Peterbilt roared to life, the lone headlight beam angled crazily. There was a smoky haze he hadn't noticed until the high beam pierced it.

Abigail belted herself into the passenger's seat, unaware Dust was in the sleeper, hidden in the shadows. "What the hell are you waiting for, mister?"

"Christmas," David said, but put the rig into first gear and rolled the truck forward. Each time he shifted, the transmission complained, making noises he'd never have guessed were possible. Before the invasion, he wouldn't have driven his baby ten feet without getting something like that fixed.

But this was the end of the world.

CHAPTER FOURTEEN

DAVID DROVE across the courtyard and through the gate like it wasn't even there. The crossbar snapped like kindling. The chain-link gate was knocked off the rails and he ran over it. It caught on his axle briefly, further insulting the truck that was his pride and joy.

He looked for the guards, surprised he hadn't been blasted out of the driver seat already. The alarm was definitely for something other than a prison break. Several of their attack ships hovered, then jumped into the air.

Looking like nothing so much as a cross between helicopters and jet fighters, these ships rode thrusters with intense blue flames.

Two human guards watched him fearfully as he rumbled down the road. He let off the gas, intending to pick them up.

"That's Ed Campling and Pat Smith. They're just security guards. They don't know what they're doing," Abigail said. "I think they're supposed to keep the bad aliens out."

"They're all bad," David said, changing his mind and standing on the gas pedal.

"You're not going to stop for them?"

"We didn't go back for anyone else."

"But you gave them a choice, and they all stayed," Abigail said, clearly frustrated. "I just hate this." Tears filled her eyes, but she looked like she wanted to punch something.

David slowed for the first corner, passing mounds of cow manure where cattle could stand to stay dry if it rained. Now, two of the big alien guards stepped onto the road. They held weapons but seemed distracted—probably unauthorized snack they'd made of a cow.

Looked like they'd decided to block his truck. He could run them over, but he wasn't going fast enough to stop them from shooting into the cab.

Letting the truck roll on its own, he grabbed his rifle, opened the door, and stepped out onto the ladder to the roof. He held on with his left hand and pulled the rabbit gun to his shoulder with his right, hoping he could hold it tight enough to shoot accurately.

The Ruger had almost no recoil. It also lacked knockdown power. He aimed for the eyes of the nearest alien and pulled the trigger. The tiny bullet riccocheted off the alien soldier's visor. He aimed at the throat of his adversary this time, stroking the trigger several times and was rewarded by gouts of blood and the alien staggering back.

The other alien, still loopy from its feeding fest, raised his weapon. David fired the rest of the ten-round magazine at its throat and face, then tossed the rifle to Abigail. He swung back in and stomped on the gas.

"Abigail," he said, "I'm going to ask you some questions and I want immediate answers."

She nodded.

"That means you're gonna have to talk," David said.

"I'm sorry," she said. "I'm a little rattled."

He started with something easy. "How old are you?"

"Seventeen. I'm a senior," she said.

"You have any injuries?" he asked.

"Do you mean, did they bite me?" she asked, shrinking away from him defensively.

"It doesn't matter unless it means you're going to collapse and I don't know how to help you," he said, confused by her reaction.

"I'm not injured. That's probably one of the reasons they let me work for them. I don't get sick much and I didn't get hurt."

"I don't have time to fuck around with this," David said. "So I'm just gonna straight out ask you. What are you so worried about? Why can't you just tell me what the problem is?"

"I didn't want you to throw me out. People change after they get bit. I might've been too afraid to try to escape, but I'm definitely too afraid to go back."

"You think I'd abandon you if I thought you were bitten by them—infected or whatever?"

She nodded, clearly terrified.

He glanced at the mirror. There was a lot of activity around the feedlot.

"I wouldn't have time to stop and dump you out anyway," he said. "Do you know what the alarm is for?"

"I think they're being attacked," Abigail said. "They've got problems with some other... nonhumans. There's more than one side. It's like these guys are cops and the others are serial killers or something."

David wasn't sure what to do with that. They all looked murderous to him.

"None of them are good," Abigail continued. "But some of them don't have any self-control at all. They're the ones who go on feeding frenzies. That's a crime or something with them." Her frustration showed. "I don't know. I just hear them talk in their weird hissy voices. It's all really confusing."

"You're doing great, kid," David said. "I'm asking you hard questions. You just tell me what you think, and I'll sort it out later."

At that, she opened up, like a dam had broken. She explained how she came to be a prisoner, what the rules were, how she had wanted to escape but didn't dare and dozens of other things, her story rambling and in no particular order.

The Peterbilt wasn't a stealth vehicle. The slower he went, the quieter his truck was. He avoided coming to a stop or making sharp turns, navigating access roads—some paved, others covered with gravel.

"I'm sorry, I didn't mean to dump all of that on you," Abigail said. She gazed around, still unaware they weren't the only two people in the vehicle. Dust was still in the sleeper.

Ships flew tight patterns overhead, looking for something. Searchlights sliced the night sky.

"Hey, Abigail, can I tell you something and you promise not to freak out?" David asked.

She shifted uncomfortably, trying to stay out of arm's reach. "Okay," she said tentatively.

"I have another passenger," David said. "Dust, you can come out. I want you to take a look at this and tell me what you see."

The runaway emerged without a word, never blinking as she evaluated Abigail.

"Oh, hi," Abigail said, clearly unsure how to process this new development. "You're not from around here, are you?"

Dust ignored her. "The aliens at the cow place hadn't acted like they were panicking. Maybe they're just really disorganized."

"Take it further," David said.

"Maybe they're afraid of something," Dust offered. "They have to have enemies."

The girl tapped her finger on her chin as he drove.

She's holding back, he thought.

They passed a farmhouse, smaller and shabbier than Abigail's home. There were several single-wide trailers on the same property, one of which was well maintained and two falling apart. The vehicles were older. The yard around the main house was overgrown.

What concerned him was the open field beyond it. It sloped down to a pond between what passed for hills in this part of Kansas. The moment he saw it, he thought it would be a good place to ambush an enemy.

"Keep your eyes open," he said.

What happened next was strange. Aliens ran toward the farmhouse, straight through the middle of the ambush zone. They moved quickly and with confidence.

David pulled over and parked—keeping the high ground and hoping no one noticed him almost a half mile away. What he saw were shapes, figures running that he assumed were aliens by the way they moved.

What made it weird was they appeared to be smaller than any he'd encountered until now. He wouldn't rely on that impression, but wasn't bad at judging distance and the size of objects. Terrain features and a few of the trees and windbreaks offered scale.

The aliens that attacked him and the guards at the feedlot were enormous. These were human-sized, perhaps smaller.

"It's a trap," Dust murmured.

Abigail started to tremble. "The small ones are the worst."

David should leave, back up the narrow road if he had to, but do whatever it took to get out of here. "What do you mean?"

Abigail hugged herself. "I've heard about them skinning people alive—digging around in people's organs like they're looking for something. That's what I heard. I never saw it."

Three squads of the larger aliens opened fire on the smaller ones, cutting down the first dozen without mercy. Then they closed in and threw what looked like nets over the ones trying to escape.

It was over quickly. What he didn't see was the big aliens feeding on the small aliens.

That could be important, he thought, *or completely irrelevant*.

"We need to get out of here," Dust said, alarm rising in her voice.

Abigail's whimpering turned into a scream. She rubbed her arms and hugged herself, trying to warm up. He felt the cold and remembered what he had seen at the first highway checkpoint.

Whoever or whatever the bigger aliens were, they had ways to immobilize their victims from a distance.

"Yeah, that feels bad," he said. "I hate it when the cold comes."

He slammed the truck into reverse and backed up, using

his mirrors to guide him. The speed he chose was reckless, especially when he started going down one of the gently sloping hills. Peterbilts weren't made to back up like that. He hit an intersection, cranked the wheel, and spun it around like he was in an action movie. The tires hopped across the gravel, struck the pavement of the road he wanted to use, and shook the truck and everyone in it violently.

He struggled to get into gear. The big rig was holding up like a champ, but everything had its limits.

"Some of them got away!" Dust said, surprised.

David looked up and saw several of the smaller aliens running away. Two of them were taken down by what he had assumed were attack dogs until he realized the *dogs* were flying. The last escapee vanished into the distance while the pursuers struggled with the ones they captured.

David got the truck moving, found another side road, something the farmer had made—he would probably get stuck if it was even slightly muddy. He emerged onto a two-lane blacktop, driving slowly to get across the ditch.

Back on the highway, he nursed the Peterbilt forward. It replied with more of the sounds he didn't like.

He tapped the dashboard. "Just hang in there, girl. You're doing great."

"We're going to need that Hellcat," Dust said.

"That's why we're going to Wichita as soon as we reunite Abigail with her family," David said.

He caught movement in his mirror and realized he'd picked up a stowaway.

The creature was indeed smaller than the others. He pretended not to see the alien but kept track of its progress. Before long, it was hunkered down between the wheel well and the trailer coupling.

David eased off the gas, gradually shedding speed, then stopped as fast as he could and jumped out. He should have been looking right at the creature. Dust and Abigail leaned out to watch with growing alarm.

"What are you doing?" Dust demanded.

"I saw one hitching a ride," David said. Movement flickered in the corner of his eyes and darted to the front of his truck. There, frozen in fear, was a humanoid creature about five feet tall, maybe a little less. Slender and light on its feet, it had yellow and black eyes that looked startling against its coal-black skin.

"Human," it said in a gravel-rough voice. "Ysik no hurt human."

"I'm David. Is that your name? Ysik?"

It snarled, barring its teeth.

David had a keen eye for body language and something wasn't right. He moved, positioning himself in front of Dust and Abigail.

"Human no hurt Ysik. Ysik no hurt human," it said, bobbing its head up and down and repeating the snarl.

"Listen, buddy, if you're trying to smile at me, just stop. You look like you'd eat a cat if you could catch one," David said.

It held up hands with its claws extended. "What cat is? Cat is human? Human cat?"

"No. Forget it. Get out of here. The big guys are hunting for you," David said, pointing at the sky. Ships still scoured the landscape, searching with powerful spotlights.

"Fosk-ha. Fosk-ha hurt humans. Fosk-ha hurt Ysik," the little alien said.

David looked away, just for a second, and the creature was gone, already in the next field.

Abigail leaned from the window. "Can we get the hell out of here, mister?"

He went around to the driver's side and climbed behind the wheel. "Call me David. Or Osage. Or Brad Pitt. Anything but mister."

"You're no Brad Pitt," Abigail said, looking him over.

"Don't make it ugly, kid. Let's get you home. I've got places to be."

CHAPTER FIFTEEN

DAVID MADE his way back to the Brighten farm. He knew before they got there something had gone wrong. His first reaction, his gut instinct, said the aliens had retaliated. He hoped that nothing he'd done—or failed to do—had doomed Travis and his family to this fate.

Meanwhile, he had Abigail to deal with. She was probably going to lose her mind when she realized they were gone. He thought about just turning around and leaving. He wished he could ask Laura. She was better at psychology and understood victims. She'd know whether seeing carnage at the farm would be cathartic or would just make everything worse.

How would I feel if I were in her shoes? he wondered. *I'd want to see it all for myself. Then I wouldn't have any questions.*

"I don't see the pickups," Abigail said, her words full of dread. "And I smell smoke."

He knew she might panic. Everyone had their threshold, and he'd seen her start to lose it more than once.

He forced himself to remember that a seventeen-year-old

wasn't a seven-year-old. With a parental waiver, she could join the military and travel the world learning to kill people.

"Can I take you somewhere else? Do you have other family around here?" David asked.

She shook her head no. "Everyone came here, to our farm."

David turned off the Peterbilt, hoping he could get it started again.

"I'll stay in the truck," Dust said. She'd been even quieter than normal around Abigail. Whenever David looked at her, she was cautiously watching the farm girl.

"Can you go see?" Abigail asked, misery twisting her expression. "I'm not sure I can take it."

The teenager wanted to go inside the house, probably believing it was her duty, but she didn't have the courage. She'd been through a lot.

"I'll let you know when it's clear," David said.

"Are you sure?" she asked. "I mean, I can do it." She started to get out of the truck.

David held up his hand for her to stop. "I don't think there's anyone here. Something made them leave. They would've stayed if they had a choice."

That wasn't what he was thinking, but he wasn't going to say more. A young girl at the end of the world, captured by aliens and rescued by a stranger, she probably thought she'd done something to get her entire family killed. Or that they hadn't thought she was worth staying for and left her behind.

She was going to be a hot mess for a while.

David opened the door, mentally preparing himself for a bloodbath.

"Aren't you going to take the rifle?" Dust asked.

"Keep it with you, same as last time," David said.

"I still don't know anything about guns," Dust said.

"I do," Abigail said, taking the Ruger 10/22 from her and checking the magazine was loaded properly.

As he neared the house, he could tell that *something* happened. Windows were broken out and doors torn from hinges. He walked the perimeter, looking for surprises.

The southwest corner was completely gone. He hesitated, unsure what to do next. Instinct warned him that time was of the essence.

Afraid that Abigail would change her mind and barge in on something horrible, he climbed through the rubble. What had been a mud room was now nothing but splinters and tangled up screen doors. The kitchen was a wasteland of broken dishes and destroyed cabinets.

He searched for bodies or blood smears but saw nothing. Farther into the house, things looked more normal. Room by room, evidence suggested the Brighten family packed up and left.

He found Abigail's room—boy band posters on the walls and a vanity with enough makeup to stock a department store.

At the foot of her bed was a backpack. He unzipped the main compartment and looked inside without disturbing anything. Someone had taken the time to fill it with items she would need to survive for several days.

There was also a .357 revolver and a scoped rifle.

Lying next to the backpack, a sealed envelope had Abigail's name, Abs, printed on it.

He heard her footsteps coming down the hall. When she came in, he nodded toward the supplies. "Someone left you a hand cannon and a deer rifle."

"The revolver is my older brother's. He always teased me, said I couldn't shoot it because I'm just a girl," she said, still too stunned to be upset that she had been left behind.

"Can you?" David watched her, ready for some first rate hysterics but not expecting it for some reason.

"Can I what?" she asked.

"Handle a .357 magnum," David said. It had been a while since he'd fired such a weapon.

"It's got the rubber Pachmayr grips. It fits my hand pretty good. I've shot that one once or twice, but it's been a while." She was stalling, not wanting to face the truth.

"Get your stuff," David said. "You can come with us until we figure out where they went."

She and picked up the envelope. "Looks like my brother's handwriting."

"I'll give you a minute."

Clenching her jaw, she turned away, waving dismissively. Her shoulders shook. David had never seen a girl fight for emotional control until his sister went through her first breakup. That had been bad. But his sister's tears had soon turned to pleas that he'd promise he wouldn't smash the guy's face for taking her virginity then dumping her.

But that was years ago, and he needed to do something for this stranger now.

"Abigail."

She jerked away from his outstretched hand, sobbing through tightly clamped lips. Her face reddened and tears streamed. When pacing didn't make her feel better, she leaned against the wall and slid to the floor.

David didn't know what to do. Talk or keep his mouth shut? Offer comfort or keep his distance. Helpless, he sat on a chair close to her and waited for her to need something.

She seemed to appreciate his decision.

"Do you have sisters?" she asked.

"One. She's a cop."

Abigail wiped her nose on the back of her hand. "I bet you're a good brother."

"No complaints so far. Or not too many."

She laughed for a second, then went back to fighting back tears. He reached over, patted her on the shoulder, and decided that was enough. She didn't know or trust him.

"You'll be okay," he said. "You can stay with us until we find them."

She nodded and got up, found some tissues, and blew her nose noisily. "It started right after I milked the cows."

CHAPTER SIXTEEN

"I'VE BEEN GOING to my grandparents' place before track practice for three years," she told him. "They've got two dairy cows and some horses. I sweep out the stalls, check the other animals, put down hay, make sure all of 'em are watered, then milk the cows before work."

David leaned back and listened. A warm feeling passed through him. She was smiling at the fond memories and he was seeing a piece of domestic life he'd never imagined.

"There's a red SVT Cobra Mustang 5.0 up in McPherson I'm saving up for." She blushed for reasons David could only guess at.

"What year?" David asked.

"Ninety-seven," she said. "It's a one-owner vehicle. My Aunt Nancy's neighbor's mother is a schoolteacher who bought it new. It's never been driven over sixty and has less than ten thousand miles on it."

"Did the schoolteacher drive it regularly?" David asked. "It's not good to let them sit too long."

Abigail nodded, eyes drying. She scooted forward and

sat cross-legged. "It's mine for six thousand dollars if I can pay cash and keep my grades up."

"I thought you worked at the feedlot," David said, casually glancing at the window, wondering if Dust was getting impatient. Would she be in the truck when he came out?

"Only on weekends," Abigail said. "Until this happened."

"What do they want? Who are they?"

She shrugged. "I don't know much."

"You have more experience with them than I do," David said. "They attacked my truck when I was trying to turn around on I-70. The only other time I've seen them face-to-face was right before you and I met."

She glanced down, embarrassed maybe, then reversed tack. Climbing to her feet, she looked ready to argue. "My family was coming for me, weren't they?"

"They were," David lied. "But I convinced them I was good at this sort of thing."

"Are you?"

"We didn't get caught, did we?"

She hugged herself and looked away, unsure.

"What do you know about them? Tell me what you can."

She gathered her thoughts, then stopped pacing. "I'll tell you as I see it, but you have to promise not to treat me like a kid. If you don't believe this crap, keep it to yourself or don't ask me to talk about it."

"I'm listening," David said. "And from what I've seen in the last thirty-six hours, anything is possible."

"Okay. Here it is. The soldiers and lower cast—that's what my brother called them—only drink animal blood. Doesn't matter if the animals are dead or if it's cold, but they like it better fresh out of the animal's arteries. There are, I don't know, rebels or something that also take blood from any mammal," she said, talking fast and making points with her hands like she was in a debate class at school.

David had expected more girl-ness. From what he could tell, this farm kid went to school, worked two jobs, ran cross country, and was on a forensics squad or something. Busy kid, but still a kid who wasn't as grown up as she thought she was.

"My dad and his brothers did most of the risky stuff— meeting with them and asking questions, but also snooping around and spying on them." She started pacing again, rubbing her arms like she was cold. "Their leaders only drink blood from humans."

She stopped abruptly, held herself hard and stared at her feet as the tears came again.

David was about to ask her if she needed to take a break when she whispered, "I saw them take Mr. Jagger and suck him dry. They just tossed him aside like a used up husk. I saw... I saw..."

"Abigail." David moved toward her.

"I saw Mr. Williams ripped apart."

David gave her a hug and thought she might as well be his little sister right then. She trembled so violently he thought she was going to hurt herself. He patted her back and waited for her to cry it all out.

"Thanks, Mr. Osage," she said when it was done. "I need to use the bathroom and get cleaned up before we go."

"Okay, Abigail."

"My brothers and friends call me Abs."

David laughed and it felt good. "Okay, Abs. Yell if you need something."

When he went outside, he walked softly through the house, listening carefully.

Should I have taken the guns from her? he wondered. *No, she's not a quitter. She wouldn't hurt herself.*

He walked across the front porch and down the steps, hoping he was right.

"Where is Abigail? We can't leave her here," Dust said.

"They have running water. She wanted to clean up," David said. "You and I need to talk."

"I can't tell you much."

This surprised David. He'd expected angry denials, maybe even an attempt to flee. The girl wasn't what or who she claimed to be. That was what his instincts told him.

"Start from the beginning. Tell me everything," he demanded.

She shook her head. "It doesn't work that way. You don't just get what you want because you're meaner than everyone else."

"You're one of them," he accused.

"Go to hell."

He wished he'd taken more time to think this through. As he stared into Dust's impassive face, he realized was about to accuse a young woman he was protecting of being a bloodsucking alien.

"Is that true what Abigail said, that people who get bitten by these monsters are changed?" he asked.

She crossed her arms—standing her ground when he thought she would retreat or run away. Trying to wait her out failed, so he changed tactics.

"Travis and his family were surprised you survived the bite," he said. "He told me about some kind of change, an infection that kills most of its hosts."

She held his gaze but said nothing.

"You're one of them," he repeated.

"I'm not."

"Then why didn't you get sick?" David asked, struggling to remember all of Travis's descriptions. "What about the other aliens—you could be one of them. Maybe you're something different, not from around here. Give me something to work with. I'm trying."

She didn't deny anything.

"I need the truth. Am I on the wrong side?" he asked.

"What are you talking about?" She backed away, something he now expected each time he confronted her.

"If you're one of them, am I on the wrong side? Am I selling out humanity by protecting you?" he said, tasting bile and hating himself. The words refused to stop even when he wanted to take them back.

"Do whatever you want!" She stormed away. "I didn't ask you to protect me!"

He ran after her, grabbing her arm. "Wait."

She yanked free. "I don't need your help."

"You know that's bullshit, Dust. You're hurt and alone."

"What do you care?" she shouted. "I wish I'd never seen your truck. I thought you were different, but you're like everyone else."

"Just stop. Talk to me. Make me understand," he said, breathing a sigh of relief when she stopped to face him.

Long moments passed while they stared at each other, too angry to speak and too desperate to actually leave each other.

"I'm not one of them, not like you think. Can you accept that?" she asked.

David thought about the question. "Just give me something to work with. I'm really trying here. It isn't every day the Earth is invaded."

"My situation is complicated, and I don't know how to explain it."

"I've seen a lot of impossible situations and been forced to make hard decisions." David was almost talking to himself, thinking of times and places he didn't want to remember. "Try me. I might be more sympathetic than you assume."

"Do you know what it's like to be a test subject?" she asked.

"I know what it's like to be locked in a cage." He thought of Agent William Boyne and the incident at the Salina refugee camp, wondering who the man worked for and what they had done to Dust—or if she was just making this up to manipulate him.

"I can't explain. Or maybe I just don't want to explain," she said. "But I'll swear on anything you like that I won't hurt you or the farmer's daughter."

David thought about it, knowing from the look of her that he wasn't getting the full story now. Her promise had to be enough. "That's good enough for me, for now. But we're not done with this conversation."

The relief in Dust's expression was so genuine that David wondered how he could have ever thought she was anything but human. Of course she was on his side. Of course he could trust her.

Abigail emerged from the farmhouse a changed person. Gone were the tears. "Did I miss something?"

"It's nothing. David's a jerk," Dust said.

Abigail shrugged as if to say 'whatever.'

David recognized the strength of her resolve. She strutted

down the stairs wearing hiking boots, low-rise jeans, a cropped shirt under her older brother's black and gold letterman's jacket, and the .357 revolver holstered on her hip. She had her blonde hair pulled back in a tight braid. The scoped rifle was strapped to the backpack her brother had left for her so that the barrel pointed down—less likely to get water in the barrel if it rained or something. David had seen hunters carry their packs this way on the wilderness trails of Colorado. He wasn't a hunter, but he loved to hike by himself, and the hobby had put him in contact with hunters, both at lodges and on trails.

"I think she's after vengeance," Dust said quietly.

David wasn't sure if Dust had meant to be heard, but he'd been thinking the same thing. He needed to get this show on the road.

"Load up whatever you want to take, but once we get to Wichita, there *will* be less space. Decide what you really need," David said.

"I've got this," Abigail said, touching the pistol with her fingers while staring straight ahead without blinking. She didn't wait to be invited to the truck but climbed in like she owned a piece of it. David and Dust followed. He fired it up, the straight pipes blaring into the falling night.

None of them spoke for a long time. He left the radio off. The only sound was the occasional static on the CB radio. He wished someone would give him some news, shout triumphantly about the Armed Forces sending the invaders back to hell or wherever they came from.

It felt like only hours before that he'd been talking to Gummy Bear about strange lights in the sky. Now the entire world had changed.

Gravel sprayed up behind his tires, striking the mud

flaps and the undercarriage of his vehicle as he raced along the narrow dirt road back to the interstate. He didn't like the way it was vibrating and knew that the truck's days were numbered.

He reached forward and patted the dash, reassuring the truck. She was a tough old war horse, and they'd been through a lot together. Abigail and Dust watched him with slightly different expressions.

"What do you want from me?" he asked.

Dust weighed him, making some sort of decision that was probably more important than he could understand. Abigail's response was more awkward. She shrugged and turned away.

He drove into the night as fast as he could push the semi-truck. The sound of the highway was music to his ears.

From the Park City exit, he saw evidence of fighting in the night. A trio of the turbine powered helicopters like he'd never seen crossed above Wichita. Each craft shone down a spotlight and fired nearly invisible energy pulse weapons at unseen targets. Drones zipped just above treetops. Something about them was wrong—like they weren't fully mechanical. *Which meant what?*

David thought the primitive tactic was strange until he realized it was a trick. The three craft with spotlights were each flanked by two others that flew without illumination of any kind.

Surface-to-air rockets launched from residential neighborhoods. Before they climbed halfway to their targets, the alien ships backed out and veered away. Then the stealth ships unleashed a hellish barrage of pulse weapons.

"Did they hit anyone?" Abigail asked, leaning forward in her seat.

David didn't answer. Secondary explosions told the story well enough. He slowed the truck, pulling off the interstate the first chance he had.

Wichita was completely flat, and there were trees in most of the neighborhoods. David wasn't able to see exactly who was fighting back or calculate their survival rate.

Alien attack craft continued to patrol the night, hovering over some areas, firing at pockets of resistance, but always searching for targets.

One group turned their turbines downward without warning and climbed straight into the sky, then accelerated to the west.

"I don't think going into the city is a good idea," Abigail said.

"She's right," Dust agreed.

"We need a new vehicle," David said. "It doesn't have to be my baby, but the truck is done. If we can get to my storage unit, life will be a lot easier for us during the post alien invasion apocalypse."

"But you want your car," Dust confirmed.

"I do," he answered. "Neither of you have to go with me. This will be dangerous. But so is going back the way we came. There aren't any safe places now."

"So you might as well have your car?" Dust said. "Is that how you make decisions?"

"Yeah. Why the hell not?"

Abigail touched the butt of her pistol. "I'm with you. Those assholes took my family. They crossed me, and I've got something for them."

"Your family ran to save your brothers and sisters and cousins," David said. "Don't get your heart set on dying to avenge them." The words came out before he thought about how she might take the news.

"Same thing," she said, face flushing red. "The invaders took everything from us. I have lots of reasons to shoot someone in the face."

"Settle down. This isn't a video game or a movie. You're pissed, but you've never killed anyone and it isn't so easy."

"And you have?" Abigail asked.

David parked the truck in a grocery store lot and got out without answering.

Abigail and Dust followed him.

The local power grid was down. Only a few massive alien ships were illuminated by blue security beams. David spotted strange power conduits running along street curbs and into gutters.

He led the way between a row of houses just before an alien ground vehicle rolled past them. The wheels were rimmed in energy. Twin turbines propelled it forward. He thought the turbines could be turned down to make it another type of jump vehicle.

Rotary cannons poked from a turret on the top.

"Don't move," David said.

Dust rolled her eyes. "I was thinking about going for a jog. Or maybe I could just run into the street and wave my arms around for no reason."

"He said don't move. That means shut up too," Abigail said.

David edged to the corner of a ranch style track home and watched the alien patrol vehicle continue until it was several blocks away. "Let's go."

"Why can't we take one of the cars parked along the street?" Abigail asked.

"Most of them are new enough to have car alarms," David said. "My storage unit is only a mile or so from here. We're sticking to the original plan—get my stuff and head northwest to find my brother and his family."

"What about my family?" Abigail asked, anger and fear in her voice.

"Where do you think they went?" David asked.

"My uncle—the successful one, Dad calls him—runs the beef packing plant in Dodge City, and he knows a lot of farmers west of there, all the way to the mountains. We had a big family argument right before they took me to the feedlot to work for them about whether the aliens wanted the packing plant. There are ranches and feedlots near Dodge, but my dad thinks they're not interested in animal processing since they only seem to want to drink blood. He said these sons-a-bitches didn't come all the way across the galaxy for a good burger."

David thought about that. He didn't see how they could sustain their large physiques with a liquid diet, even if it was blood. "They have to eat something."

"They slurp down a really disgusting black gruel," Abigail said. "I've seen it. Watching them spoon it down is almost worse than when they jab their disgusting feeder tongues into the cows. I'm about to throw up just talking about it."

David heard another vehicle approaching and guided Dust and Abigail behind a hedgerow.

A police car rolled slowly past their position, shining a spotlight that missed them by inches.

"What the hell was that about?" Abigail asked. "That was a freaking cop. Why wasn't he fighting aliens?"

"Some cops are fighting back," David said, hoping it was

true. He knew that if anyone was going to give the invaders the middle finger, it was his sister up in Chicago. "But it looks like others have switched sides. A lot of people do that when an occupying army is too strong. They're trying to survive, just like the rest of us."

"Dad says everyone should be fighting back," Abigail insisted.

David wondered how she would feel if she learned her idol had nearly taken a devil's bargain for her release. She was still talking, so he didn't interrupt. He tried to pay attention while also watching for more cops or aliens.

"I'm sorry, it just makes me mad. Every day I was working for them, I was planning what I would do when I had guns and a fast car," Abigail said. "I just thought it would be different out here."

"Don't worry about it. I know a thing or two about cops," David said.

"You do?" Abigail asked, surprised.

"He's on parole," Dust said, moving beside David.

"Was."

Dust kept most of her attention on the farm girl.

Abigail stared at her blankly.

"It means he was in prison. He's got a criminal record," Dust said.

"That's not the only reason I know about police procedures," David said.

"Why were you in prison?" Abigail asked. She was both fascinated and wary.

"Driving too fast," David said, then led them down a dark street. Someone had broken out the streetlights.

CHAPTER SEVENTEEN

CREEPING through residential neighborhoods on foot reminded David of his youth, with and without his siblings. Laura had always been game for adventure. Charles had only come with them once and he had ruined it for everyone. He'd been too paranoid, too cautious, and wracked with guilt from start to finish.

Dogs barked as they crossed a front yard. Dust glared at them in the darkness, her eyes brighter than normal.

"Shut up, you stupid mutts," Abigail hissed.

David motioned for his partners in crime to relax as he led them onward switching to the other side of the street because someone's lawn sprinkler was inexplicably still working. The grass had been mowed recently, something he thought might have gone by the wayside given current events. It was weird to see burned-out shells of vehicles next to chalked murals of Disney princesses. The invasion was still a fresh wound here.

"There are dogs barking all over the city, not just here. Listen."

"Why are they doing that?" Abigail asked. "We have a lot of dogs. I know what they get up to at night. These aren't acting right. They're scared. You can hear it in the way they yelp."

"Maybe they don't like this brave new world." David watched the area for a minute longer, then approached the storage complex. At the gate, he swiped his wallet and was admitted. As soon as the gate slid away, they hurried inside and disappeared between rows of storage units.

No one spoke. The sound of airships and sporadic gunfire created an eerie background music to their sojourn. The feeling of unreality was stronger than ever.

David opened the garage door and entered. He pulled back the tarp on his Dodge Hellcat. Despite all that was happening, he grinned. The powerful mixture of nostalgia and excitement was infectious. Abigail walked around the car and whistled. Even Dust, who didn't seem to care about cars one way or the other, smiled more than she had for several hours.

David opened the trunk and took a quick peek at his camping gear.

"You keep that stuff in your car all the time?" Abigail asked. "Why don't you have a pickup truck or something if you like to camp?"

"This gets me to any KOA park in North America. I'm not trying to impress anyone with my mountaineering prowess. I just like a bit of nature when I have time for it," David said. "We'll need more food, but this should get us started. You brought guns, and I brought a sleeping bag and band aids."

"What now?" Dust asked.

"Run around the corner and relieve yourself. There's a

public restroom. If it's locked, give a yell. I'll break the door open. I can't say when we'll be stopping again," David said, then checked the tire pressure and oil. Dust and Abigail hurried out, leaving him with just enough time to Armor All the leather seats and the dash.

"Shotgun!" Abigail called out when the girls returned. She bounced in the front seat and whistled again at the gleaming interior.

"I like to have it showroom ready before a cross-country sprint," David joked.

"It's got that new car smell, for sure."

Ten minutes after that, they were rolling down the street, while watching in every direction. Wichita, a city of about four hundred thousand people, looked like a ghost town. Only the searchlights and gunfire broke the illusion.

"Shouldn't you turn off your headlights?" Dust asked.

"Too obvious. If we get stopped, we'll look guilty," David said. "But I'm not going to stop. And I don't want to hit anything in the road."

"Like what?" Dust asked.

"Debris. Barricades. Bodies." His short answer ended the conversation.

He was glad they didn't argue the point. His heart pounded in his chest. The adrenaline of a street race followed by a potential police car chase flooded his system. This time the stakes were far higher than either of those unlikely events. He had two innocent people counting on him not to get caught.

Memories of the alien guards at the feedlot and the attack at the turnaround on I-70 chilled his blood. He gripped the steering wheel tighter as images flooded his mind. Alien commandos, tall and grim. Their high-tech armor making them impervious to attack. On their helmets had been the symbol. They had moved with purpose, and he suspected it was to capture him. *Or the person by his side. Dust.*

He committed the color of their armor and the smallest details of the symbol to memory. That was something he learned early at El Dorado Prison: know how to spot your enemies and never assume they're gone just because you can't see them.

There were no cars on the road, which made it impossible to be inconspicuous. He estimated that they had only minutes before one of the jump ships came to investigate his movement.

"Here comes one!" Abigail said, pointing out her window.

David gradually accelerated, hoping he could make his move without prompting them to make theirs before he was ready.

"Another one is coming from the other direction," Dust said, her words clipped.

David raced down Rock Road from 37th Street North, gaining speed by degrees, knowing exactly how fast he could take the on-ramp five blocks ahead. Fast food row, storage units, and strip malls lined each side of the four-lane street.

"We're not going to make it to the highway." Abigail's breathless words came true as an alien ship jumped the overpass and dropped low enough to block the street.

David stomped on the accelerator, jerked the wheel a millimeter to his left, then shot around the ship as it slid sideways a beat too late to ram him. He felt the tires grab and the suspension adjust. It was all coming back like he was still in that final car chase before everything went to hell.

Abigail was right, however. He'd dodged around his adversary but was now traveling a hundred and ten miles per hour, far too fast to negotiate the on-ramp. With no other choice, he continued into the city and tried to lose his pursuers in the neighborhood.

This time they were all flying. It was a lot more challenging than escaping one police helicopter and some underpowered Police Interceptors—cop cars one day, taxi cabs the next; Ford hunks of junk with prisoner cages that smelled like puke and bad decisions.

Spotlights shone downward from fast moving alien ships as he weaved through neighborhoods with twisting streets and lots of cul-de-sacs. He drove through a yard and onto a walking path barely wide enough to support his wheels, then cut his lights. The car slipped under the large looming trees.

"Cross your fingers. If someone is out for a late-night jog, we're going to smear them across the dirt," David said.

"What about bad guys and barricades?" Abigail shot back.

"That would also suck."

"You're going too fast," Abigail complained, clutching the armrests as they bounced along the path. "Maybe we should get back on a real street."

"All in good time." David didn't like their chances. These pursuers wouldn't disregard a chase if it became too dangerous. He really hoped there was a curfew that kept the midnight pedestrian population down. While he was at it, he hoped the entire invasion was a mistake and everyone would just shake hands and part their intergalactic ways.

The car engine growled and the tires hummed as he steered around a narrow turn in the bike trail.

In the front seat, Abigail grabbed the dashboard with both hands and clenched her teeth. He glanced in the back to see Dust gripping the seat in front of her with one hand, pressed the other against the little side window, and jammed her legs down to the floorboard for maximum leverage.

Tree branches slapped at the windows of the modern-day muscle car. It'd been a while since this part of the park had been trimmed. David laughed without much humor. Why had he assumed this shortcut would be in the same condition as it had been before he went to prison and subsequently built his trucking career?

Abigail squealed when something big thumped against the window. It might've been a thicker branch, but David wasn't sure. When he eased off the gas pedal, the exhaust pipes of the Dodge growled during the downshift. He looked for a turnoff, found one, and emerged near Wichita State University, the city college that had changed so much he barely recognized the place.

Not that he had attended the institution. He'd driven through the neighborhood hundreds of times and maybe cut through the campus once or twice. It was hard to remember exactly.

This he did remember. Last time he rode through campus, it didn't have a spaceship parked in its center. The immense craft was as tall as a skyscraper, with conduits snaking into the asphalt all around it. Even from a distance, he could see something strange was happening here. Like a giant had shoved its toys aside, cars and trucks were crammed near the buildings to make space in the main parking lot. Lights flickered up and down the height of the ship.

"What are you doing?" Dust asked when the light turned green but he kept his foot on the break.

Down the street was some sort of checkpoint. The vehicles were more familiar than the turbine drop ships or the bigger vessels that seemed to be routed into the ground now. Those at the roadblock had huge wheels and thick armor, but were still as alien as an eight-foot-tall humanoid wearing movie armor with a feeder tube in place of a tongue.

Shadows moved under the remaining streetlights. *Those big bastards are on foot*, he thought, going car-to-car searching all the vehicles they'd stopped. Their weapons had a distinctive shape. Angry shouts floated on the wind. Gunfire cracked; silence followed.

David's heart raced. He told himself that he didn't know what had happened, and it was stupid to worry about it now.

Keep moving. Keep thinking. Ride this thing out until we know what's happening.

"That looks like trouble." He nodded toward the roadblock. "I don't see any activity around the big ship there. The campus roads twist and turn in there, I think, and I'm hoping we can wiggle our way through, then pop out on the north side of the campus. From there it's about a mile on surface streets to reach the highway again, this time southbound until we catch Highway 54. We'll head west if we're going to look for your family, Abigail."

"Okay." The farmer's daughter's voice wavered.

Dust shifted uncomfortably, her silence more unnerving than a complaint.

He slow rolled toward an entrance, then began curving

his way through the university, moving ever closer to the towering spaceship. There were no obvious guards, which he thought was strange. Shadows flickered near the base of the huge structure.

More aliens, he guessed. No way in hell he was driving close enough to confirm.

Drones came racing around the tall ship, scanning it from top to bottom and then bottom to top. Cables streamed behind them, looked more like tentacles than cables. He stopped his brain from thinking about what that could mean. Too fucking strange to deal with.

All he cared about was not getting any closer to the ship —or the things near it.

An access road led him around the north side of several buildings. Each time he thought they were going to escape, he ran into a change in his very limited knowledge of the geography. There had been an entrance that was no longer there, victim of a new baseball stadium parking lot.

"Is something wrong?" Dust asked.

"I've mostly seen this place from the outside," he said. "And that was years ago. I thought we could get out right there. This road should have led right to sorority row."

"You know that, how?" Dust asked.

"I was young once. Might have crashed some parties."

"Just pop the curb," Abigail suggested, shifting in her seat several times, talking over Dust without seeming to think about it. Her nervousness bothered David. The inside of the car was small, and they were sharing the space during a difficult ordeal. He winced every time she drew her feet up under her, imagining her shoes scuffing the leather interior. "Just get us the hell out of here."

He shook his head. "Not worth it. We follow the road

until it dumps us onto the street. It can't be that far. It's not like we're at UCLA or something."

When he finally saw the exit, he turned without second-guessing his luck but not before he saw a closer view of an alien starship. The view entranced him. He almost pulled over and stopped the car.

"Keep going," Dust whispered. "This is not the time to ask for a guided tour."

"Yeah, right. It just looks so alive. Full of lights." He turned onto the street and was relieved there wasn't another roadblock on the north side of the block. He turned left and made his way west on 21st Street until he reached I-135 and headed south.

There was no need to fly up this on-ramp at full speed. He took it slow, paying careful attention to a police car that had been cut in half by alien gunfire. Scorched holes were punched through its exterior, definitely caused by something more destructive than bullets. He wondered if the driver of the car had survived. There didn't seem to be a body behind the wheel or anywhere around it.

Not that he was stopping to examine the scene carefully.

"I'm picking up the pace once we get onto the highway," he said. "But I'll try not to draw any attention until I have to. You better put your seatbelts on if you haven't already."

Neither of the young women argued.

They encountered no problems for several miles. There were a few vehicles on the road, mostly police cars. Had they switched sides? he wondered. Maybe they were they just getting by, biding their time. Or maybe they'd sold their allegiance to humanity to save their own skin.

North and east of his current location, there were airships still searching for him. He'd gotten away, this time, but he wouldn't get lucky again. Resisting the urge to put the pedal to the metal and go for broke took all of his will power. He felt the need for speed but understood being invisible was better.

Or maybe they hadn't been looking for him at all, but someone or something else. It didn't matter. All he wanted was to be gone.

"Why aren't they chasing us?" Abigail asked. "And why are those police cars just driving around like they're on regular patrol?"

"I don't know," David said, not about to share his recent thoughts on the subject. "I'm just glad they're not stopping us."

He assumed—hoped—that the officers had merely bowed to their new overlords to keep the peace and act as a layer between murderous oppression and civilians. David thought he understood that decision but couldn't quite articulate it. As David passed another watching cop car, one of the officers looked over and made eye contact with him. The man's expression was grim, his pallor sickly like he hadn't eaten for a while or was extremely hung over.

After that brief stare, the man pointedly ignored David in the muscle car.

"I think that guy sold out," Abigail spat. "What a gutless coward."

"Just be thankful he didn't stop us. He could make our lives really difficult if he is working for them. I'll bet if he is helping them, he's doing the bare minimum to keep them from killing his family," David said. "He looks like he's been poisoned."

"With what?" Abigail asked.

"I don't know. It's just a hunch. I've seen a lot of junkies in withdraw. You can get drugs in prison, but they're expensive and the supply isn't steady unless you're a trustee in the medical wing."

It was strange to drive in such a quiet city. The occasional chatter of gunfire was distinct, but otherwise it looked like someone had flipped a switch and turned the city off. While lights shone in a few of the houses, there was little vehicle traffic and nothing flying that didn't belong to the invaders.

"Here comes one," Dust said, pointing to the south at about the same time David took an exit ramp to the highway.

Three additional ships joined the one Dust had spotted. A second later, they had formed a V formation and accelerated with breathtaking speeds. When they passed over David's car, a sonic boom followed.

He continued to drive, watching them for as long as he could but keeping most of his attention on his immediate surroundings.

"There must be a battle someplace," Abigail said. "I bet they're going after our fighter jets." She looked at David in the rearview mirror. "Do you think our fighter jets can beat them?"

"They caught us by surprise." He'd meant to say more; he'd wanted to explain how the military would later adapt and overcome. But the words just didn't come out. As awesome as F-22s were, he didn't think they stood a chance.

But what do I know?

Fatigue pressed down on him. It wasn't a good time for weakness, but the feeling didn't surprise him. It took a lot of energy to remain on high alert. Sooner or later, adrenaline wore off.

He relaxed his hands on the steering wheel and kept the

speed reasonable, about eight miles per hour since there was no one to block his lane or give him the finger. Before long, he was heading out of town.

Abigail shifted yet again. "I thought I'd feel better when we put the city behind us, but I don't."

David didn't comment. He looked at a broad field on the south side of Highway 54 about a mile west of Wichita. He'd driven by it hundreds of times in the past while taking loads out to western Kansas. Gone were the hay bales and barbwire fences to keep cows in. Now it was a refugee camp surrounded by a maze of chain-link fences. None of the guards were human.

Men, women, and children were poked, prodded, and driven into different sections of the hastily built facility. He continued to drive but took one last look in his rearview mirror. What he'd assumed were chain-link fences were something different. A blue sheen pulsed around the edges of the thin barrier, focused on the top and corners. No human factory had produced those fences.

"Should we help them?" Abigail asked, sounding very young and unsure.

"Maybe later," David said. "But probably not. We need to go before one of those drones comes after us."

Abigail grimaced. "I don't like the drones. They remind me of big, flying spiders."

In the rearview mirror, Dust's expression was unreadable. She turned away, casting her gaze back toward the concentration camps run by aliens who drank blood.

CHAPTER EIGHTEEN

CHARLES WAITED until his girls were asleep and then went to find his wife. She'd volunteered to help new people with orientation, which wasn't her style. She worked hard but only to advance her career and provide for their family. Her generosity had always been aimed at people she knew and cared about, never at strangers.

Handing out blankets didn't come natural to her. He was surprised she was spending so much time doing it.

"Have you seen Emily?" Charles asked Raymond Powers, the project leader now in charge of domestic supplies.

"No, was she supposed to be here?" Powers asked.

"No, it's not the shift she volunteered for," Charles lied without knowing why. "I thought she came up here to get her handbag."

"Who carries a handbag in a bunker like this?"

"You don't know my wife," Charles said, forcing a smile. "A woman just doesn't drop her Chanel because the world is ending."

He didn't know where to look next. Emily had left him a note. Now he wished he had it with him to check. After a while, he found himself back at work.

The company's largest meeting room had become a command center. People he'd never seen before worked at computers that had been wheeled out and turned on right after the attack.

Henry walked toward him, bypassing several of the workstations, his face flushed and hair a bit wild.

"Charles, where have you been? We are about to see the joint force counterattack," Henry said.

"I didn't know I was supposed to be here," Charles said, eyeing his friend's suit, rumpled but fancy. The man was even wearing the kind of high dollar cologne Emily liked to buy.

"Someone should have told you what was happening," Henry said, guiding him toward the front of the room where they would have a good view of the wall screen.

"Have you seen Emily?" Charles asked.

"I did. She was on her way through here to give out blankets or something," he said. "She was pissed she couldn't stay for the show."

"Why shouldn't she?"

"This is top secret stuff. You and I are here due to our expertise in gaming strategy," Henry said.

"Oh. That makes sense," Charles said, still overwhelmed by the activity of the place. There were military contractors and more than a few high-ranking leaders from all five military branches.

"Those men are liaisons from the Armed Forces," he said, pointing out a few stern-looking men. "If we come up with good ideas, their jobs are to make sure our strategic and tactical solutions get implemented in the real world. Cool, right?"

"Yeah, it's great," Charles said, spotting Emily walking quickly out the door back toward the new arrival orientation area where she was supposed to be passing out blankets.

"That pisses me off," he said.

"The liaisons?" Henry frowned.

"No, Emily. They have her doing common labor when she would be more help to us using her mind. She should be here."

"Oh. Yeah, you're probably right, but there isn't time to argue the point. This is happening now."

Guards checked identification badges. Charles felt as though his presence was tolerated, not invited. All the company's power players were here. The government and military types conferred with them frequently. He stood near one wall with Henry, watching and waiting.

"This room is now secure, and everyone still here is bound by the strictest confidentiality clauses of our contract with the US government and her allies," a man standing at a podium said.

"What we are about to see is the first real fruit of our efforts, a major counterattack from Earth's strongest military coalition. We're calling it the EMC for now, the Earth Military Coalition. Take notes, but keep your voices down unless called on."

Someone dimmed the lights, and a view of the North Pacific appeared on a screen. Three fleets he had never imagined working together converged on what looked like an alien oil rig.

The platform was half starship and half drilling platform.

Squadrons of alien fighters and high-tech blue water ships patrolled an area covering hundreds of miles.

The scene repeated on other screens, one for the North Atlantic, South Pacific, and one in the Mediterranean Sea. The human ships looked small from the altitude of the drone footage—one of which went off-line almost immediately. Several tense but quiet conversations happened, and a new drone was activated to cover what was occurring in the North Pacific.

"Fingers crossed," Henry said.

"I'll cross whatever works," Charles answered, breathing life into one of their lame jokes from college.

Henry laughed. Charles felt better.

Patriot missiles launched from several ships in the North Atlantic Fleet. Moments later, the same happened from each of the other EMC battle groups.

Charles felt ill at ease. Henry was acting oddly, and he wasn't quite sure what type of conversation to make while watching the end of the world on high-definition video screens.

Sirens sounded on ships to warn their crews before Tomahawk missiles launched one after another. Dozens of ships attacked simultaneously. The sky became a tangle of vapor trails heading for the alien ships. Some struck without causing visible damage. Others smashed alien jump ships from the sky. The most common fate of the cruise missiles, however, was getting vaporized by energy beams.

Fighter squadrons raced in, dropping out of the clouds with the sun at their back whenever possible. The pace of the dogfight was too fast to track. Voices in the command room argued, shouting and pointing at individual victories or defeats. Charles heard someone crying. When he looked to see who it was, all he saw were people cursing and slamming their fists on desks.

Three of the newcomers raced toward a British aircraft carrier, took aim, and sliced it in half as they passed over its deck. The death squadron turned toward American ships, destroying everything they encountered. One took damage and turned away from the fight, but it didn't look ruined to Charles.

The pace of the battle slowed. After several defeated launches of missiles, nothing happened, and the civilians and military personnel alike were anxious.

"What's going on?" Charles asked, though he had his own suspicions.

"I wasn't in on the planning, but I've talked to some people," Henry whispered. "They had some stealth fighters that were supposed to be part of this. They didn't show."

"Maintaining air superiority against this type of enemy seems like a tall order," Charles observed. "They shouldn't have planned on that happening. Optimism can't replace hard reality."

Henry nodded but his eyes were focused on the screens. Stealth fighters appeared, but were vaporized just as quick. It was difficult to see exactly what had taken them out. Some were struck by nearly invisible energy beams while others were engaged by high-speed fighter aircraft that seemed to drop out of orbit. One reconnaissance drone gave visuals on a truly massive fleet of alien jets that lifted off the ground like Harrier jump jets, but these behemoths were far larger and more varied.

"We're definitely not going to win," Charles said. "Not that I blame these strategy planners. They actually have done fairly well with what we have."

"Really? I'm not willing to accept that," Henry said. "The EMC had every resource on the planet available to them and this is the best they can do? Somebody has to be held accountable."

"I'm sure somebody will. Probably, the ones holding them accountable will be the alien overlords." Charles had meant this as a joke, but Henry went pale. Something changed in his expression that Charles didn't like.

It was in that moment that he saw his friend, always the best athlete and the smartest and handsomest man in the room, was a coward. His mind couldn't process this defeat and was grasping for any way to save himself.

All of a sudden, Charles realized there was only one man he wanted by his side. His brother. They'd never gotten along. David was sometimes a barbaric asshole with way too much testosterone fueling his decisions. But right now, Charles despised Henry as weak even though the man physically towered over him.

I'm in the wrong place, he thought. *With the wrong people.*

Charles's eye caught movement. Off to the side, the highest-ranking military officers were leaving the room, taking their aides and bodyguards with them. He hadn't noticed a change at first because there were still Navy, Marines, Army, and Air Force personnel running the battle. With so many people in the room, a covert exit was possible.

"I'm not surprised they're bugging out," Henry said. "For all their talk, these warrior types are pretty gutless, which really screws us. We need to do something. Need to look out for ourselves."

Charles observed the CEO of Warfighter Games and several others stepping back from strategy tables and leaving through side doors. Security guards blocked a man who tried to follow them, not giving an explanation but merely raising one hand in the universal gesture of warning to come no farther.

"Looks like our benevolent leader is going with them," Charles said.

If Henry had seemed pale before, now he looked like he was going to be sick.

"I need to find my wife and get back to my kids," Charles said.

Henry gave him a strange, slightly panicked look. "What? Oh, of course. Go find Emily. I'm going to stay here for just a little longer. I need to talk to some people."

Charles patted him on the shoulder, intending to reassure his best friend, but feeling him tense unexpectedly. Not knowing what to do with the observation, he just smiled awkwardly and left the room.

———

CHARLES ENTERED the small family dorm room he'd been assigned as part of the Warfighter Games design team. Cara and Debbie threw down their coloring books and rushed him, wrapping him in hugs.

Charles felt better than he had in days. "I thought you liked your coloring books?"

"We do!" Cara said.

"I like them the most!" Debbie argued.

"Where's your mother? She can't be taking another shower. We're almost out of water rations," Charles said, thinking aloud.

"You're loud-thinking like Mommy doesn't like," Cara said.

"Daddy does that, sweetie," Charles said, hugging each of his daughters again.

"He's not supposed to," Debbie said.

Cara nodded in very serious agreement. "He's not."

Charles laughed. For some reason, his eyes were rimmed with tears. "Sounds like Mommy is done with her shower."

The girls grabbed their coloring books. "Can you help us until Mommy's done?"

"Anything for my little angels," Charles said, and he went to work with the blue crayon. He tried not to think of the naval battles that had gone so poorly.

Emily took longer than usual. She was spending more and more time grooming recently, which made no sense to Charles. The bathroom was small, her makeup kit a fraction of what she maintained in their five-bedroom home in the suburbs.

He thought she looked pristine as an angel when she finally came out—glowing skin, bright eyes, and a wonderful smile for him and their girls. The utilitarian robe wasn't exactly lingerie, but he thought she looked as sexy as always—too good for him by several orders of magnitude.

Still, despite all her beauty, she also looked sad and stressed, and ready to be done with this ordeal.

"You girls get in bed," Charles said. "Mommy and Daddy are going to talk in the hallway."

"Are we?" Emily asked, sounding annoyed by the suggestion.

"I haven't seen you all day," he said, even though he knew that wasn't exactly true.

She leaned forward and kissed him gently on the mouth, eyes half closed. Emotions smoldered when she drew back to give him a sleepy look. "Okay, Charles. Let's have some quality time in the hallway."

He held the door for her. Moments later, they were leaning on a wall facing each other with their arms crossed.

"How was your day?" he asked.

"Frustrating," she said. "It took me forever to even get started. And then it was drudgery."

"I thought I saw you in the command center," he said.

She sniffed. "They ran me out of there. All I wanted was to cut through the room and get to my workstation, which wasn't where I thought it was."

"This facility isn't that complicated." Charles studied her reaction, not liking the way he was feeling.

"I'm sure I will learn my way around. None of this makes sense to me. Why are we hiding underground when the military is up there fighting for us?"

Charles didn't understand her question. The battle above ground didn't need unarmed and untrained civilians messing things up. His job, and that of his family, was to stay out of the way and help in other ways.

Yet his intuition said this place was a death trap, not the high-tech bunker it purported to be. The incongruity of facts and feelings tortured his rational mind.

"We need to leave," he said, not knowing he was going to make the radical decision until the words were already out of his mouth.

"Stop saying those things out loud," Emily said. "I ran into Henry earlier and he told me breaking the rules is going to get people forcibly evicted from the shelter."

"That sounds like something Henry would say," Charles said.

"What is that supposed to mean?" She stood away from the wall, angry enough that her cheeks were burning.

"I was allowed to witness a major counterattack against the invaders," Charles said.

"Which you're not supposed to tell me about, I'm sure."

"Do you want me to hide things from you, Emily? Lie to you? Do you think we should endanger the children just so we can follow all the rules?"

"Is this Charles Osage I'm talking to, or David? I love him because he's your big brother, but you can't act irresponsible like he does. We have a family and these are dangerous times."

"That's why we need to leave," Charles said, pitching his voice low. "I saw several important people in the company and the generals leave when things started to get dicey during their most recent operation."

"Those men and women probably have other responsibilities. I would bet my next sales commission they are already at another bunker just like this one putting people at ease. They know better than to scare everyone."

"Listen to me, Emily," Charles said. "I'm having my feeling."

This gave her pause. He rarely listened to intuition, but there had been incidents during their years together when he listened to his heart and miracles happened. "Like the day I proposed to you. And that time we took Cara in for an unscheduled checkup and probably saved her life."

Emily shifted uncomfortably. Heat rushed to her face and she crossed her arms, doubting herself more than he'd seen in a long time.

But she rallied quickly, and he knew that changing her mind now would be like moving a mountain. "Listen,

Charles. I never wanted to be in this bunker, but now it's the only place that is safe. I've been asking around, and people have been telling me their stories. Things are really bad outside. We are not taking our little girls into that chaos."

Charles wanted to argue but understood he needed hard facts to change her mind.

"Why don't we put this aside for now?" she said softly. Then she hugged him, burying her head on his shoulder.

He relaxed into her embrace. He wanted to cry. Arguing with the love of his life was the hardest thing he'd ever done, and he didn't want to do it anymore.

"I love you," he said.

CHARLES HELPED EMILY PUT the girls to bed, then went back out. It was a hard decision because for an hour the relationship had felt fresh and alive again. He hadn't realized there was a problem until the joy of the emotions hit him.

Now he was worried but didn't understand why. He laughed a little crazily as he walked down one of the long hallways. She couldn't leave him now, could she? They were in this together until the end. Where exactly would she go if she did dump him?

Don't be a jealous idiot.

She could have any man she wanted and not just because she was gorgeous. She was charming and loving and made him a better person. Who didn't want that? She could be the queen of the world with the snap of her fingers.

Stopping at the bottom of the stairwell, he tried to remember where he had been going. Pacing back and forth was another habit that Emily didn't like. He'd been walking off is nervous energy with no real destination, he realized.

This was one of the nonessential levels. Everything had been mothballed and locked up. The hallway stretching away from the stairs was dimly illuminated by emergency lights.

His first thought was that this could be his new sanctuary, some place he could pace all he wanted without bothering anyone. He started to get excited, imagining the creative new ideas he would generate this way.

As it turned out, there was no need to pace back and forth because he could walk the block, taking the first left and then the next and so on. He was halfway around the loop when he heard the voices.

He stopped, then felt guilty for listening.

The voice of Patrick Kingston was easily recognizable. He was from the Midwest with a voice like the ringmaster for a traveling circus. But he'd either been trained as an orator or had picked up a formal style that concealed his native dialect.

Charles recognized at least two other voices from high-level board meetings but couldn't put names with faces to them just by the sound.

Thea a hissing clatter of words interrupted the argument and turned his blood to ice.

His mind went blank. He wanted to run but couldn't remember how. Cold pain seeped into his nerves. After what felt like several minutes, he was able to press his back against the wall and hold himself up with effort.

What would David or Laura do?

The sound of his rushing blood filled his ears. His heart

pounded noisily. He'd never experienced anything like this, and it scared him. At the same time, it felt pretty good.

The hallway was still empty save for the dim emergency lighting every twenty or thirty feet. Each LED lamp in the ceiling made a small circle on the floor below it. The elevators looked so far away, they might as well have been part of an Alice in Wonderland landscape.

He pressed his ear to the door and listened.

The hissing voice spoke English, but he couldn't understand it. The door was too thick and the accent too bizarre. At times he was certain that the most important words would be out of his auditory range no matter how close he stood by the source.

"You're a terrible salesman, Drailen-Foek-ha. I still don't see what's in it for the human race," Kingston said, his voice strong and confident.

Charles thought Kingston was an amazingly good choice for the company's ambassador. The man didn't seem rattled by confronting an alien invader. *Probably because he's a self-absorbed imbecile who advanced his career by taking credit for other people's ideas*, he thought sarcastically.

The *warm, fuzzy* feeling was ruined when he understood what the creature growled back in response.

"Benefit for humanity. Rewards for you. Some of your people. The blood power of this planet must go to the Fosk-ha."

CHAPTER NINETEEN

OFFICER LAURA OSAGE stared at a ceiling like none she'd imagined seeing in real life. Hospital lights glared downward, as cold and harsh as the monsters who had poisoned her.

David wouldn't lay here like this. He'd fight back—tell the motherfuckers to go straight to hell.

She didn't want to move. That would be like admitting all of this was real. She hated normal hospitals, and this place was so much worse.

Thinking about the last few days caused her to cry, which was even less dignified while lying on her back. She lacked the energy to curl into a ball.

"Are you comfortable?" asked a thin alien so tall she nearly laughed in a strange combination of wonderment and horror. Laughing and crying at the same time was clear evidence she had lost her mind.

"Why can I understand you better than the others?" Laura asked.

The alien smiled and, like a tree bending in the breeze, sat down beside her. "I have worked very hard to know your language. In my profession, I need to know more than just how to give humans orders."

"Are you a doctor?" Laura asked.

"The term is adequate to describe my purpose."

Laura believed it was a male but couldn't be sure. The blue of its skin seemed softer than any she'd yet seen. Of course, the warriors she'd encountered had been full of battle lust, flush with excitement and whatever they used for adrenaline.

"Is this one of your hospitals?" Laura asked.

The alien bowed his head then raised it, his expression gentle.

Laura studied him, confused. "What are you doing?"

His brow pinched. "I am nodding to demonstrate that I understand your words."

"No, you're not."

The alien hissed in frustration, or that's what Laura interpreted the noise as. "What am I doing?"

"You're bowing your head." Laura's back ached. The bed felt more like an autopsy table than a place to convalesce.

"Does this mean something different from a nod of agreement?"

"Yeah, asshole, it does." She twisted to get comfortable, realizing she had been bound to the bed but now the restraints were loose.

"I must warn you, I know this word. It is not respectful. Do not speak thus again."

"Why do I have my own room?" she asked.

Just then, there was a commotion in the hallway. The

doctor, or whatever he was, rushed out. She caught a glimpse of him running into the room across the hall with frightening speed.

A woman cried out for mercy, screaming that the pain was too much. "Please, just let me die!" she sobbed.

The alien doctor hissed and shrieked like a hurricane blowing through a keyhole. Laura's body clenched, bracing for an attack. Another voice, a human one, joined the commotion, promising he could calm the woman.

Laura listened to the arguments with dread, her stomach twisting in knots. Then the alien doctor promised the unseen speaker to let the woman have one more round of the treatment before other steps were taken. She didn't know what that meant, but had a hunch that she'd rather die than find out for herself.

When her door opened, she closed her eyes as if she were asleep. Judging by the many footsteps that crowded into her room, the argument had made its way there. Aliens hissed their demands. A human begged to give the patients time. Humans could survive the blood transfusions, a man insisted. Some needed more time, that was all.

The doctor leaned close, breathing on her neck. She wanted to lash out, hit him as hard as she could, and then scramble off the bed and flee.

He started making a sound that she could barely hear but that grew slightly louder as he examined her from head to toe. It was like a purring sound crossed with insectile clicking. She hated everything about the noise.

Eventually, the doctor stood and said something to the others. The aliens left the room. The human argued, but was silenced with a hiss.

"She is not asleep or in danger," the doctor said. "Leave us."

The man who had been advocating for the humans stood silently. Laura wanted to open her eyes and see who it was but didn't dare. After a few long seconds, she heard him leave.

"Why do you pretend to sleep?" the alien doctor asked after the door clicked shut.

She opened her eyes and stared at the ceiling. "What was he talking about, blood transfusions?"

"It is an incorrect term. He does not understand as much as he thinks he does. In time you will understand the blood power of this planet and its creatures. All you must know now is that you survived an attack from one of our warriors. This could mean you will be privileged among our servants."

Laura twisted onto her side and vomited bile. Each convulsion aggravated a headache that had been lurking just below the surface of her awareness. She thought she had a fever and the room wouldn't stop spinning.

"I am Aon-fosk-ga, what you call a doctor. You may also think of me as a scientist and an overlord."

"Those are two different things in my world," Laura groaned.

"Not any longer." The alien sat up straight, and it was then that she realized he had been holding her left wrist to take her pulse. "The rules have changed. If you want to survive, then you will follow them."

"That's a pretty bold assumption considering what you've done to my friends."

"Do you want to help those who remain?"

Laura knew what was coming next. She wished she had a way to argue against the inevitable logic. The commando who had first captured her said something along the same lines, that she could make like easier for humans.

"The creatures of Earth cannot stand against us," Aon-fosk-ga said. "They must be ruled. Those who resist will only hurt themselves. We must find those among you who can keep the peace. Are you not a peacekeeper?"

Laura closed her eyes away turned her face away.

"One of the soldiers bit me," she said, changing the subject. "Why did he do that?"

The doctor pulled up a chair and sat near her, leaning forward earnestly. Some of the alien's body language was uncomfortably strange, but there were commonalities between humans and these Fosk-ha.

"We have traveled farther than you can imagine. Many of us have never seen a planet in our lifetimes. The ships that we use to travel the galaxy are far more advanced than you can understand. Earth is a jewel, a biosphere with great power that you take for granted. We need it because we have been away too long," Aon-fosk-ga explained. "We must go even farther if we are to survive. This is just a way-stop. We only have two options: nourish ourselves physically, mentally, and emotionally or find one of the Dustvarians capable of navigating a translation starship."

"You should've done that before you left whatever cosmic shithole produced you," Laura said.

"I cannot disagree. If we find a Navigator, then much will change," Doctor Aon-fosk-ga said.

LAURA LEFT the hospital three days later, feeling almost human despite how strange Chicago had become. There were a few buildings that hadn't been scorched, perforated by pulse blasters, or smashed apart during the invasion, but most of the damaged structures had been replaced by slim colony ships.

She looked at the two-inch-wide band on her wrist, checking the instructions. Ignoring the sleek bracelet was dangerous. Last night, she'd stayed awake after curfew and suffered electric shocks, which did nothing to ease her into dreamland. The night had been miserable from start to finish.

After that, she paid attention to what the paper-thin device put on her itinerary.

It couldn't read her mind, which was a relief. Most of the second day after her bite had been spent contemplating what the thing was and how she could get rid of it.

The band did three things so far as she could tell: sampled a few molecules of her blood every five minutes, broadcast her location to the alien overlords, and put rules and instructions on a view screen. Right now it was telling her where her new apartment was located and ordering her to go there for "grooming, consuming nutrients, and sleeping."

I can't live like this.

Chicago now resembled a science fiction movie poster. The aliens had swept the slate clean in some places, creating expansive landing fields where there had been factories and warehouses before. Above the skyscrapers were air lanes for Fosk-ha craft that moved like antigravity ships. She heard their engines and pieced together memories of the chaotic first day.

One blue-lit craft touched down on a landing strip like a star coming to rest. These ships were far more advanced than what humans could manufacture, she knew, but the basic technology was something humanity might imitate and master given enough time. This led to another, more unsettling thought. How long would it be before humans were blasting off on a ship like that to conquer some other alien world?

Men and women barely spoke as they walked to work. The few children she saw walked in groups supervised by human—or human-looking—adults and a black-armored soldier. A Fosk-ha soldier stared down at her. On his chest a silver badge on his chest—a letter A in a circle that was itself in a box. She'd seed this more and more often and didn't know what it meant.

The band on her arm vibrated, indicating she was disobeying orders. She turned onto a new street, typing quickly on the wrist screen in an attempt to convince the device that a course correction was required for her to reach her new domicile.

The idea of a shower, a meal, and a good night's sleep wasn't wrong—she just needed to have a look around first. Chicago was her city. There were things she needed to do.

Street by street, she cataloged everything she saw. Instinct warned her not to write anything down, not to take pictures, and not to look at one location for too long. She doubted they'd installed an invisible body camera, but it was a useful paranoia to foster. Even if they couldn't see through her eyes, they could see a lot.

As she studied the new cityscape, she realized that the alien ships and pre-fabricated structures were situated strategically. The invaders had done this before. The shock and awe phase of their attack had been devastating. Their occupation protocols were beyond anything done in human history.

She thought about what Doctor Aon-fosk-ga had revealed. The Fosk-ha were intergalactic travelers on their way… somewhere. Could she send them on? What would they need to leave Earth alone?

She passed one Fosk-ha soldier as he stepped from an alley, wiping blood from the front of his chest plate.

"You missed some, champ," she said, knowing it was a bad idea to provoke some bloodthirsty freak she'd never met.

"Why do you talk to me? Are you chosen among us? Have you not been instructed?" he said, stepping closer.

At well over seven feet tall, the Fosk-ha warrior loomed over her. She thought they were shorter out of their armor, but still freakishly huge and strong. Her heart raced and her vision narrowed.

She forced her awareness outward as she had been trained since the Academy. There were normal sounds—cars, crosswalk announcements for the hearing impaired, and air conditioners. No human planes, helicopters, or drones flew, and at the moment, all the alien aircraft were grounded as well, leaving an empty silence.

"Show me your control band," the soldier ordered.

She tried to guess his rank, but the symbols made little sense. His pauldron only had a single, uneven line that she assumed meant he was a low-ranking foot soldier. But what if the marking indicated he was an officer, a lieutenant perhaps?

With no other choice, she proffered her arm, pretending

to be calm and in control of her fear. Inside, her body was doing all it could to prepare her for a fight to the death. Adrenaline could be fun. *Could be*. This definitely wasn't.

"You are almost to your dormitory," the soldier said, clearly disappointed. "And you are marked loyal to the Fosk-ha."

Laura said nothing.

"This means I cannot feed on you." He shrugged. "But be warned, things change. When you fall from grace, your blood will taste twice as rich. For the Fosk." He saluted the sky by twisting his fist upward and retracting it like a giant doing the last move in a karate form.

After she watched him go, she followed the prompts from her arm band. The vibrations had become more and more insistent as time passed. Icey numbness grew in her fingertips and toes, then disappearing the moment she stepped toward her dormitory.

She couldn't see it yet. The wrist band told her it was around the corner, one block over. When she turned, the sight took her breath away.

Lines of Chicagoans ambled toward the tall, prefabricated Fosk-ha dormitory that was thirty levels high and growing through a complex scaffolding that reminded her of a metal spider's web.

The people looked neither happy nor unhappy. She caught a few of them glancing around.

Good. Don't quit, she silently urged them. Keep your eyes open. Never surrender.

The mantra felt hollow. She wasn't exactly kicking ass and taking names. Why should the good citizens of Chicago fight back when she was rolling over like a trained dog?

The Fosk-ha wanted her to keep her job, police her own people in exchange for preferential treatment. A week ago, she wouldn't have considered the devil's bargain. With no kids or spouse to worry about, she would fight in the resistance.

What resistance? She longed for signs of a rebellion. Where were all the good ole boys with their end-prepper arsenals and four-wheel drive trucks?

Laura Osage had nothing to lose. Her brothers had to take care of themselves. She had sworn an oath to serve and protect. Did that mean appeasing the alien overlords to minimize violent reprisals against civilians, or going to ground and fighting back with hit-and-run tactics?

Tears filled her eyes as she thought about David. He was so proud of his truck and definitely not the guy to submit. He'd fight just to be an asshole. *Is that what I should do? Even if it gets more people killed?*

A guard waved her into the building. Digital signs near each elevator provided instructions—by name. The invaders knew everything about their conquered subjects.

At the end of a tubular hallway, she walked through steel door that opened at her approach. Though small, the apartment was larger than she had expected. A cell would have fit her mood.

"Welcome, Officer Laura Osage. I am Robert Bob, your artificial assistant," said a voice.

She turned to the screen in wonderment.

"Can I be of assistance?" Robert Bob said.

"Your name is Bob Bob?" she asked.

"That is incorrect. Robert Bob. Our name generator indicated both names were acceptable and pleasing to humans," the vaguely human avatar answered.

"Bob is short for Robert," she said, not sure why she was explaining this to a computer program written by aliens who were here to enslave humanity, drink their blood, then continue their merciless spread across the galaxy.

"Processing," Robert Bob said. "I see. You are correct. This is most humorous."

"Fucking hilarious, Bob Bob."

"Would you like to call me Bob for short?"

She walked to the refrigerator, stepping back when it opened automatically. "I'd like for you people to leave Earth and never come back."

"Of course. However, orchestrating such an event is beyond my abilities," Bob said. "My file says you were injured during first contact and then treated in one of our human-centric hospitals. Do you require further medical services?"

"I'm good," she said, examining the food and drink choices in the ultramodern refrigerator.

"Processing," Bob said.

"What are you processing, Bob? I said, I'm good."

"Human idioms, especially in your language, are illogical and often require careful consideration."

"We didn't invite you to take over our planet." She pulled out a pre-made sandwich and a jug of orange juice.

"On the contrary, you did."

"What?" she spat the word like it was a curse.

"Earth is far from other habitable worlds. We would not have found our way to this system had there not been a call to us."

"Tell me all about that, Bob." She sat on the couch, leaning back with one leg crossed over the other as she ate the sandwich and drank the orange juice.

"Processing."

"Of course. Listen, it's really rude to drop a clue like that and then hold back. If you want to be a good personal assistant or whatever you are, then spill it."

"Spill it?"

"Tell me everything. And by the way, this is a really good sandwich," she said, feeling better than she had for days.

"The Fosk-ha believe they have the right to exist. The Ysik believe otherwise and seek to eliminate us from the universe."

"Sounds like my kind of aliens," Laura said, finishing the sandwich with a huge bite.

"Be careful, Laura Osage. This is a false assumption on your part. Why do you think they would feel differently about humanity? Help them destroy us and your people will be next," Bob said.

"Are you brainwashing me? And don't say 'processing.'"

The avatar smiled awkwardly. "There is no need for brainwashing. You ask good questions and I am authorized to provide answers to most if not all of your questions."

"How can we destroy the Fosk-ha and these other aliens, or at least make them leave us alone?" she asked without thinking.

"Your question has been flagged as seditious. It will be reviewed by a Fosk-ha administrative council," Bob said. "To answer it, you must develop better technology, unite as one people, and learn to fight properly, while making alliances with alien races that are less likely to dominate and destroy all of humanity."

Wow, I'm surprised he answered.

"Where can I find these pro-humanity aliens?" she asked,

pitching her orange juice container into the kitchen trash can.

"Nice shot, Laura Osage."

"Are you going to answer me?"

"There are none. My apologies, Laura Osage. Humans have nothing to offer other sentient races known to the Foskha," Bob said.

"Bullshit."

"I am not sure how that pertains to this conversation," Bob said. "Do you have another question?"

"Can you look a little more like Chris Hemsworth?"

"One moment."

"Scratch that, Bob. I don't want you to ruin him in my head," Laura said. "Who called your people to Earth?"

"Access denied."

"Figures. And here I thought we were going to be friends," she said, massaging her aching lower calf where she'd been bitten.

"We are friends, Laura Osage," said the avatar who now vaguely resembled the god of thunder.

"No, Bob, we're not. A friend would help me."

"Does your injury require attention?" Bob asked.

She turned away from the screen but doubted she was actually hiding the injury from the computer. It probably had cameras in every conceivable location. Her captors had built the place, after all.

Removing her boot, rolling up her pant leg, she stared at the damage. It wasn't as bad as it felt. The rate of healing disturbed her. "Why did I survive this bite?" she asked, staring at the large white mark surrounded by a circle of smaller marks.

"Unknown. Some humans survive. Others die screaming. A few change into something we have no name for."

The last statement worried her. "Am I changing into something you have no name for?"

"Your body's reaction to the venom that is in all of us—the symbiotic virus enables us to survive long journeys—will take time to reach the final stages of transformation."

"What happened to the woman across the hallway in the hospital?" Laura asked.

"She did not survive. Her nervous system consumed itself."

Laura attempted to read the emotions of the computerized assistant, then laughed. "Remind me not to play poker with you."

"Pardon my lack of understanding," Bob said. "My programmers underestimated the disorganized nature of your thoughts."

"It's fine, Bob. I'll try not to confuse you, but you have to keep up. Why did the woman die? Why didn't I suffer the same fate?"

"We would like to know the answer to these questions as well," Bob answered. "Until that discovery is made, it is my duty to warn you of certain changes you will experience."

"I don't think I'm going to like this," Laura said, standing to pace her apartment. She strolled wall to wall, turning sharply and balling her fists as if getting ready to fight someone twice her size.

"None of the chosen has been pleased with their new metabolic requirements," Bob said.

Laura groaned. "Don't tell me you turned me into a space vampire."

"Very interesting. This was a concern of other chosen as

well. We were surprised that you had a name for such things, even if inaccurate and fantastical."

"Don't call us chosen. That'll piss me off. It sounds like something from a bad movie."

"Would you prefer to be called the infected?" Bob asked.

Laura laughed maniacally.

"Is something wrong?"

"Everything's great," she said sarcastically. "What are my new metabolic requirements?"

Her stomach twisted, and she felt a bit faint, which was unusual for her. If dread could be physically manifested, this was it.

"You will need to consume blood," Bob stated. "There are many complicated reasons for this change. Primarily, you will be able to eat our nutrient paste after tapping the blood power of this planet."

"Nutrient paste?" Laura had been worried before, but now she realized she'd unknowingly accepted the devil's bargain by surviving the alien bite. The idea of drinking blood appalled her, but the nutrient paste somehow seemed worse.

"Your first dose will be tomorrow. But first, you'll have to consume the blood of an earth creature."

Laura frowned. He'd said that so causally, like drinking blood wasn't a big fucking problem for her. "What if I refuse?"

"You will die painfully."

"Is that what happened to the woman across the hall in the hospital?"

"No. She was unable to tolerate the changes. Her body rejected itself," Bob said. "The degeneration always starts at the nerve endings and proceeds rapidly to the brain. Extremely painful."

Laura hugged herself and stared out a small window toward a Chicago she barely recognized. Tears ran down her cheeks. She'd cried more in the last few days than she had her entire life.

CHAPTER TWENTY

THE NEXT MORNING, Laura ate breakfast and dressed in civilian clothes, tucking her off-duty pistol in the back of her waistband before covering it with her shirt. She received instructions on her wrist monitor to report for work and wondered what the police department would look like post invasion.

She took the subway and carefully watched people. The crowd acted more normally than what she had witnessed when she left the hospital. A few spoke about the invasion in whispers, seemingly terrified of being caught. These men and women posted what to Laura were obvious lookouts and stopped talking when she moved too near them.

They didn't trust her. That was annoying but at least they weren't pretending none of this had happened.

Others complained about bad relationships, shitty bosses, and the performance of their favorite sports teams. There had been no games since the invasion but that didn't stop diehard fans from speculating on teams and players.

At the first terminal, she saw signs of overt disobedience.

One of the worst aspects of leaving the hospital had been the sight of Chicagoans passively going about their days without even looking at their alien overlords. The frightened faces on the subway grated on her nerves for reasons she couldn't articulate.

What she saw in the downtown terminal, however, was something else.

Two alien soldiers wrestled a protest sign away from a man standing near the stairs. They seemed utterly confused that he would do this. She couldn't understand their conversation from this distance but thought the long-haired white man was doing his best to explain the concept of civil rights to the Fosk-ha soldiers.

They shoved him for his efforts and aimed their weapons at his face. He was going to get himself killed. A couple bystanders grew angry and shouted at the aliens from a safer distance. Additional Fosk-ha guards arrived, followed by a pair of police officers from Baker Sector. She recognized them but didn't know their names.

It broke her heart to see the resentment of the crowd. The cops, as usual, were the bad guys. Didn't these idiots realize their lives were only worth the blood in their veins? Someone had to keep order or there would be serious reprisals from the conquering force.

The realization was like a punch in the gut.

We lost.

That's not supposed to happen.

But it did.

By the time she was off the subway and heading toward the stairs, the incident had resolved itself. She missed the details of the confrontation but saw one of the bystanders had been knocked unconscious and was being dragged away by two black armored aliens. The crowd dissipated rapidly. She thought she could taste fear in the air. Or maybe that was her own adrenaline pumping sour chemicals into her mouth.

She continued on her way, eventually reaching the station. There weren't many officers on duty and they greeted her with sullen nods. The women's locker room was empty. She opened her padlock and got dressed.

Boots, pants, and T-shirt went on first, then her ballistic vest. It fit looser than she remembered. She put on her uniform shirt over top of it and finally her duty belt. She switched her off-duty gun with the Glock 17 from a lockbox inside of her locker. There were a pair of seventeen round magazines on her belt with one magazine in the weapon. She charged it, then added an extra bullet to top off the magazine in the gun.

Brock Green greeted her when she stepped into the hallway. "You look like shit."

She wanted to ask him if he'd been bitten but didn't dare.

"Sorry about Sans and the others," he said.

"Yeah, me too." What else could she say?

"When I didn't see you after the invasion, I thought you were probably dead," Brock said as they walked to the squad room. "I heard some rumors that they captured you and tortured you."

"That is a good way to describe it. Not totally accurate, but pretty close." She studied officers they passed and wanted to scream at them. The station had always been a loud place with people trash-talking and swapping stories. Now everybody acted like they were on death row—barely speaking as they watched everything about everyone in the station, including friends they'd known for years.

Brock sidestepped a pair of officers taking a prisoner toward the investigation section, then hurried to keep up with Laura. "I wonder what that guy did?"

Laura didn't bother speculating on the cause of the man's incarceration. She was more interested in talking to Brock. "Did they give you the 'help us protect humanity from themselves' talk?"

He went pale, looking around to see if anybody was watching or listening. Then he pulled her into the cafeteria and closed the door behind them. Very carefully, tears welling in his eyes, he rolled up his left sleeve and showed her a bite just like the one she had on her calf.

"Don't tell anyone," he said, a look of desperation on his face. "I don't want to get burned at the stake or whatever it is they do to vampires."

"You're not a vampire." She looked around to make sure no one was in the room they had noticed.

"They made me drink blood!" he whispered, full of self-loathing.

She was stunned. What she dreaded was about to come true. Who would be her first victim?

She would throw herself from the parking garage. Or eat the barrel of a gun. Drive her car off a bridge. But she wouldn't become one of them.

"I'm sorry! Don't tell anyone, please!" Brock pleaded.

This wasn't the man she remembered. He'd always been one of the hardest working cops she knew—not necessarily happy all the time, but never moody or depressed. And certainly never one to beg.

"Shut up. Just shut your mouth and calm down," she snapped, looking at the door. People were laughing at something unrelated in the hallway.

When he had control of himself, she guided him farther into the cafeteria, away from the door. Kneeling, she rolled up her pant leg and pushed down the top of her boot to show her own wound.

The scene happened in slow motion. She couldn't hear anything. It was like a dream where she was trying not to move but couldn't stop her hands. A loud hum filled her ears. Spots danced in her vision. It was like getting choked out in a jujitsu match.

Brock changed back into the man she knew, more concerned for her safety than his own. He faced the front of the cafeteria, shielding her from the view of anyone who walked in. "Cover it up. You could have just told me. Man, we are really fucked."

"Only if you lose your cool," she said, straightening her pant leg and standing. "We can't be the only ones this happened to. The question is how do we find out who they poisoned and who they didn't?"

"Poisoned. Is that what they did?" he asked, bewildered.

"That's how I think about it. You know more than I do. They made you drink someone's blood."

"It wasn't from a person. They told me only high-ranking aliens get that privilege." He chewed his fingernails, something she'd never known him to do. He wasn't a nervous person by nature.

"Let me get this straight. They forced you to drink blood from an animal or from a bag? Was that why they were raiding the Red Cross blood bank?"

He hooked his thumbs into his duty belt and looked like he was trying his best not to throw up. "Rats."

"What?"

"They make us drink rats' blood. It's part of the pecking

order. We're worth about as much as a rat to them, so that's what they feed us." He nodded at several men and women entering the cafeteria. "Let's go. We're going to be late for squad."

"I can't do that. What happens if I refuse?"

He grabbed her arm and pulled her out into the hallway. H waited until they were to answer. "You can't refuse. From what they told me, it will drive you crazy to resist. You still have to eat normal food and water, but now you're addicted to drinking live blood. Eventually, there is this black sludge you have to consume… at least, that's what I heard."

"What's the point?"

"You don't age, for one thing. That's why they need it. They have to live a long time to travel from one world to the next. Even in cryo freeze pods, they need something to extend their life. I think they consider the blood in the Red Cross banks alive, or close enough that they can make it work. But until they found us, they had to keep victims breeding on their ships so they could replenish a couple of times a year while the rest of them stayed in cryosleep. They do it on shifts."

"How did you learn all of this?"

"You know me, I listen more than I talk. Or that is what I did before all this happened." He glanced at his watch. "We're out of time. The squad room is filling up and if we talk outside, we'll draw a crowd."

She knew he wasn't wrong. Other people would want to know what they were gossiping about. Even now, she saw eyes turn toward her and Brock as they approached the squad room.

"Let's go inside and get this over with," she said.

"Sergeant Hemmert will put us in a two-officer car if you ask him," Brock suggested.

"Good idea. Put the blood-sucking traitors to humanity together. What could go wrong?" she said, and they ducked into the noisy room.

Human civilization was on the ropes, about to be knocked out and down for the count, but that didn't change how her friends and coworkers acted.

"Laura, where have you been? I heard you were on one of those ships getting violated by alien science—with probes and stuff," Officer Sedona shouted from across the room. He held up his fist like he might be putting his arm into something slimy.

"Tell us all about it, Sedona," she said. "Did you get the VIP treatment too? How's your ass or did they just jam in three fingers?"

Sedona and his friends laughed, then expanded the joke.

Boys, Laura thought, and left them to their fun.

She found Sergeant Hemmert at a squad table near the front.

"Hey, Sarge, mind if I double up with Brock?" she asked.

"Please do," Hemmert answered, holding the roster in one of his large hands. "Brock has been worthless since the attack. I know you hear me, Brock. Did you think I was trying to spare your feelings?"

Brock laughed awkwardly, choosing to sit at the squad table rather than answer what was most likely a rhetorical question.

Hemmert stepped closer to Laura. "How are you doing? All joking aside, you were listed MIA for the first day and a half."

She pitched her voice low. "I'm doing okay. First day

back. What the hell is going on? Are we living in Occupied Chicago now?"

"That's exactly what this is. The chief and the mayor came to every squad meeting yesterday and explained the aliens were in control of the city and that they wanted peace. Our job, they said, is to provide that. The chief promised that we are only expected to conduct business as usual but most of it has been riot control and infrastructure stuff. Guarding reconstruction efforts, mostly. I'll cover more of what's expected of us in squad. You're not the only person who just got back."

"Thanks for the head's up, boss."

"You never answered my question," Hemmert said, holding his gaze on her when it was clearly time for him to step behind the podium and begin.

"I'm all right. Spent a night hiding in the sewers after Sans and the others were killed. More time in the hospital. I'm worried about my brothers but don't see what I can do for them from Occupied Chicago."

"We'll catch up later. I'll put you in a car with Brock on patrol. Let you drive around and see what's changed since the invasion," Hemmert said.

"Thanks." She took her seat, listening to the start of the shift squad meeting without taking notes. There wasn't a lot of information. The key takeaway was that disobeying the alien overlords was a good way to disappear.

"I'LL DRIVE," Laura said.

"That's why I don't normally volunteer to ride two to a

car with you. You never let me behind the wheel," Brock said.

"That's 'cause I'm the best driver on the department," she said, loading her gear into the trunk, then checking the shotgun, traffic control flares, and first aid kits.

"How do you figure?"

"My brother started teaching me when I was ten."

"In stolen cars, I heard."

Laura faced him. "Sort of. He didn't explain where the cars came from when I was young, but later he told me he'd won them. Then lost them. The street racer crowd he rolled with was pretty wild."

"I heard he went to prison," Brock said, leaning on the car as they talked.

"Get in. There are probably calls holding," she said, then logged into the laptop mounted between the driver and passenger seats.

"I understand if you don't want to talk about it. Every family has a black sheep."

"How do you know I'm not the black sheep in our family?" she asked, giving their kit one last check.

"If you've done something worse than get sent to prison, I never heard about it," Brock said, turning the computer toward him to read the pending calls.

"How did you get bitten?" she asked.

"I was wrapping up the DV call when the dispatcher put you and the others out in trouble. The scene was chaos by the time I arrived. We were running and gunning all night, responding to what we thought were run-of-the-mill disturbance calls but turned out to be alien attacks."

Laura listened, wanting to ask questions but holding back until he was finished.

"They are not all the same. Did you know that? Some aliens attack without mercy, drinking blood than killing their victims. Others take prisoners. Some Baker Sector guys told me there are at least two races of aliens. Rumor has it they could be rivals," Brock said.

Laura drove the perimeters of her beat, then started checking alleys and vacant buildings she knew were trouble. "Damn, Brock. There are a lot of people here."

Most people slipped away when they saw the patrol car, but some stared at them with unreadable expressions on their faces.

"That is creeping me out," Brock said.

"What do they want?" Laura asked.

"It could be they are still in shock. I'm no psychologist, but how long does it take the average person to admit aliens are real, and they just took over Chicago? I wonder how we are doing in other parts of the country."

Laura drove to the stadium lot and parked with plenty of open space around them. She wanted to see anyone who approached. "I need to make a call."

"Does your phone still work?" Brock asked, amazed. "I've only encountered three people who can still get service."

Already nervous about using the phone, she dialed her big brother and let it ring. "I guess we'll see what happens," she said to Brock as a heavy metal song played in her ear.

"Who are you calling?" Brock asked, starting to get nervous.

"My brother. If you want, you could ask him about prison," she said, wondering if a Fosk-ha response team was already on the way to deal with the unauthorized call. The rules were explicit: no unauthorized communication was allowed with any type of device.

They never explained how they would monitor or enforce this mandate.

"You shouldn't risk it just to contact family. Everything we do has to be for a good reason from now on. We're playing death chess here, not checkers," Brock said.

Laura laughed. "Death chess. I like that. My brother might be able to help us escape."

"Escape? What the hell are you talking about? There is no escape. We have to follow their rules and help who we can, when we can. That's it. Nothing else is worth the risk."

"No one is going to see it that way. If we work for the Fosk-ha, we're traitors to humanity, no matter how we justify it," she said as she abandoned the attempted phone call.

Brock shook his head. "I know it sucks, but we need to get with the program."

"Well, he didn't answer so you're off the hook. Are you going to report me to our blood-sucking alien overlords?"

"Don't be a bitch," he said, clearly miserable. "We've been friends since the Academy. I'm not turning you or anyone else in. But that doesn't mean I'll stand by and let you get yourself killed."

"I know, Brock. This is just hard to get used to."

"You should get rid of that phone. If they find you with it, we'll both get fed to their warriors," Brock said.

"You're right," she said rolling down the window. "It doesn't work anyway."

When they were crossing a bridge, she pretended to throw the phone at the same time she brake-checked her partner, tossing him forward against his seatbelt. During the moment of distraction, she slipped the phone inside her shirt.

"Sorry," she said. "There's still a lot of debris in the road."

He shifted uncomfortably. "I'm glad you pitched it. Safer this way."

"I already regret it. Not knowing if my brothers are alive is going to drive me crazy."

He frowned. "Everyone lost family. We can't save all the people. Aren't you the person who taught me that?"

She remembered the conversation he was referring to. During their first few weeks, Brock had started renting hotel rooms for homeless men and women, rescued several dogs from animal shelters, and applied to be an emergency foster parent.

"That's different," she said.

"Maybe it is, maybe it isn't. But there is only so much we can do. One mistake and we'll get more people killed than we will help. Let's learn the rules before we start breaking them."

CHAPTER TWENTY-ONE

LAURA WENT to the CVS Pharmacy and purchased a small box of lancets normally used to prick a finger for blood testing. Last year, she had a partner who was diabetic. She'd seen him check his blood sugar often. This gave her an idea she couldn't let go, which was good because she had to do something.

There is no way she was sucking blood out of a rat, not for aliens or anyone else. Besides the fact it made her feel like a freak, everything about it was disgusting. Nightmares about rats staring in her face and breathing into her mouth had kept her up most of the night.

Brock Green refuse to talk about the experience. He was a day ahead of her on the assimilation sequence. His experience was causing him to lose weight and most of the color in his face—which pissed her off. These alien sons-of-bitches were ruining her friend. Once happy, energetic, and hardworking, Brock was now skittish and paranoid.

Laura refused to give up until she figured some things out; she had a job to do. Like it or not, she was working for the enemy to keep the peace in Chicago. Humans needed to recover, regroup, and start planning a resistance.

The precinct headquarters she'd been reporting to for almost five years was cleaner and more orderly than ever. The overlords demanded it. It was like they were still living on a starship that needed to be kept in perfect working order at all times.

People she'd known for years barely spoke to each other. No one looked angry or unhappy, but she thought they were. Maybe they were scared. Confused, ashamed, lost.

Everyone was affected. Her own face showed signs of sleep deprivation. She had dark circles around her eyes and a random twitch that she didn't like. Mirrors had never been her friend. She'd rarely enjoyed looking at herself, or hearing a recording of her voice, or whatever. That was just the way she was wired and didn't worry about it.

Everyone had their insecurities. What was she going to do, cry? The world was ending, and that was a big enough problem for anyone.

She was as hungry as she'd ever been. True to what her alien rulers had promised, normal food didn't metabolize well without blood supplements. She thought there should be a way around this. If these highly advanced star travelers couldn't figure out an alternative to drinking lifeblood, how smart were they really?

Assholes.

The only explanation she got when she asked this question was that it was more complicated than she could understand. They made it sound like the blood power of Earth—of any life force world—was a mystical thing shared by all creatures in the biosphere.

"Officer Laura Osage, it is time for you to report to Aon-fosk-ga for feeding," one of the big guards said.

She complied but didn't bother nodding. The Fosk-ha bully boys expected immediate compliance to their every command. They didn't understand or care about verbal acknowledgments. The last time she replied to one of these jerks, he hissed at her and flicked his gross feeder tongue which was horrifying on so many levels.

The rooms where humans were expected to feed were in the basement, apparently. The lights were low as though the aliens had intentionally made the scene as creepy as possible. A bad feeling grew in her as they passed the loading docks near the back of the parking garage.

There was only one place they could be headed now—the temporary morgue.

Bodies were brought here for cold storage until they could be transferred to the medical examiner's facilities in another precinct building.

"What the hell is this?" she asked when they arrived.

The guard didn't answer. He merely stepped aside and allowed Aon-fosk-ga inside. The slender doctor looked her over and motioned for her to stand by the wall and wait for others. She tried not to count the cold chamber doors. If they started sliding out bodies with toe tags, she was going to freak out.

A new Fosk-ha arrived pushing a cart loaded with rat cages. The alien was big but somehow different from the warriors and the medical staff she'd encountered. He didn't look at anyone. At first, she assumed he was a slave or something similar, but she suspected the worker Fosk-ha didn't know or care that he was doing grunt work.

I have to stop assuming they have the same thoughts and

emotions as humans. The Fosk-ha worker might be content to push cages of rats and be ignored by the other aliens. *Maybe he's living the dream.*

She suppressed a crazy laugh that came unbidden. Tension grew moment by moment until it was nearly unbearable.

She counted the seconds for what seemed an eternity. Before long, however, dozens of Chicago police officers, city workers, and other civilians were standing in line to suck the blood of rats.

Laura palmed one of the lancets and waited for her chance. Her heartbeat madly in her chest. This wasn't going to work. She knew it wasn't. But she had to try something.

The line moved forward. Brock Green was near the front. He leaned into the cage, pull the rat forward, and did something she couldn't see. Moments later, the animal squealed and then scurried away from him.

She couldn't look away from the scrawny rodent and realized she was running her tongue around her sharpened canine teeth. They must have done that to her while she was out. Bitter saliva coated the inside of her mouth. Her heart pounded in her chest.

The rat's red eyes searched for a way to escape the cage. Its long tail flicked and its whiskers twitched. After a few moments, it crawled into the corner and curled up for a nap.

Several other humans repeated the procedure, two of them throwing up afterward. Another passed out and was taken from the room by angry guards.

One young woman refused and was dragged away screaming.

I can't believe they're trying to turn me into a rat vampire. Her turn arrived, and she was terrified.

It took all her willpower not to look around to see if she was being watched more closely than the others. It felt like she was. How could they not sense her deception?

When she leaned into the cage, the rat stared at her just like it had in her nightmare. The smell of it made the scene real.

She grabbed the scrawny animal, feeling how it trembled like its heart might explode. With the animal in her left hand and the lancet in her right, she jabbed her thumb and let the blood smear onto the side of the animal. Then she rubbed some red liquid around the edges of her mouth.

The terrified rat squeaked and squealed then ran into its corner where it refused to take a nap. It darted back and forth like it was ready to fight or flee.

"Sit down and shut up, you little bastard," she muttered.

The rat, not being trained to obey commands, ignored her and continued to spaz out. The guard approached her and stared down angrily.

"I must've bit it too hard," she said, trying to look innocent. She pointed at the blood on the corner of her mouth.

The guard hissed a snort and stomped away—probably to report that she should be executed or worse.

Other humans were led to their rats and forced to feed. She wondered if any of her human companions were faking it. From the look in their eyes, she doubted it. They were far more terrified of the alien invaders than they were of the rodents.

Her stomach rebelled as she returned to the squad room to get ready for her shift. Not being able to easily digest food was going to be miserable. She needed to find somebody with an antidote or something to help her get through this.

And she had no idea who that person was or where they could be found.

———

"IT'S MY TURN TO DRIVE," Brock Green said, already loading the patrol car.

Laura didn't argue. She felt distracted. The scene in the basement morgue with the rats wouldn't leave her mind. There were a lot of reasons she didn't want to drink the blood of animals, or people, God forbid. A big part of it was guilt. It just felt wrong and unnatural.

Despite the fact that she'd faked it, she still felt the same guilt. She'd always been an animal lover—not a fanatic but empathetic of people-friendly creatures like dogs and cats and other pets. Now she felt like she needed to join PETA and stage some sort of rat rescue.

There were other questions that weighed on her mind. Where were the humans these aliens were feeding on? Were there humans who had already made the leap to feeding on each other? What was the purpose of all this?

"Are you ready?" Brock asked.

"Sure. I just don't like riding shotgun," she said, avoiding his gaze.

When they were both in, he started the car and drove away from the precinct headquarters. "You didn't bite the rat."

She watched him drive. He'd made the statement without looking at her. It hadn't been a question.

"How'd you know?" she asked.

He shook his head slightly as he made a left turn but still

didn't look at her. "I've known you for a long time. Believe me, these jerks will figure it out before long."

She didn't know what to say. Of course he was right. They were all in a bad spot and she was only making things worse for herself.

Brock didn't say anything for a long while, his lips pressed in a thin line. Then, "You're probably disgusted that I did it."

She watched the sparsely populated neighborhood they were patrolling. "I can't afford to judge you or anyone right now. To be honest, I'm still trying to figure things out."

"If you'd seen how they swept aside our military and what they did to people who resisted during that first stage of the invasion, you wouldn't be playing games with the Fosk-ha. I saw one of them latch onto a woman and drain her until I didn't even recognize she'd been human. She shriveled up to nothing. Another of the Fosk-ha shot him in the back of the head and yelled at the other soldiers around him."

This caught Laura's attention. "Why do you think he did that?"

"I don't think they were supposed to start feeding until they did their jobs," Brock said, a sour look on his face as he remembered the scene.

"That could be important. We look at them and think they're all united, one alien race dedicated to our destruction."

"They don't want to destroy us. They want to feed on us. I don't understand or care why. I just know that I wish I was dead or had never been born," he said. "I'm jealous you were able to skip your first feeding. I wish I had at least tried to resist. But you'll know what I'm talking about soon enough. In a couple of days, you'll be looking forward to biting the rat."

"I don't understand why they're forcing us to become like them."

"Because they're probably going to take us with them as blood-bags when they go to the next world they conquer, and we won't survive the journey without the longevity the blood power will give us."

Laura shivered involuntarily. Her friend knew more about the invaders than he let on. Who had he been talking to? How deep in was he?

Can I trust him?

"Did you pack a lunch?" Brock asked.

"As ordered," she said, holding up her wrist monitor.

"Next time pack all the food you can. Your refrigerator will be restocked automatically while you're on patrol," he said, parking the car.

She was about to ask him what the hell he was talking about when he went to the trunk and lifted a cooler out.

"The Fosk-ha feed us because they need us to keep the peace. We're critical occupation workers now. As for the rest of Chicago… not so much," Brock said.

Laura took one handle of the cooler and Brock took the other. They walked toward a school that had been turned into a refugee camp. Men, women, and children who'd seen their homes replaced by Fosk-ha generation ships huddled against each other looking tired, dirty, and hungry. Alien guards sat on their ground vehicles watching impassively.

"I only have one cooler today," Brock told the people who surged toward the cooler. "Same rules apply. No pushing or shoving. We'll look for more food and water, then come back in a few hours. If the Fosk-ha see disorder, they'll expect us to bang some heads. And if we don't, they'll start dragging people away."

The leaders of this group promised that they understood and helped keep the potential mob under control. People touched Brock's arm like he was a saint or an angel and cried when the food and water was gone.

Laura handed over her meager lunch.

Brock glared at her.

"What?" she asked, offended at his scornful expression.

"You have to feed yourself first. If you show weakness because you're starving yourself, they'll have you on twice-a-day rats," Brock said.

"Good to know. Thanks for the warning," she said, watching families divide up the sandwiches Brock had given them.

"Let's roll. We might be able to find more for these people," Brock said.

"Why aren't they raiding grocery stores and pharmacies?"

"That happened for about five minutes. Then the Fosk started blowing people's heads off with their energy pulse rifles." Brock paused at their patrol car, facing her and speaking quietly. "We are completely beaten. You haven't seen the brutality these monsters are capable of. They're not human. They don't think like we do. Their moral code, if it exists, is nothing like we understand. Don't get them confused with humans because they walk on two legs and speak our language."

"You're right," she said. "Let's get back to work."

CHAPTER TWENTY-TWO

THINGS WENT DIFFERENTLY at the next camp they approached. Night came early as an unusual volume of Fosk-ha ships descended toward the landing fields on the south end of the city. They were moving slowly and were bigger than any Laura had seen so far.

She stared transfixed at the lights of their launch bays. Smaller vessels zipped out on patrol.

"When those return, they will send out maintenance drones," Brock said. "Mostly they repair their colony ships and terraformers, but they fix our stuff as well. I've seen them obsess over fixing things that really isn't to their benefit. I still don't know what that's about. Maybe they feel guilty for ruining our planet."

"A lot happened while I was out of commission. Didn't think it was that long," Laura said, returning her attention to the neighborhood they were entering.

"The first night was the worst," Brock said, slowing the squad car. "Looks like there could be trouble this time."

He stopped, one hand on the gear lever as though he

might throw the vehicle in reverse. Streetlights had been smashed out by vandals. There was no movement, which was suspicious. At this time of night, there should've been somebody out and about. It felt like an ambush.

Laura pulled a small pair of binoculars from the glove box. They weren't night vision capable like the one Sans had used on his drug houses before getting slaughtered by alien invaders, but they had decent magnification and gathered what light there was—which was creepy because most of it was the red glow of the ships landing several miles away and with buildings obstructing the direct line of sight.

"I wish we'd gotten here sooner. This is camp twenty-eight. They don't even have a building for shelter. It's like a park with tents and boxes. There's a couple dozen porta-potties on the north end of the field and a decorative pond I think people are drinking out of," Brock said.

"Why didn't they get one of the new buildings?" Laura asked. "Or why can't the Fosk-ha maintenance drones fix them up something from the apartments damaged during the invasion?"

"Camp twenty-eight is full of troublemakers," Brock said distractedly. He slipped the squad car into drive and rolled forward slowly.

"I see movement." Laura shifted in her seat so that she could watch the mouth of an alley they were passing. Shapes darted across dim light sources from the next street.

"I'm going to turn around before I park," Brock said.

Laura checked her Taser, pepper spray, and gun. "Good idea. It's not too late to come back in the daytime. My wrist monitor is telling me we were expected back at the station thirty minutes ago. I'm not excited about learning the punishment for coming in late."

The bricks started flying before they could park and get out with the supplies they'd gathered. Two thumped the vehicle near her door as Brock backed up to turn around. After a short pause, projectiles rained down on the trunk and back window, smashing it to pieces.

Brock threw the car in drive and stomped on the gas pedal. "It looks like they don't get the supplies we found for them."

Laura didn't say anything. She'd faced mobs before and hadn't liked it. This was about ten times worse.

BROCK DIDN'T SHOW up for work the next morning. She asked the Fosk-ha guard that watched over the police squad room. The exchange took a while but eventually the alien explained that Brock had a bad reaction with his rat.

"I am also to advise you that skipping your feeding will have consequences," the Fosk-ha guard said.

"I woke up with woman troubles," she said, hoping the lie worked on Fosk-ha males as well as it did humans.

This guard only gave her a cold glare through his helmet visor—as usual.

At first, the opaque visors had annoyed her. There was something impersonal about speaking to someone twice your size that wouldn't even reveal his or her facial expressions. But now she liked it when they had their helmets on. Some of them tended to flick out their tongues, as if they yearned to latch onto her throat and drain her dry. The helmets prevented that.

She thought they knew this mannerism was disturbing to humans and did it on purpose—their version of sick humor.

Her partner wasn't the only one missing in the squad. She sat next to Olivia Norton, a third-generation cop she'd never gotten along with before the invasion.

"We're a little short-staffed this morning," Laura observed.

Olivia's hostile stare was worse than usual. Her eyes were red from lack of sleep. They were also wet, like she had been crying in frustration and could start again at any moment. "You're one of them. Don't fucking sit next to me."

Laura couldn't formulate a response. She'd assumed all the cops working for the Fosk-ha had survived a bite and were rat vampires like Brock and the others. She didn't consider herself a full member of that club because she was still faking her blood feedings.

"I didn't ask to get bit." *Bitch.* Laura left off that part.

"Whatever. You could have killed yourself afterward." Olivia's eyes were dry now, her rage growing with each exchange.

"I think I tried."

"You think? You either did, or you didn't." Olivia nodded at two other cops as they sat down.

Laura sighed. "I threw myself into a drain. Tried to escape. Their bio-drones dragged me out. Then… then I'm not sure what happened. It was a fucking nightmare," she said, barely talking to Olivia now. The words felt strange on her lips. Brain fog dulled her thoughts. She wondered if she was feeling the lack of metabolic efficiency for the first time. *Because it sucked.*

"She hasn't drunk blood yet," Roger Mains said. "I've seen what happens when they don't. We should report her. She's dangerous like this. When she breaks, she'll become one of the wild ones they hunt down."

"What are you talking about?" Olivia asked.

Roger kept his eyes on Laura as he answered Olivia's question. "She won't be able to control herself. They don't tolerate that because, from what my Fosk overlord explained to me, the wild ones ruined entire worlds before this. Swept over them like a plague. Unchecked, they go into a feeding frenzy and spread like a disease. That's why you've seen Fosk hunting other Fosk."

Olivia stared her down, both fists clenched. A small group of cops gathered around, clearly ready to act. It wasn't an overt display of aggression toward Laura. At least two cops held back, acting as lookouts in case an alien moved close enough to overhear the conversation. There was normally at least one in the room.

"Who's going to do it?" Olivia asked but kept her gaze on Laura.

Cold sweat broke out. *What is she talking about?* Laura wondered.

Roger took control of the team. "No one. Not yet. I need to think about it."

A tremor ran through the group. Whatever the group of cops had just decided, Laura could tell that no one was happy about it.

When they all left, Laura felt hollow. She'd thought the moment the aliens took her to the rat feeding room had been the lowest in her life, but she'd been wrong. These people had been her friends. Now they hated her worse than they hated the alien invaders.

Sergeant Hemmert entered. He looked tired. Conversations died as he took the podium and began the squad meeting. There weren't any jokes. He didn't call anyone out as a rookie or a crotchety old bastard. He just announced the notice-to-appear date needed for certain citations to be written, then started reading a list of incidents that had happened during the previous watch.

No one took notes. When he was done, he made assignments and sent them out.

Almost everyone was directed to ride as a single officer unit because they were so short-staffed now. Laura spoke to no one. She loaded up her squad car and headed out on patrol.

There wouldn't be any supply deliveries today. She was smart enough to know how dangerous it was heading to one of the camps by herself. She called Brock, but he didn't answer his phone. That was when she realized she didn't even know where his new dormitory was. Some of what the aliens did to control their subjects was almost diabolical in its subtlety. Everyone had been completely removed from their old lives and put in new places where they could barely interact with each other without supervision.

That needed to change. Maybe she would never be accepted in Roger and Olivia's group, but she could start building a team of people who didn't accept this new status quo.

What she really wanted right now was to talk to David.

Time passed slowly. She didn't witness people breaking laws, at least none that she was willing to enforce. At first, she'd seen drunkenness and been angry. Getting hammered wasn't going to fix anything. The last thing humans needed to do was turn on each other and continue old feuds.

That made her think resentfully of Olivia and the others. They were on the same team. What the hell had she done for them not to trust her? She'd probably been one of the first people to fight the aliens, might've even killed a couple of them.

Her night was about half over when she turned her car onto an access road that had recently been built. Where there had once been a shopping mall, there was now an expansive field filled with parked alien ships.

From a distance, the landing pad looked like it was made of asphalt. This close, however, she could see that it was some kind of thick material that was neither steel nor concrete.

She parked her car and walked to the edge. Kneeling, she examined it closely. Construction materials weren't exactly her area of expertise, but this seemed like it was made of rigid metal threads woven together.

She touched the material and received a pleasant zap. She flinched back, fearing she was going to be electrocuted, but the energy didn't affect her the same way. She wasn't even sure that's what it was.

It was, however, some sort of field keeping the woven material rigid. Perhaps this meant the surface could change its density to absorb impact if needed.

She also realized there were several layers to the material. The landing field was several feet thick and made of several alloy weaves. Each was a slightly different color, and the middle layer pulsed with bright blue dots.

She backed away and observed the area from the shadows. It wasn't long before she realized she wasn't the only human in the area.

Olivia and several others were approaching one of the ships, moving like a SWAT team. She knew Olivia, at least, lacked the training but was always gung ho. It was possible the others had military experience or tactical training she didn't know about, but to her, they looked just like a bunch of kids living out a video game fantasy.

They were going to do something to one of the ships.

She wanted them to succeed in destroying all the alien vessels but knew without a doubt they were making a serious mistake that would have deadly repercussions for everyone.

"Why the hell did I come this way?" She stood from where she had been examining the landing field. A feeling of dread washed through her. If the tech for the alien landing pads was light-years beyond anything humanity had, what hope did those fools have in carrying out their mission?

Not an ice cube's chance in Hell.

They were too far away for her to shout at. Maybe she could run toward them waving her arms, but that didn't seem like the best solution either.

In the end, she decided to throw herself under the bus. She hadn't memorized all the alien rules but was fairly certain human vehicles weren't allowed on the landing area. She jumped back in her squad car, turned on the lights and sirens, and raced on to the launch pad, easily outdistancing the self-proclaimed commandos. Before long, she was between them and the nearest ship.

A swarm of bio-drones descended on her car. At first she wondered what they were going to do and thought they might break out the windows and stab her in the face with their tendrils. She was surprised when several of them locked onto her wheels, wrapping the axle, and causing the vehicle to stop as everything locked up.

The largest drone landed on the hood and stared at her with about five hundred eyes. It hissed words she didn't understand. Her best course of action was obviously not to move.

Glancing in the mirror, she saw Olivia and the other would-be commandos retreating from the area, and she briefly felt relieved.

After what seemed like forever, Hahn-fosk-hon, the alien who had first bit her, arrived. He looked sad and disappointed. Several of the aliens now secured the area around the ships. There was an armored ground vehicle and two jump ships.

"What are you doing here, Laura Osage?" the alien captain asked.

"I thought there was a danger to the ships, so I responded to help."

"Danger? From what?"

"Human rebels. I don't know who they are so don't ask."

"You are so loyal to us that you would interfere with your own people?" Hahn-fosk-hon's expression seemed skeptical. Several strides away, other senior aliens watched but did not interfere.

"Don't overthink it. I didn't do it for you. They would've gotten themselves killed," she said. "They won't thank me and neither will you, so why don't you just go to hell?"

"You assume that we haven't been to this place you call hell," Hahn-fosk-hon said. "Someday I will explain the cold fire of space travel and what it will do to you. Then you will learn that such words are not to be used lightly."

CHAPTER TWENTY-THREE

DAVID PUSHED the Dodge Hellcat to triple digit speeds on Highway 54 headed westbound. Dust slept in the passenger seat, jacket wadded up against the window. Abigail slept in the back, occasionally making whimpering sounds. He clenched his jaw each time she cried out against nightmare attacks.

The sooner he reunited Abigail with her family the better. Dust was a mystery. Her survival of the bite and some of the things she said convinced him she wasn't just a runaway hitchhiking to escape a bad home life.

He had a couple of different objectives. Staying alive was at the top of his list. Avoiding apprehension was a close second.

What he'd seen on the highway and in Wichita made him think this wasn't going to be easy. The invaders had technology he couldn't understand and could barely imagine. They ran regular patrols with ground vehicles and also with the oversized jump-jets he'd first seen on Highway 70 at the turnaround point.

Small towns and rural areas were different, but even there he spotted drones or automated sensor clusters. The invaders had thought of everything and had the numbers and the technology to enforce their will over all of North America.

David didn't want to believe that was possible. The middle of the country—from Texas all the way to North Dakota—was full of wide-open spaces and low population density. From what he knew of the invaders, they sought out human victims. The High Lord douchebags reserved feeding on humans for themselves and their favorite servants.

Logically, they would first take out strategic objectives and then control large population centers. That left the middle of the nation barren. If he was lucky, maybe he could find a small band of freedom fighters out here waging guerilla warfare on the Fosk-ha sons-a-bitches.

That's what he was gambling on—redneck bullheadedness.

The problem came when he approached Dodge City. The infamous town didn't have the largest feedlots or meatpacking plants in Kansas, but they were significant. More so than the ones near Wichita where'd he picked up Abigail.

There were bound to be more aliens between here and Seattle, but he hadn't expected what he discovered.

Alien superstructures were visible before he saw Dodge City. If his memory served him correctly, the towering machinelike buildings the invaders constructed were erected near feedlots.

"Dust, are you awake?" he asked.

She pushed herself away from the window and faced him. In the back seat, Abigail still hadn't woken up.

"Is there going to be trouble?" Dust asked.

"There's always gonna be trouble, but I think this is worse than normal," he said, pointing toward the horizon where the alien superstructures loomed.

She studied the images for a long time without speaking.

"Well?" he asked.

"Those look like something the aliens built."

"What do you think it is?" he asked, evaluating her answer carefully. She was different even if she wasn't one of the invaders.

Visions of bluish skin with crystalline pock marks and ropey veins across their muscles filled his memory. Tall, lanky figures. Flashes of bloodsucking tongues.

Meanwhile Dust looked so normal. Human. He couldn't imagine her being one of them.

"Some type of terraforming operation? Drilling rigs? Might even be a dormitory or generation ship they've landed here," she said. "I'm just speculating. Maybe I read too much and watch too many movies."

"Right. I'm sure that's where you get all these crazy ideas."

"We can't get past them on this road," Dust said. "Is there another way?"

"Maybe. But not during the daytime. All the side roads are gravel. It'll throw dirt plumes twenty feet high. We'll need to find someplace to hold up for the rest of the day and make a run for it after the sun sets."

"That makes sense," Dust agreed.

Abigail sat up, wiping sleep from her eyes. "What makes sense?"

"Nothing. Go back to sleep." David needed to focus on what he was doing.

"You don't have to be a jerk about it." Abigail rubbed sleep from her eyes.

David found a double grain elevator right alongside the highway as was common in this part of the country. There was no house or trailer near it. He guessed whoever worked here lived in one of the farms a few miles away.

Between the elevators was a drive-through where trucks many times larger than the Hellcat could fit. He pulled into the shade and cut the engine. Listening to the engine rattle and tick as it cooled soothed his nerves. It had been too long since he pushed one this hard. Road grime and splattered bugs covered what had been waxed and shined to showroom perfection. Until now, he'd only taken it out when he was home from a job and the weather was nice.

Buying the car had been on his bucket list, something he'd always wanted—a fast car that was totally impractical. Now that his truck was destroyed, this was his *everyday* vehicle. He hoped he'd be able to keep it fueled from abandoned gas stations or farms between here and the Northwest.

It felt good to get out of the car, stretch their legs a bit. Dust sauntered toward the front of the hiding space, looking out at the highway that ran past the grain elevators. Before the invasion, this had been a convenient place for harvest crews to store wheat. It was a co-op like he hadn't been to one for a long time. Places like this were all over the state, abandoned in favor of larger food hubs in other parts of the country.

Abigail leaned on the car. "I like your car. It's faster than my Mustang, I bet."

The one she'll never get to buy now that the world has gone to hell, David thought.

"Yeah, I never thought I'd get to drive it like that," David said, the feel of the steering wheel still in his hands. "Not a trooper in sight these days."

"I can't believe I fell asleep." She ran one hand along the frame. "I think now I want a car like yours someday when this is all over. Someday, I'm going to be rich and famous. Then I won't have to work two jobs and go to school."

He shrugged. "Anything is possible."

She crossed her arms. "Do you think we're going to find my family? I spent most of this trip wondering how I'd do it on my own, without you and Dust. What if I had to survive solo?"

"You think you could?"

"If I had to. We need to be ready for anything, don't we? That's the way I was raised. I bet you don't know how to milk a cow or skin a buck." She tossed that last challenge with some Kansas farm girl attitude.

"Nope." Dust shrugged. "How hard could it be?"

Abigail laughed, seeming younger and more relaxed as the emotion flowed out. "Girl, you've got a lot to learn!"

Above them came the hum of an alien aircraft. David moved to the front of the loading and unloading area where Dust was watching them, standing in the shadows like it was an old habit. He hoped the invaders didn't turn their advanced technology his way. They probably had night vision technology and thermal imaging that would render his attempts at stealth a farce.

"Those ships are like the ones that shot up your truck," Dust said. "What did you call them, jump ships?"

"Something like that. They take off horizontally but are really fast once they decide which direction they want to go." David looked at Abigail. "What do you know about their ships? You had to work close to them for a while. Did you learn anything we haven't talked about?"

"I know that the pilots of those ships get special privileges. Wasn't able to figure out what that meant, but I'm assuming they eat better. Maybe get slaves or something."

The topic clearly made Abigail uncomfortable. David was curious but didn't push the issue.

"They're going to pass near us," Dust said, watching the squadron as they turned over a low hill and sped past a farmhouse.

"Of course. Why the hell wouldn't they?" David growled.

"Shouldn't we hide inside the building?" Abigail asked, already headed toward the large bay doors leading to the interior of the towering grain elevator.

David shook his head. "Get in the car. We might have to make a run for it."

Dust agreed with Abigail. "We can't outrun those ships."

"I don't want to be stuck here. What if we end up having to fight them? Do you think we have a better chance if that happens?"

Abigail's eyes widened in panic. She gripped her holstered pistol hard. "This sucks!"

"We can stay out of sight for a while." David eyed the teenager and her pistol. "But this isn't a good place for a confrontation. If they spot us, don't move. Don't even think about moving. When it's time for us to make a run for it, I'll decide and I'll drive."

All three of them climbed into the car and scrunched down. Seconds later, one of the drop ships appeared in front of the drive-through area, its guns facing them. Dirt and grit flew up behind it from its powerful engines. It had short wings that were ringed with some sort of energy field. Looking at it gave David a headache.

It shifted side to side, turning slowly as though scanning the area, with special attention to the car parked where there should be a large grain truck.

David didn't move. He heard Abigail squeak, but then her uncharacteristic timidity quickly became aggression. She turned the corner from flight to fight in an instant. There was no way to predict what she might do if things got rough. He hoped she would listen to him. As for his hitchhiker, something warned him that she was the one to worry about.

"How are you doing, Dust?" he asked, less able to read her body language.

The young woman looked serene, like staring down drop ships was nothing new to her.

She knows what this is, he thought. *She knows what that ship can do, but isn't saying.*

The ship faced the car and stabilized its position, churning up dust and grit.

"What's happening, Dust?" David asked, his hand aching from how hard he was gripping the steering wheel. The mad pounding of his heart was unbearable. He hadn't been this worked up since he was fourteen years old and about to be pulled over for the first time.

"How would I know?" she asked, eyes never leaving the alien attack ship.

"Don't bullshit me," David said. "We don't not have time for games."

"Fine. I'm guessing the pilot is communicating with headquarters. But I'm not a mind reader and I don't have one of their radios."

"Why would she know anything about these aliens?" Abigail asked.

David ignored the farmer's daughter, choosing to stare at Dust instead.

"Back at the turnaround, you kept saying you were sorry. The feds have a team of special agents looking for you. Level with me, Dust. What's going on?"

"There is too much to explain," she said, shifting nervously in her seat. She had one hand on the door handle like she might pop it open and make a run for it.

"What are you doing, Dust? Let go of the door," David said.

"No one has ever tried to protect me. no questions asked. You don't deserve to be captured." She shoved the door open and ran.

The airship wavered, then tipped forward to activate its engines. David and Abigail shouted as the backwash rocked the car; grit filled their mouths. The wind staggered him but at least Dust was far enough away to make a run for it. She looked small as she sprinted toward the waving wheat field.

Three black-armored commandos dropped out of the ship and ran Dust down like an animal. The ship rolled away and circled the scene.

"You can't leave her!" Abigail said.

"I know!" he shouted and worked himself up for the fight of his life.

"I'm scared," Abigail said.

"Me too."

"What are we going to do?"

David cursed. If he thought about his next move, he'd never make it, so he didn't waste time screwing up his mental space. It was time to jump into the mosh pit and hope for the best.

David smashed his foot down on the accelerator, cranked the wheel, and spun the car around to chase Dust and the aliens out the other side of the co-op building. The force of the turn slammed Dust's open door shut.

A second after that, he rammed the bumper of his low mileage, nearly paid off Dodge Hellcat into the back of the nearest alien soldier. The force flung the eight-foot-tall humanoid past Dust and the others.

David twisted the wheel, fishtailing his beautiful car the other direction. This time the rear quarter panel banged against the second alien super commando, flinging him through the air.

Abigail aimed her revolver at the last of them, but David shoved his hand out to keep her from firing. "I'm rolling down the window!"

David said one thing, but did something else. All he wanted was to spare the glass. The mindless instinct felt ridiculous but there was no stopping it.

He reached across to fling open the passenger door again. The moment it swung wide, Abigail leaned across the seat, aimed, and started shooting at the same time the alien soldier pivoted to deal with the unexpected threat.

"Oh shit! Oh shit! Oh shit!" Abigail grunted as she pulled the trigger. Her adversary fired back, his energy rifle blasting a hole through the trunk of David's car. Sounds were weirdly muted to his hearing, but the smell of expended gunpowder was so powerful he could taste it. Time dragged. His vision focused on the son-of-a-bitch aiming a deadly space weapon at the car he still owed twelve thousand dollars on.

One of Abigail's bullets caught the alien in the throat, right where two pieces of his armor were joined with a dull mesh. The impact caused the freak to lower his weapon and put the other hand over the wound as it sprayed blood across the Dodge.

David whipped the car around again. "Get in, Dust!"

Dust dove into the front seat. "You don't know what you just did," she said.

David sped away, not waiting for the ship to start shooting. He hit the highway, already doing sixty miles per hour. Seconds later, he had the Hellcat well over one hundred.

"You can't outrun the ship," Dust said breathlessly. "And even if I you do, there will be others."

David didn't respond. His speedometer hit one hundred and forty-three miles per hour and kept climbing. The ship appeared in his rearview mirror and started gaining. He thought it was charging its weapons. The air around the barrels shimmered with the distortion of a heatwave as blue light glowed brighter and brighter.

That can't be good.

CHAPTER TWENTY-FOUR

"YOU HAVE three and a half hours of personal time that must be used outside of this dormitory," Robert Bob said.

"Wow, Bob Bob, that's generous," Laura said, putting her pistol back together and then organizing the cleaning kit. She couldn't stop thinking about Roger and Olivia's rebellion. Had she done the right thing?

Every time she thought about it, her gut twisted. There wouldn't be another chance to do the right thing, and that was going to torture her for the rest of her life.

Such was her preoccupation that she barely realized the opportunity before her. The Fosk computer assistant was giving her a free pass to run amok in the city. It seemed like a cruel joke.

"If you had a sense of humor, I'd be laughing," she said. "I think I'll pass. No offense, but it sounds like a trap."

"Of course, Officer Osage," her computer assistant said. "Shall I report your noncompliance now or at the last possible moment? It would be a shame for you to clean weapons that don't need cleaning for another three hours."

Laura looked at the omni-directional speaker in the center of her kitchen counter. Sometimes it felt like an electronic eye watching her. "Are you serious? I am *required* to get out of this cage?"

"Your domicile is an apartment, not a cage. More to the point, we have studied your people for over fifty Earth years. Our scientists have concluded that without recreation, humans become emotionally unstable and dangerous."

"Interesting," Laura said, already making plans in her head. "Does everyone get this kind of consideration, or just your useful slaves?"

"I am not programmed to answer this question."

"Didn't expect you would be." Laura clipped an inside-the-pants holster in place, then secured her off-duty weapon there. She adjusted her T-shirt to maintain a layer of fabric between the gun and her skin; she hated sweating directly onto the weapon. Lastly, she pulled on a short jacket that just barely concealed the weapon.

"You have less than three hours," Bob said. "Please pay attention to security alerts and remain within one mile of this building."

"One mile? Are you serious? That's a waste of my time."

"Rules are rules, Officer Osage," Bob said in a close imitation of Laura's voice.

"Don't use my own lectures against me." Laura had often used this line to calm men—and a few women—long enough to slap handcuffs on them. It didn't feel great to have the trick used on her.

"Officer Osage, please leave your domicile at once. No more delay. You may access a list of approved activities via your wrist monitor if necessary."

"No need." Stopping at the front door, she looked at the

thick band where old timers wore watches. "Can I leave this behind during my alone time?"

Her wristband vibrated, then displayed a message: *That is against rule 719-1-a14, Officer Osage.*

"Of course it is." She turned off the viewscreen and left the building. If Bob wanted to harass her, it could vibrate and beep. The device was better than the organic drone thing that had latched onto her originally, but not by much.

At first, she just walked. People treated her differently when she was out of uniform. Not that this was a street party. No one gathered in groups larger than nine without a Fosk-ha supervisor, because that was a rule. Most people avoided eye contact. Those brave souls who acknowledged her presence never used five words if four would convey their sentiment.

She wanted to find members of the resistance and communicate without alerting her overlords. There had to be a way to make up for how she had foiled the attack on the airfield. The task seemed impossible, but she had to believe in something. She needed hope.

A squad car rolled down the street. She kept her eyes on the concrete in front of her feet until it was almost past her, then looked to see who it was. Neither man inside was familiar, but she saw what she'd feared since the moment she spotted the vehicle.

They were like her, and from the healthy sheen of their skin, she thought they hadn't been faking their rat feedings.

I need to find the resistance, make contact while I'm out of uniform, establish trust. Brock was only one person, and that wasn't enough to do anything. There wasn't time to deal with these guys even though they seemed up to no good.

She watched the squad car stop near an alleyway. Pedestrians changed course and soon the street was almost completely empty. Her instinct to avoid the cops was as strong as it was irrational. Why not talk to them? No one else knew what she was going through. Why even try to blend with civilians? They hated her as much as they hated the Fosk. No one ever got what they wanted. She'd set out to find the underground resistance but found two traitors to humanity just like herself. If she was smart, she'd start making friends with people who were in the same situation.

Unfair, but it was what it was.

She was about to head home when the officers got out of their car. One was blond, the other dark-haired. The blond cop disappeared down the alley. His partner scanned the street, then followed him.

"That wasn't suspicious at all," she muttered, then hoped her wrist monitor didn't record her response.

Wind ruffled her hair. The city seemed quieter than normal. The street was almost empty.

"What are you shady assholes doing?"

She hoped their furtive behavior made them part of the resistance, but that wasn't what her instincts told her was happening. Getting the drop on them proved far easier than it should have. Their poor situational awareness annoyed her even if it allowed her to creep down the alley and see what they were doing.

The second officer stood watch while his partner talked to a kid with a dog crate. She moved closer each time the lookout failed to remain vigilant. If these guys were fighting against the aliens, she didn't want to be part of their weak-ass operation.

But that wasn't what they were doing. Of course not.

I had to find these jerks instead of someone with a clue.

She moved closer, stopped, moved closer still, and selected a dark shadow to hide in.

"These aren't rats," the dark-haired officer said. "You told me you could catch rats."

The kid backed away, but in Laura's opinion, he had more spine than the cop. For a thirteen-year-old, he had a hard look in his eyes. "Dogs are easier to catch than rats. They come right up to me."

"I don't need dogs, I need rats," Dark Hair said.

"Fucking report him for something, disobedience or a curfew violation," Blond Hair said. "That might earn us an extra ration."

"I've got this, Ron. Just calm down. The kid just doesn't know what's what, is all."

The kid backed away, gripping the dog crate. "You told me you wanted rats, and that you weren't going to kill them. You said I could keep them and eat them later if my family got hungry."

"That's what I said." Dark Hair moved forward, backing the kid toward a wall. He signaled his partner who abandoned his post to help trap their quarry.

"Relax, kid. We're not going to hurt you. Just let me look at this dog," Dark Hair said.

"A dog will do," Blond Hair said, licking his lips once, then shivering as he took a step forward.

I can't fucking watch this, Laura thought.

The blond cop yanked the dog crate away from the kid. The animal inside whined in panic. "Give me that."

He didn't wait for compliance, but shoved the kid in the face and pulled open the crate. For about a moment, it looked like Dark Hair would protest, but then he was helping his partner get the animal out.

Blond Hair yanked it away and held it up like he was going to eat it in one bite instead of sucking its blood and letting it go.

"Hey! Assholes!" She barely realized she had stepped out of the shadows with her off-duty pistol drawn. It was like watching somebody else in a dream. She'd never been a planner like Charles or able to knock people down like David, but she knew how to improvise.

"Who the hell are you?" Dark Hair asked.

Laura flashed her badge with her free hand. "Internal affairs. And you're screwed if I report you. Give the kid back his dog and get back to work. I don't want to have to tell you again."

Dark Hair held up his hands, negotiating like a seasoned beat officer. Blondie backed up, the mutt whimpering in his arms. The cop looked both panicked and starved, and not in the least bit sane.

"Hey, we just needed a little something to get us through our shift," Dark Hair said. "I didn't even know it was against the rules. It's not like we are rampaging after humans."

The kid was pressed flat against the wall now, backing up but refusing to leave without his animal. Laura wondered if it was a pet or just a stray he had trapped. Either way, it didn't matter.

Blond Hair growled, stepped forward, and flung the dog aside. It tumbled, then scurried away with the kid chasing after it. "She's not Internal Affairs. I've seen her in the squad room."

And then he lunged at Laura so abruptly that even Dark Hair was surprised. He wasn't trying to scare her or subdue her or teach her a lesson; he was going for blood. If he had looked crazy before, he was now a maniacal caricature of his former self.

Laura retreated, tripped, nearly fell. She didn't have a weapon out. The use of force guidelines she'd been taught over and over since the Academy slowed her response. In her mind, this was clearly a no-shoot situation.

He grabbed her by the throat. She slammed her left forearm across his wrists, breaking his grip before he established a good hold. But he also stumbled backward, looking about as graceful as a clown tumbling down a flight of stairs.

Her mind was catching up, telling her to shoot him, but her hand was already smashing the pistol across his forehead.

"Stop!" Dark Hair shouted.

He was moving, edging toward her left flank like the Academy defensive tactics instructor had explained could be a weak side for some people. She wanted to believe he was still the calm one, but he was making sounds she didn't like, growling and hissing.

Blondie came at her again, right before she had her balance. She retreated one more step and hit him in the mouth with a straight left. Blood sprayed out in a vertical halo briefly illuminated by a distant streetlight. One second it was red, and the next black shadows fell around them.

Striking while retreating was a trick she'd learned in fourth-grade Tae Kwon Do class. She'd been kicked out of the tournament, but her brother David had laughed all the way to the car and told her that was a pro-MMA move she had.

"You're dead!" Blondie screamed, pressing forward harder than ever.

Dark Hair lunged at her from the left, forcing her to change directions and move quickly to create distance.

Gripping the gun with both hands, she took a shooting stance. "Stop or I'll shoot!"

This got their attention. They had their own guns, but didn't draw them.

Her heart pounded madly. She felt like she was running a sprint and desperately wanted to get on her radio to call for help, but she didn't have one.

Dark Hair raised his hands, back to negotiating. A half smile that Laura found extremely irritating creased his face. He looked like every sleazy fast talker she'd ever met. *How the hell did I think this was the trustworthy one?*

At about the same time, Blondie finally drew his weapon, gripping it with both hands. She hoped his hands would start trembling like hers were, but if he was freaking out, she couldn't tell.

"Everyone, just stop," Dark Hair said. "Look around. We're out in the street."

"Drop that gun, you stupid bitch, or I'm gonna of shoot you in your cute little face. I'll be totally justified and you'll be dead." His voice was cold, his stare hard.

"All right," she said, the words tumbling out of her mouth almost too fast to understand. She lowered her gun a foot, then all the way to her side. "I give up. I'm putting it back in the holster. You can cuff me and take me."

"Drop it," Dark Hair said.

"Come on, man. Would you drop your personal gun on the concrete?" She edged back one step, which Blond Hair didn't seem to like, but fuck him. "We're on the same side. I'm a feeder like you."

"Fuck that. Don't call us that," Blondie said.

"What the hell are we then?" She screamed the words, truly frustrated and ready to yank the gun up and start shooting. "You know this sucks for me too, you fucking jerks."

"All right, all right," Dark Hair said. "We have to take you in. Look around. We're in the street now. People are watching. If we don't hook you up, we—and by we, I mean the entire police department—is going to lose face and our jobs will be even more impossible. Just holster the damn gun and let Brian slap the cuffs on."

"I'll cover her while you cuff," Brian said, still aiming at her head.

Laura slipped the Glock into the holster. Brian lowered his gun an inch. Dark Hair pulled handcuffs from the back of his belt as he stepped forward.

She twisted on the balls of her feet and sprinted away. They came after her, but it was too late. Initiative mattered, and she had it in spades this time.

They shouted but didn't shoot. One ran to the squad car and raced around the block to head her off. She didn't look back. This was a game all three of them had played before and she had to win.

"Hey, you!" said a voice as she ran down a side street listening for Brian's pounding feet and the car racing to the next intersection.

A woman stood on the steps of an older apartment. The door was half open. All the lights were off. She waved for Laura to get inside.

How the tables have turned, kid. She would have laughed at being the fleeing felon ducking into a house—a situation she'd cursed many times when on the right side of the law. *Don't think about it like that. They are the bad guys, not you.*

She barely looked at the people who helped her, choosing to head out the back door as soon as the way was clear.

The trip back to her apartment dragged on forever. She checked her wrist monitor over and over, waiting for instructions to report to her alien overlord for immediate execution. The only thing that happened was that a countdown timer appeared and beeped at her every five minutes.

No alarms went off.

Bob didn't order her to arrest herself.

No death squads were waiting for her when she opened her front door.

Good to know, she thought. Maybe they couldn't spy on her every second, because that adventure should have set off some alarms. She wondered what would have happened if she'd started shooting.

CHAPTER TWENTY-FIVE

THIS TIME, Charles stood in the hallway alone. The pieces wanted to fall into place. Only his resistance kept the solution beyond his grasp. David and Laura had always teased him about his confidence, overconfidence they called it. But he was good at puzzles, always had been.

Computer coding came natural to him. He saw problems on a different level. That was the reason David had called him to ask about raiding an alien stronghold. The thought still troubled him. His brother was probably dead, too brave for his own good and unable to protect everyone from bullies. Maybe it was admirable, his brother's behavior, but more likely it was just a character flaw that would get him killed, no matter how tough he was.

So when a solution was there but he couldn't see it, it was because he was getting in his own way. Why wouldn't Emily accept the fact that Warfighter Games was in over its head?

The door opened. Emily stepped into the hallway. "Are you mad at me?" she asked.

"I'm not angry."

She pulled him into a hug. Tears formed in his eyes. Nothing was supposed to happen like this.

"I don't want you to worry about the company," Emily said. "Henry says things are getting better."

"They're not getting better, and I don't give a shit what he says."

She pulled back and looked hurt. "I thought you two were friends."

"Why are you talking to him about this anyway? When did you talk to him?" Charles felt the pieces moving. The resistance inside of him grew stronger than ever.

"Don't get like that." Emily turned to face the empty hallway.

"Like what?"

She mutely shook her head.

"You know I hate it when you do that," he said. "And what do you mean, like what?"

"I married you because I didn't think you were one of those jealous types."

A piece of their relationship puzzle clicked into place. They'd had this discussion before, but this time her posture was different. She wouldn't face him, not completely. Her body language was a series of half measures.

Silence grew between them like poison. He wanted to speak his mind, he tried to force the words out, but his tongue wouldn't work.

Emily hugged herself and refused to look at him. She looked guilty and unhappy and annoyed that he wasn't saying something.

"You were going to leave me," he slowly said, hearing

the words that seemed to be coming from someone else. "But no one expected an alien invasion. Lucky me."

He laughed crazily, and she glared at him. Gone were the consoling hugs and soft touches that she used to keep him off guard.

"I can't believe this," he said.

"Don't be ridiculous." She was finally arguing, denying the truth. "Think about the girls. Don't let your irrational jealousy scare them."

He wanted to punch the wall and shout at her. With great effort, he spoke in the calmest voice he'd ever directed at her. "I've never been jealous. We both know that. Maybe I should've been."

"What the hell is that supposed to mean? I've always been faithful to you."

"Until now."

"Fuck you, Charles." She shouldered past him and went inside, closing the door behind her and turning the lock.

AN HOUR LATER, she let him in. "No arguing. The girls are asleep."

Charles nodded, looking her straight in the eyes in what seemed like the first time in forever. She'd been crying. He felt like he should've been doing the same and wished his eyes weren't so dry. Things like this weren't supposed to happen when the world was ending.

The two of them relocated to the tiny kitchen just off the small living area. They stood near each other, speaking in whispers.

"I'm sorry, Emily. I overheard Kingston talking with an alien," he said, then rushed on before she could voice the skepticism written all over her face. "I was walking downstairs in one of the closed off areas. You know how I like to pace and talk to myself when I'm thinking. I came to a corner, and I heard them, clear as I can hear you right now. We need to start thinking about other options."

"What kind of options, Charles?" She sounded annoyed but at least she wasn't shutting him down completely.

"Right now, they have us cut off from the rest of the world. If I can't get access to unfiltered news, nobody can. That worries me. After hearing Kingston negotiating terms with an alien in secret, it scares the shit out of me."

"Watch your language, Charles. The girls are sleeping, but what if they're not? I don't want them picking up bad habits like that."

Charles worked through a few of his favorite equations until he fought down the urge to debate the nonsensical idea of the girls picking up bad words during their sleep. "I need to go outside, make contact with anyone who's seen these things face-to-face. Maybe there's someplace we can go."

"Like where, Charles?" Emily said, a note of hysteria in her voice.

"My parents' place in Colorado. It hasn't been rented for a while, but it should have basic provisions. Mom and Dad wanted anyone who stayed there to be ready to be snowed in, no matter the season. That's just what we need."

Emily frowned. "You want to take our children and drag them hundreds of miles through a war zone with no guarantee we will have a place to stay whenever we get there? Absolutely not."

"I'll go. Once I have a few things figured out, I'll come

back to get you and the girls," Charles said, not quite believing his own words.

She stared at him, looking more scared than ever, then finally nodded, wide-eyed and uncertain. Charles felt like a jerk because he was glad she was afraid. If she hadn't been upset, he would've thought she was just getting rid of him so she could run off with her lover, whoever he was.

"I love you, Emily. I wouldn't do this if I didn't think it was the only way to take care of you and the girls," Charles said. "At first, I one-hundred-percent believed the right decision was to stay in the bunker. But everything has changed. I'm sure about this, Emily."

She nodded and allowed him to hug her. He held on for as long as he could, then silently packed up a bag and slung it over his shoulder. Looking at Debbie and Cara was hard and nearly undid him. He kissed them on their foreheads, and they gave him sleepy hugs.

"Daddy's going on a trip," he said. "Don't tell anyone. It's a secret."

"Okay, Daddy. We'll wait for you. Just come back as soon as you can," Debbie said.

Cara nodded her agreement.

He gave Emily one last hug, then left before he cried.

The halls were empty. His ID badge opened every door he came to. At first, he'd been worried there was no escape, and that they were locked in this place like an underground prison.

Getting out will be a lot easier than getting in, he thought.

He took the stairs, then loitered in the lobby to make sure he hadn't triggered a security alarm. The next thing he knew, he was outside breathing fresh air.

Which was amazing. Scary as hell, but fantastic and

wonderful too. Working underground hadn't bothered him much. He remembered telling David about his office and practically feeling his big brother's dread. Neither of them had like confined spaces growing up.

There wasn't much civilian traffic, pedestrian or otherwise, moving that night. He saw strange vehicles in the distance shining spotlights down into the city, probably searching for someone. The military may have been defeated, but plenty of regular people had resisted the occupiers.

He shivered, rubbed his hands together, then zipped up his jacket. With a little hop to adjust the weight of the backpack, he began striding down side streets, putting as much distance between him and his overlord captors as he could. It was a hard thing not to think about his wife and children. But he was doing this for them.

It's the only way.

Gunfire and explosions thundered in the distance. He headed in that direction despite his misgivings. An hour passed, and he never found where the battle had occurred. Dread ruined the excitement of his adventure. If he couldn't find evidence of something as important as a gun fight, how hard would a real mystery be to solve?

Eventually, he arrived at one of the bus stations, not sure if he wanted to get a ride across the country or to just find a decent map. Either way, what he saw worried him—blood smears near the doors of vehicles, glass broken out, drag marks. One of the tires looked like it had been chewed on by something big.

The invasion hadn't been without casualties. Nor had the time afterward, from what it looked like. Evidence of death was everywhere.

There were never bodies, only smears of blood. Maybe the victims had crawled away, but the marks suggested they'd been dragged away. Every few hundred meters, he saw police cars and military vehicles torn to shreds by weapons more powerful than anything his imagination had come up with.

He squatted next to one of the smoking cop cars, looking at the holes punched through the quarter panels. One went straight through the engine block. Another had deflected from a different part of the motor. Without more data or specialized training, he was just guessing this had been done by the invaders.

But there was plenty of evidence of Earth weapons in the fight—scorch marks from explosions, bullet holes in concrete and windows.

Next to the bus terminal stood a police station. It was locked up tight and aliens stood guard alongside human officers. Charles backed away, hid on a side street, and rethought his options. He shouldn't have been surprised but the sight of it had him wanting to piss his pants.

This wasn't supposed to be easy, he thought and pulled out the first of several cell phones he had in his bag. One by one, he plugged them into his laptop and deactivated their GPS functions. Then he took them apart, examined each component, and made them as safe from cyber hacking as possible.

He was nervous to make the first phone call and found himself wondering what David would do. So despite the inconvenience of it, he packed everything up on an impulse and moved to a new hiding place. That seemed like something his street-savvy big brother would do—stay on the move, keep the enemy guessing.

"I can't believe I'm even doing this stuff," he muttered,

then opened the first throwaway phone to make a call. Laura didn't answer, but there was a funny sound when he broke the link so he disposed of that phone immediately. His second try was to David. It rang and rang until he hung it up and relocated. To try again.

Suddenly, leaving the Warfighter Games company didn't seem like such a good idea. He repeated his most reassuring arguments to himself, but knew in his gut they wouldn't let him back in. And if they did, it would only be once, so he had to do whatever he was going to do now.

The only way he was going to stay sane was to keep busy, so he kept trying to call his siblings. First Laura, then David. He crushed phone after phone beneath his heel.

By the time he admitted his experiment was a failure, he was hungry and needed a place to sleep. He wandered into alleyways, avoiding cops, aliens, and shadowy figures that moved furtively through a city he used to think was safe.

―――

CHARLES KNEW something was wrong the moment he woke up. For starters, he was sleeping outside curled up in the doorway to a coffee shop like it was going to open and serve him breakfast. The sign on the door read "Closed for Alien Invasion."

"There's nothing like truth in advertising," Charles said.

He was starting to enjoy the apocalypse, even if he was a bit confused, seriously hungry, and in chronic need of caffeine. The few reports on the outside world claimed most people were still living and working as normally as possible. If that was the case, they were doing it someplace else. The world around him was frighteningly lonely, but not a single person had told him to stop talking to himself. If he had a thought and wanted to hear the sound of it, he just spat it out. It was a judgment-free zone.

He gathered his meager belongings and looked up and down the street, hoping the feeling of wrongness would pass.

"You're not very good at this, Mr. Osage."

Charles turned in a circle, frantically searching for the source of the voice. It sounded close. He finally picked up an image reflected in a window and realized that Halloran, the security supervisor who had accosted him earlier, was standing just around the corner from the entryway to the coffee shop.

"You scared the crap out of me." Charles moved into the street so that he wouldn't feel cornered in the alcove.

"I scared you? Think how I felt when you started talking to yourself. Awkward," Halloran said. "Do you have any weapons?"

"Where would I have gotten weapons?" Charles asked. "And what are you doing here? Last I checked, I was free to leave the bunker if I want to."

"Yeah, but why would you want to?" Halloran asked.

"I'm starting to wonder that myself." Charles was cold, hungry, and wishing the coffee shop was actually open. He needed something to get him going. Even the crap they served in the Warfighter Games programmers' lounge would be welcome right now.

Halloran, Charles realized, had an M4 on a sling that hung in front of his body like he was playing Warfighter: The Red Massacre. Their conversation about what he had to do to become part of the security team came back to him in a rush. This man was a high-speed operator, definitely a member of the military special operations community—possibly a Navy SEAL or Delta Force operator, but to Charles's imagination, he had the aura of a Force Recon Marine.

"Penny for your thoughts, Mr. Osage," Halloran said, then gazed up and down the street as though scanning for threats.

"I'm thinking you could *make* me go back if you want to."

Halloran shrugged, more concerned with their environment than with good manners. "Doesn't matter what I want. It only matters what my orders happen to be."

"That doesn't put me at ease," Charles said. "What are your orders?"

Halloran stared him down. "They're flexible. You don't get to my level unless the company trusts you. But I would ask you not to put me in a bad situation."

"That doesn't make me feel better."

Halloran shifted his weight, his right hand gripping the gun on the sling. "Are you going back into the compound?"

"Will they let me back in?" Charles needed this piece of information for his meta-analysis. It was a good thing the security chief was here, even if it was also a bit disturbing.

"Probably, if I vouch for you. And I might. But only once."

Charles turned away and headed in the other direction, trying to watch the man out of his peripheral vision. The security chief fell in beside him. "This is your decision then?"

"You have a problem with that?"

Halloran shrugged. "You're not tough enough to survive

out here. I've taken my team out three times, and I'm telling you, it's bad."

"Where is your team?"

Halloran acted like he didn't hear the question. Instead he stepped aside, rifle at the ready, and aimed it down a dark alley like something was there. Then he relaxed.

Nice theatrics, Charles thought. *Very convincing.*

He studied Halloran a moment longer than seemed safe, wondering if he should make a break for it. "Tell me about the chain of command in the Warfighter Games security team. Can I give you orders?"

"No. Not until hell freezes over."

"I had to ask. I came out here to contact my family, and I'm not going to let you stand in my way," Charles said. "If you're going to try to drag me back or shoot me, you might as well do it now."

"Part of my job is keeping you out of harm's way. So for now, I'll watch your back. But if I get an order to bring you in, then I'll bring you in."

"Is part of your job spying on me?"

"As a matter of fact, it is. The problem is that I'm not smart enough to know half of the things you're probably going to get into. I'm good at watching and listening, but that's the extent of my spying skills," Halloran said. "And when my bosses give me the order, I'll slap zip ties on you and take you back to the compound. Just so we're clear."

Charles analyzed the security chief like he was a non-player character in one of his games. What was he here for? What quest couldn't be completed without his help?

"What makes sense in this scenario?" he said, facing Halloran.

The man raised one eyebrow. "Talking to yourself? What would Mrs. Osage say?"

Charles flinched but pressed on. Everyone in the company knew his quirk. "Chris Halloran, Level 1 Security Supervisor for Warfighter Games, has all the marks of a man recruited from military SPECOPS teams. He's strong as hell, probably runs marathons for fun, and games with the best twelve-year-olds on the planet. Not many people ever beat the Red Massacre."

"All true. Also great with the ladies," Halloran added.

"He's also here against orders, which leads a rational and scientific mind to ask why."

"I like it when you talk about me in the third person like I'm not standing right here."

"Why *are* you out here, Chris Halloran, Level 1 Security Supervisor?" Charles asked.

Halloran gave him a hard look.

Charles waited.

"I have instincts." Halloran took a moment to sweep his eyes over a nearby building. "And there are some things I want to check out. How about we don't talk about this anymore?"

A police car turned a corner a second after Halloran pulled him into a doorway. Charles was ready to drop his lame efforts to interrogate the man, but thought of his siblings. Neither of them would've let this guy off the hook.

"Tell me the rest or I'm going to flag down that cop and see which of us gets in more trouble." Heart pounding madly, he took a step forward, ready to dash into the open. "You're in this at least as deep as I am, I think."

Halloran hesitated about two seconds, cursed under his

breath. "The aliens drink blood. I told my team I would look into it."

Silence. Disbelief. Charles couldn't process the man's sincerity. It wasn't every day he saw one of the most dangerous men on the planet go pale with fear.

CHAPTER TWENTY-SIX

CHARLES STRODE across the Westlake Center with Halloran falling five or six strides behind him. "It's cleaner than I expected."

Halloran grunted noncommittally.

He's got excellent hearing, Charles thought, filing the information for future reference. "I thought there'd be trash blown around or maybe some burned-out cars."

Halloran moved closer but also swiveled as he walked, always looking for some kind of threat. It was just something the man did—*while holding a machine gun.* "There wasn't any fighting here. It's not good ground. Too open. No chokepoints to funnel the enemy into. If our enemies were dumb enough to mass here in the center and we had the high ground to fire down on them, that would be something."

"If they were camping," Charles said. He rarely played the games he designed, but when he did, getting ambushed by adversaries hiding motionless in the shadows drove him nuts. It was a viable strategy, but took the fun out of the contest. Getting sniped three seconds into the scenario sucked.

The one time he'd tried the strategy, some twelve-year-old kid with ten thousand hours of first-person gaming under his belt had tossed grenades into his position.

"Just like that." Halloran laughed. "Keep your eyes open. We haven't seen a patrol for a while. I heard something that might have been a city bus. There are some people still going to critical infrastructures jobs. Eventually we'll run into them."

"Is that how it was the last time you came out with your team?" Charles asked.

"There were more people doing more things," Halloran said quietly. A minute passed and no pedestrians or vehicles appeared. "We're good for now, I think. Hell, maybe someone finally got the balls to organize an effective resistance."

"Better than the military?" Charles was curious. Something else had happened here, but he didn't have enough data to put the puzzle together. All he knew was that he had a really bad feeling.

Halloran spat on the ground. "The military is gone."

They moved in uncomfortable silence until Charles stopped to draw a quick diagram in his notebook.

"Why are *you* out here, Charles?" Halloran asked. "Because apparently you didn't break every rule in the WFG book for the same reasons I did."

"What do you know about these creatures?" Charles paused at the corner of the Macy's store and looked toward a bus that had been abandoned. He wanted answers before rumors about blood-sucking monsters terrified everyone.

"Where is everyone? Are they really aliens? There could be another explanation."

"That is more than one question." Halloran moved into the shadow of the building with his back to the wall. "And if you can convince me these bastards aren't from another star system, I'll give you a piggyback ride to the WFG compound."

"Our military isn't gone. We've combined forces across the world into the Earth Military Coalition. If Warfighter Games is so important, why isn't the EMC defending Seattle? *If* these are aliens, and *if* Warfighter Games is vital, it would make sense to defend the Pacific Northwest. All I've seen out here is a ghost city," Charles said.

He'd thrown that out as a kind of test. He wanted to know if Halloran had seen the EMC naval defeat. He wanted to know what kind of propaganda the company was feeding their armed guards.

"You probably know more than I do, Mr. Osage. We were told the initial battles were a draw and several governments and corporations had entered into negotiations with the invaders from a strong diplomatic position."

"Do you believe that?" Charles asked the question while thinking of the secret meeting he'd witnessed in the darkest basement of the compound. The memory reminded him of why he was out here risking permanent separation from his wife and children. He could still hear Kingston kissing the strange alien emissary's ass.

Halloran laughed bitterly. "I did twelve years in the Army before taking this job. I know when I'm not getting the entire story. But—and this is a big but—knowing everything isn't always good or necessary."

"I like to know everything," Charles said. "I'm surprised

you can operate with that degree of ambiguity. That takes a true Renaissance man with an open mind and a high level of intellectual courage."

"That's me," Halloran said with a crisp laugh. "The Renaissance Man."

Charles felt anger creeping through him, which he hated but couldn't always control. "Don't bullshit me."

"When I brought my team back from our first recon mission, there were some people I know from way back who had questions, the kind they didn't want our employers to know they were asking."

"Keep talking."

"Every time I brought my team in, someone asked me if the aliens really drank human blood." Halloran gave him a hard look, as if daring him to argue.

"I haven't heard that rumor," Charles said, already dismissing the rumor as more fearmongering nonsense. "Now, you and your team will have researcher bias, which means—"

"I know what that is, Mr. Osage." Halloran led the way down another street, avoiding a work crew at the end of the block. They turned a corner, and the security officer stopped abruptly, staring at a sign covered with graffiti.

"Is that one of their signs?" Charles asked.

"Apparently, the invaders want our pets," Halloran said. "So, Mr. Osage, do you have any cats or dogs we need to take to the pet deposit facility?"

"No. Why would they want our pets?"

"Maybe they came to Earth because they saw all the cat and dog videos on the internet."

Charles laughed.

"Maybe they drink more than just human blood."

That quickly killed the mood. Charles sobered at that, and told himself people would believe anything if they were frightened enough. It wasn't Halloran's fault. No one had enough data to draw rational conclusions.

———

"THERE ARE PEOPLE UP AHEAD," Halloran said. "Work crews. One cop. I don't know how they will react to us."

"What are you talking about?"

"Let me show you the rest." Halloran led Charles to the corner, put a hand on his shoulder, and motioned for him to peek around the edge.

"You're paranoid," Charles said, "but I guess that's your job."

What Charles saw next changed his world completely.

The ships he had seen fighting the EMC combined forces had barely seemed real. This was different. The ship was parked like an old-school rocket, towering above the surrounding buildings. Cables pulsing with light snaked into the ground. He saw movement on every level of the ship, but no details. His first thought was that when this thing lifted off, it was going to incinerate half of downtown Seattle.

Guards stood at ramps leading into the immense ship.

"Those guards look big," Charles said, wishing his voice hadn't gone hoarse for no reason.

"They are," Halloran said. "And their armor is more advanced than anything I've seen—and I still have my top-secret clearance. I'm ready for your alternative theory anytime, Mr. Osage. Tell me these guys aren't aliens."

"Something's happening," Charles said. There was a

thundering noise just at the edge of his hearing—something ominous like a stampeding crowd. Glass broke from a building around the corner.

Halloran pulled him back, pressed him deeper into the doorway of a tattoo shop, and then stood protectively in front of him, both hands on his M4. "Check that door. Get ready to run."

"What's that sound?"

Halloran's voice wavered. He shifted his balance and brought his weapon up slightly higher than the low ready position. "I don't know."

More glass shattered, but this time he heard voices. Shouting. The distance was still over a block away and he hadn't expected to know exactly what they were saying, but he also understood that what they were shrieking was in no language he had ever heard before.

Charles grabbed both door handles and pulled. "Locked! Fuck."

Calm as a math teacher, Halloran handed him a pistol. "Take my place for a second. Just watch for them. Don't shoot unless you have to."

"Can you get inside?"

Halloran laughed. "I have a universal key."

He pulled a heavy knife from his tactical vest, flipped it around in his grip, then slammed the pommel in the upper corner of the glass door. Glass poured down, some of it shattering onto the sidewalk.

"The trick is to strike near the corner," Halloran said. "Hit the middle of a door like this and it just flexes. Of course, if you have to do it, I recommend wearing eye protection."

Charles flinched as he realized Halloran was blinking

furiously and trying to get something out of his left. Eye. "Shit, are you okay?"

"I'm fine." Halloran growled deep in his throat, something Charles remembered his brother doing after breaking his leg in a motocross accident. "And worse comes to worst, I'm right-eye dominant, so I'll still be able to shoot. Let's go."

He pushed Charles through the doorway and guarded their retreat by walking backward for several steps with his M4 ready to do some work. "That's not good."

Charles rushed into the shop, ignoring the chairs and trays of ink. Strange art decorated black-painted walls. He looked back to see what his bodyguard was worried about.

Giant figures sprinted past the broken glass door, snarling, hissing, and grunting. They ran on two legs, but were hunched over like rampaging Neanderthals. One looked right at him, eyes strangely shaped, mouth open, a snake-like tongue thrashing the air.

"Door!" Halloran shouted, then opened it, shoved Charles through, and followed.

The space was a narrow staircase leading upward. Charles ran without thinking, heard the door slam behind them, and hoped there weren't any of those monsters waiting at the top.

"Stay away from the windows," Halloran said. "Hold this door shut while I clear this floor. Looks like two rooms and a bathroom."

"Okay." Charles wedged his foot against the bottom of the door to maximize the best mechanical position for the task assigned to him. Then, just to be sure, he gripped the door handle with the idea he could hold it tightly enough to keep it from turning.

"Stay away from the windows," Halloran said again as

he moved through the small rooms with his gun pointing into each corner he came to.

"You already said that."

"I'll probably say it again." Halloran came back, nodded approval at the door-holding strategy, then pulled a small rubber door wedge from his tactical vest.

"You keep door stoppers?" Charles couldn't believe it.

"Yep. They're great for room clearing. Good way to secure doors to rooms you've already dealt with. Simple, small, and useful."

Charles nodded, wondering if there was a way to incorporate that weird little detail into Warfighter 6 if he ever had a chance to finish building the game.

"Can you wedge the top too?" Charles asked.

Halloran pulled another stopper from his vest. "Good idea."

Two seconds later, a heavy body slammed against the door, nearly breaking it from the hinges. Charles and Halloran backed away without saying a word.

"Go look out the window," Halloran said, aiming his M4 at the door as something slammed against it over and over again.

"You told me to stay away from the windows."

"Just don't get seen. I need to know if there is a balcony or a fire escape or anyway out of here. Do you know how to use that pistol?"

"I know how to shoot, but my hands are shaking."

"That will change once you start killing. Just don't shoot me. Count your rounds because you will run out faster than you think." Still facing the door, Halloran took a small step backward, then shifted to his left. A section of the frame cracked. Inhuman voices screamed through the cheap material. The deafening sound warbled and shifted past the normal range of hearing.

Charles was no soldier, but he was a student of soldiers and their tactics—that was why his games were so good. His companion was playing for keeps.

The window was a slider. Beyond it was a small balcony, mostly so the building's owner could claim there was one. Charles opened it slowly, hoping the movement wouldn't cast a reflection and draw attention.

"Oh my God," he breathed.

"What?" Halloran sounded tense.

"The street is swarming with these things." Charles gaped in horror at the dark shapes of humanoids sprinting down the street, scrambling over anything in their way, occasionally looking up. Directly across from his hiding place, two of the alien monsters scrambled onto a balcony with ease and smashed through windows.

A woman screamed. A man shouted. Seconds later, the man was screaming too. Other aliens made the climb.

"The door is coming down," Halloran shouted. "Find us away out of here or we're dead."

Charles stepped on to the balcony and leaned out for a better view. Feeling exposed, he forced himself to take his time and think.

Halloran fired three rounds, almost fast enough to sound like he was using the weapon in full-auto mode.

Charles whipped his head around and saw three aliens falling backward with holes punched in their foreheads. Halloran shuffled backward as he fired. "One, two, three... four, five... six, seven, eight..."

Bodies hit the floor. Others fell on top of their companions.

Charles couldn't look away from their faces. Mouths open, the creatures slashed the air with tongues a foot long. Teeth glistened wetly, and they hissed a language that hurt his brain.

Halloran transitioned to his sidearm, killing their attackers at a slightly slower rate as he took fractions of seconds longer to aim.

Charles looked at the pistol the man had given him, wondering if he could shoot it with a tenth of the precision the security man was doing right now, in the face of deadly, incomprehensibly inhuman enemies.

"We have to go through them!" Charles shouted as he put one hand on Halloran's left shoulder.

"I was afraid you'd say that." He dropped two more aliens. Dark blood pooled from wall to wall now. "Put some rounds into them while I reload, but don't get in front of me."

Charles pretended this was a video game where you could injure people on your team, which wasn't always the case in multi-player scenarios. He shifted to Halloran's left, aimed, and fired as accurately as he could manage. At this range, most of his rounds struck, but they weren't head shots and they didn't kill anything.

"I'm up. Stay right behind me. We're going down the stairs, then right, and hoping it leads to a back door. Let's go!" Halloran rushed forward, shooting with increased vigor.

One of the larger aliens met his charge. Halloran kicked the monster in the pelvis, knocking him backward but also slipping. Charles caught him. They both went to their knees but scrambled up, slipping and sliding in the blood and gore under their feet.

"Top of the stairs!" Halloran announced, then killed a pair of the aliens, shoving them backward with his barrel right after he put holes in them. A new group scrambled up the stairs, stomping across the bodies of their fellow freaks.

Charles pushed on his back, driving him through the press of snake-tongued monsters. Halloran stumbled once, then grunted approval as he fired his M4, shoved, shouldered, and kicked his way down the stairs. Most of them were larger than the average human. The moment Halloran stopped shooting and kicking them, the second his momentum faltered, the aliens would drag them to the ground.

One of the aliens reached over Halloran's shoulder, grabbing Charles by his shirt collar and nearly dragging them both off-balance. The creature's mouth gaped wide, teeth flashing near Halloran's left ear as its tongue darted out, stinging Charles's cheek.

Furious, he reached over Halloran's shoulder, pressed the pistol against the clawing, grabbing, biting thing's temple, and pulled the trigger. Blood sprayed over Halloran and gushed into Charles's mouth as death throes whipped the thing's head around.

He gagged and slipped on the bloody stairs.

"Fuck!" Halloran shouted.

They tumbled into a pair of aliens at the bottom, each step a disaster of slipping, banging shins, elbows, and faces. As though to add insult to injury, strong hands grabbed them and held them in place. It was feeding time, and the starving aliens were shrieking like desperate animals.

Energy weapons fired from the front of the tattoo shop toward Charles, Halloran, and their attackers. Spike-tongued aliens burst apart like gory water balloons even faster and more completely than when Halloran had three full magazines for his M4 to work with.

Four alien troopers advanced into the room, killing their own kind indiscriminately.

Halloran let his M4 hang and held up both hands when it was done. Charles imitated him.

"Why are you outside the WFG bunker?" the alien squad leader demanded.

Charles stepped between the alien and Halloran. "Research. I'm Charles Osage. This man was assigned to protect me while I looked for computer servers we might use to improve the alliance."

"Alliance?" The alien towered over Charles. The faceplate of his helmet was nearly opaque. "There is no alliance. Humanity has surrendered."

Charles bobbed his head down once, hating this game. "Of course. We call it an alliance so people won't resist the inevitable. It's human psychology, very delicate."

The Fosk-ha warrior stared at him for a long time. "Your soldier must surrender his weapons. We will escort you back to the compound."

"I'm basically out of ammunition anyway," Halloran said. "Be gentle. I'll need them back."

The Fosk-ha warriors took the weapons and ignored the words. Their leader opened his helmet, then bent to hiss into Charles's face. "This city is overrun with Ravagers. We do not control them. If you do not let us do our jobs, they will scour all life from the planet in a matter of months."

"Maybe we should work together," Charles said. "I assume you want to stop the Ravagers."

"They cannot be stopped, because your people are rare among sentient species. Like the Fosk-ha, they can become

Ravagers. There is no hope for your planet. We only wish to control the spread until we can leave for a better world," the warrior leader said.

Enraged, Charles spat, "You brought the problem, not us."

Halloran elbowed him in the gut, then asked a question to divert their attention from his insolence. "Why do any of you drink blood?"

"There is blood power in this planet. Life force that runs through your biosphere. With it, we can survive the next generation of far travel," the Fosk-ha said. "I tell you this because I respect your warrior prowess."

"I'm all about prowess," Halloran said, rolling his neck and one shoulder to work out a recent injury.

"We go now," the Fosk-ha said. "Obey our laws. Submit to our methods. We have survived many planets. Bow to us, and there may be hope for your kind."

CHAPTER TWENTY-SEVEN

LAURA FINISHED her shift but lingered at headquarters. The practice wasn't uncommon. A lot of her friends did the same thing, even if they weren't in the mood to socialize. No one had much to look forward to at home. She hadn't been anyone's houseguest, but from what Brock told her, everyone had the exact same quarters.

It barely felt like living.

Some days she was allowed to double up with Brock; other times she wasn't. They delivered food and other supplies they were able to gather, but never enough. This wasn't the Chicago she knew. The worst part was not knowing how the rest of the country was doing. The Fosk-ha media blackout was impossibly complete.

"Where do you think you're going?" a voice asked.

She turned around to see Brock following her down the hallway. "Where does it look like?"

He shrugged. "If I didn't know better, I'd say you are heading for the armory."

"You should take the test for detective," she said. Turning

her back on him, she continued toward the secure area and swept her badge across the security reader—a CPD device, not something the Fosk-ha had put here. It beeped. She pushed open the door. Brock followed her, getting up and walking beside her now.

"I haven't talked to Jameson for a while," she said. "I just started imagining him down here all by himself for the entire occupation."

"He'd be one of the lucky ones if that were the case," Brock said.

"Maybe. But even an introvert could go crazy." She reached the second door, swiped her badge, and entered with Brock. The room was large enough for five or ten people to gather and drink coffee while they procrastinated going on duty. On one wall was a barred window where Peter Jameson sat reading a paperback novel.

He looked up, narrowed his eyes, then glanced down at his reading material for a few more seconds.

"Good to see you too, Peter," Laura said.

"You wouldn't be here if you didn't need something." Peter Jameson's tone wasn't bitter or sarcastic. Rather, he sounded like he was still two-thirds into the story he'd been reading. That was just like him. If Laura had been worried about him losing his sanity, she had been projecting her own fears and doubts onto the man. He was old enough to retire but kept coming to work for something to do, which she thought meant getting out of the house for at least part of the day. Translation, he didn't need to be around his wife twenty-four hours a day.

"How's Betty?" Laura asked.

Peter put down the book without marking the page. That was one of the habits she'd noted the first time they'd met;

he didn't use bookmarks but chose to just remember where he was in the novel. "She's at home, probably making me a to-do list."

Laura smiled. "I'll make you a to-do list."

"Of course," Peter said, smiling. "Tell me why you're here."

"It's pretty wild out on the streets," she said. "I'd like to sign out a couple of extra weapons and some ammunition."

Peter gave her a hard look. "There are a lot of new rules. The big one is to not provide weapons to any resistance movement, real or imagined."

"I'm not that generous," Laura said. "My grandpa used to say you can never have too many guns or knives. Maybe I'm just feeling nostalgic, but I want to up my arsenal a little. I've had a few close calls where I didn't have backup."

Brock shifted uneasily.

"I'm not blaming you, Brock," Laura said. "I know you would've been there if you could have."

"What exactly are we talking about?" Brock asked. "Did something happen that you didn't report?"

"Something almost happened," she said, cutting off the discussion. "Made me nervous. Now I want more and bigger guns."

Peter went back to one of the racks along the far wall. Laura had hoped he would just let her inside so she could browse, but that's not the way he worked, not even before Earth was invaded by bloodsucking aliens.

A few minutes later he brought her a tactical shotgun, an M4 fully automatic carbine, and extra ammunition for both weapons and her pistol. "I have a couple of good knives and some tactical pry bars."

"I don't plan on doing a search warrant. A pry bar would just weigh me down."

"Trust me, you need one." Peter added an eighteen-inch pry bar that look like a chisel at one end to the pile. "About 500 years ago when I was riding a beat, I responded to a shooting. Turned out to be a murder suicide, but all I knew was that there was a victim down inside and the doors had been nailed shut. I kicked the hell out of it, banged up my knee pretty good. Had I been able to pry apart the deadbolt, maybe I could've saved one of them."

"Maybe," Laura said. This was the first she'd ever heard this story. "You know how it works, though. You would've just ended up saving the suspect."

"You're right. But I'll never know," Peter said. "Take the pry bar. Put it someplace on your vest if you have room for it. If not, keep it in your car where you can get to it quickly. Do you have a tourniquet and pressure bandages?"

Laura nodded. Every good beat cop carried those items, especially since there were more and more available on the internet—back when there was such a thing. She signed for the weapons and packed them up. When she left, Brock was standing near the door with his arms crossed, clearly struggling with some inner decision.

"Are you going to turn me in or something?" Laura asked.

"Maybe I should." He turned away, then back. "Were you the one who foiled the raid on the airfield?"

Laura didn't say anything, choosing instead to leave the armory and head into the hallway where Peter might not hear their conversation.

"If that was you, you did the right thing. They would've gotten killed and made things worse for everyone," Brock said. "I've been able to talk to people in other cities where the civilian populace mounted full-scale rebellions after the military and law enforcement were overwhelmed by the Fosk. The reprisals were terrible. I heard that in Seattle, they just let the wild Fosk-ha have their way with the city. It's like a horror movie up there. Is that where you want to go? To check on your niece?"

Laura spun around and backed him up against the wall, pointing her finger, and spitting her response into his face. "Maybe that's where I should go. I have a brother there, and *two* nieces. You telling me they don't matter?"

"That's not what I'm saying and you know it."

Laura stepped back before she punched him. She adjusted the backpack on her left shoulder and her grip on the gun cases with the right hand. "I don't know what happened to you."

"None of the old rules apply now," he said, growing almost as angry as she was. His face flushed red, and he clenched both fists, not to hit her, but to keep himself in check. "I'm trying to keep people alive and give them necessities like food."

"Well, isn't that noble?"

"What the hell else can we do?"

She didn't have an answer. "I don't know, but I'm sick of this place and I'm leaving."

He stepped forward about the time she dropped the pack and the gun cases. Brock wasn't a big man, but he was fit and she knew he could scrap. So before he could get a hold of her, she tore out one of her handcuffs and snapped it on his right hand. In almost the same movement, she clicked the other end of the handcuffed to a door handle.

"God dammit, Laura!"

She retreated, taking her supplies with her. He cursed and shouted at her, but she didn't look back. The only thing she could do now was get the hell out of town before this got ugly.

SHE WENT straight to the motor port and loaded her gear into a car she'd already stocked with food and travel provisions. It took all of her self-control not to stare at surveillance cameras or check her wrist monitor. If it was reporting her actual actions, then she was as good as dead. No alarms and sounded and no Fosk-ha guards had swarmed her yet.

Winning! Look at me, I put stuff in a car. I'm practically free.

She briefly wondered what Hahn-fosk-hon would say, or do to her if he found out before she was gone. The alien had spared her life. From what she'd learned, that was partly because she was genetically compatible with the Gift, they called it. She wasn't sure what it did, but thought it had something to do with their journey through space. Hahn-fosk-hon and said something about the blood power of the planet and never explained what he meant.

Laura thought it sounded evil, or the very least, deadly to the human race. She wasn't sure if they were here to stay, but the way they were tearing the planet up made her think this was basically a raid while they traveled across the stars to some inconceivable destination.

You think too much, and your imagination is out of control.

The car started, she looked in the rearview mirrors to see if any of her fellow officers were rushing out into the parking lot to apprehend her. The only good thing about the police station was that the Fosk-ha didn't come here much.

Discipline was administered in public where plenty of people could watch.

She pulled to the gate, swiped her Chicago Police Department ID card, and watched the crossbar go up. Then she drove away, obeying the speed limit, thinking about all the friends she was leaving behind, and hoping she was doing the right thing.

"All units, standby for broadcast," the radio dispatcher said on the vehicles radio. "Be on the lookout for car 22 and Officer Laura Osage. She's armed and possibly dangerous. Believed to be under the influence of seditious elements acting against the Fosk-ha and the United States of America. Contact and detain, then await an overlord."

She drove three blocks and then parked in an alleyway. With no time to waste, she climbed out of the car, pulled out the pry bar, and scrape the numbers off the rear quarter panel of her patrol car. The result was a mess of scratched paint only slightly less obvious than the big number twenty-two.

At least I tried.

She smeared dirt over her work in other parts of the car. It might not get her past a checkpoint, but it might give her a few seconds when she needed them. What she was hoping was that other cops would pretend they didn't see her. The real test would be getting past Fosk-ha patrols.

She loaded up, her heart still pounding harder than she thought it should be. It wasn't like she was a rookie stopping a car for the first time. *Just drive like you are supposed to be here and no one will even see you.*

Three blocks and two turns later, a patrol car slid around the corner at reckless speeds and blocked her path.

Brock jumped out of his squad car and marched toward

her, pointing an accusing finger at her face. "Stop right there, Laura. You're going to get people hurt. I know you think you're doing the right thing, but you aren't. They'll kill you and crack down on the rest of us."

She revved the engine, then drove forward, forcing Brock to jump back as she pushed his squad car out of her way. "You shouldn't have got out, Brock. That was a rookie mistake."

He shouted as she drove past, which only made her angrier. If he got too close, and she ran him over, that was his own damn fault now. She shouted at him with her window rolled up. "I'm leaving, Brock."

Glass exploded inward. Brock's unreasonably strong hands grabbed her shirt and her ballistic vest beneath it, then dragged her from the still moving vehicle.

I didn't see that coming.

"Don't resist, Laura," Brock said. "You haven't been feeding. I'm too strong for you."

His words barely registered. During a fight, her mind was on other things. She was a better fighter. On the ground or standing up, she'd logged more training hours. She was also meaner, something David had taught her a long time ago was important. All things being equal, the meanest son-of-a-bitch wins the fight *Take that to the bank, sister.*

Brock grabbed her throat with one hand, holding her at arm's length. She used both of her hands against his one, grabbing hold and dropping her weight simultaneously. His attack was insultingly simple and amateurish.

Her effort dragged his arm down but did nothing to loosen his grip. She twisted against the joints in his wrist and fingers, accomplishing nothing.

"I already called an overlord," Brock hissed. "Calm down. Let's talk about this so we can get our story straight."

Her curse came out as a gurgle. Still holding his hand with both of hers, she kicked at the inside of his left thigh, hoping to knock him off-balance—and if her foot continued up into his groin, that was his problem.

He twisted, minimizing the impact of the strike. She booted him three more times in rapid succession, catching him on the outside of the leg twice, and on the inside just above the knee once.

"Stop!" Brock lifted her up with both hands, then slammed her down on her back.

Stars filled her vision. The unique pain of getting hit in the head was sharp and confusing. She barely realized he'd also knocked the breath out of her lungs. This wasn't a friendly sparring match. Brock, the man she'd been friends with for a long time, had hurled her against the asphalt like they were bitter enemies. He grunted in frustration. Red splotches formed on his face. Animal rage blazed from his eyes.

Tears streamed down his face as he berated her. She didn't know or care what he was saying. All she wanted was to breathe, get out from under him, and escape. Even during her years of jujitsu training, she had never been this close to passing out. There was a good chance she was already unconscious and her mind was just trying to catch up.

Raw fear consumed her. She begged for mercy without giving a rat's ass to what it looked like. Anyone watching the show without getting involved had picked sides as far as she was concerned.

Why won't someone help me?

"I'm doing this for you!" Brock shouted.

She grabbed both of his hands again, hooked her left foot around his right knee that was in a bad place if he was trying to keep her pinned down, and then thrust her hips up and toward her left. His lack of skill allowed the technique to work. She rolled on top of him and immediately went for an arm bar.

He wasn't lying about being stronger, but that only went so far. All the years of refining her technique finally paid off. But it didn't really solve her problem. Now they were both laying on their backs with her in control of his arm—her left leg over his face and her right leg over his body as she pulled his arm between her legs and pressed her hips against his elbow for pain compliance.

He wouldn't stop shouting and he didn't tap out. The situation caused her to laugh crazily. She was so conditioned by her jujitsu training to expect a tap when the pain became too bad that it confused her when it didn't happen.

Something popped in his elbow, then his shoulder. He made a hissing sound that didn't really sound human.

The crowd was gathering but keeping their distance—making their choices. She couldn't stay in this position. When he seemed distracted, she scrambled on top of him to take the mount position. She grape-vined his legs and pulled his arm across his neck, then pushed her weight against it. Experience had taught her it was a very uncomfortable position to be in, but more importantly, it eliminated all of his leverage.

No matter how strong he was, she had him. Now she just had to talk sense into him.

"I'm leaving, God dammit!" she said. "You did what you could. Just let me go. What do they care if I leave?"

"There will be reprisals against the rest of us!" Brock

screamed at her. His face was so twisted with crazy that she didn't recognize him. He definitely had been crying. His face was covered with red splotches and he was drooling like a lunatic. Tears streamed down his face. Veins popped out every time he strained to break free.

He was right. Every time she broke a rule, someone else paid for her insolence.

But I can't do this anymore. I've got to fight back or run or die.

"You have to give up," Brock said, his words distorted by the way she was pressing down on him.

She looked up, annoyed that what little hair she had was hanging into her eyes. Her car was wrecked, but his was okay—door hanging open like an invitation. Maybe he had supplies in there she could use, and maybe not. Taking his car would mean leaving the extra weapons and supplies but she didn't have a choice.

He talked, words she didn't dare listen to. His distraction, however, was an opportunity she couldn't pass up. Jumping to her feet, she sprinted toward his vehicle.

Something grabbed her foot, and she fell on her face. The asphalt scraped skin from both hands. She twisted her hips and bicycled her legs to break free of what turned out to be her friend's hand. He dragged her back into his arms and crushed her in a bear hug.

Both of them were breathing hard. He grunted at her, trying to talk sense but mostly making horrible sounds that only pissed her off and made her sad at the same time. She headbutted him with everything she had, then managed to slip her right hand free. Whatever part of his face she'd connected with had been hard, because her bell was rung like she'd come off her skateboard in the half-pipe.

He lifted her off her feet, crushing her left arm to her rib cage with strength she never guessed he possessed. It hurt so bad she thought her spine would break and her kidneys would shoot out of her ass. Unable to reach her gun, she grabbed his baton from his duty belt and began slamming it into his head.

The first four or five times made sickening sounds that put her teeth on edge. After that, she no longer cared because she barely knew where she was or what she was doing. At one point, she desperately wanted to know what was happening to her hand to cause so much pain. And it all came back. The baton was half out of her grip, having been driven repeatedly against Brock's temple.

She paused, then went at him harder than ever, desperate to survive and furious that he'd chosen the aliens over his friends.

When they finally fell to the ground, she broke free and staggered back, needing to vomit but not remembering how. The observers faded back into their doorways and closed windows.

"I'm sorry! I didn't want to do that," she wailed, turning in hopes of finding one person sympathetic to her situation. The faces she saw were grim and horrified.

Somehow she found her way to the car and started driving. The radio put out an alert. She ignored it. The only thing that mattered now was leaving Chicago.

CHAPTER TWENTY-EIGHT

DAVID HAD SOME TRICKS. He doubted any of them would work well against this type of pursuer.

The alien jump ship rose higher into the air, canting forward with its nose down as the powerful turbines adjusted its attitude. Once it was high enough, it leveled off and directed its power aft. David saw most of this in his rearview mirror, and slammed the gas pedal to the floor.

His pursuer came on fast. The road was straight with very few places to turn off in this part of the state. Highway 54 followed the Arkansas River, which could more accurately be described as a sand bed scattered with trees. Not much of the water flowing down from the Rockies made it out of Colorado. Western Kansas was nothing but rolling prairie and a few trees in the distance.

The jump ship came close enough that he lost it in his rearview mirror. He hit the brakes and watched it fly overhead. What he wanted but didn't have was a dirt road heading off at a ninety-degree angle. Something told him that his adversary had planned it this way and caught up to him when there was nowhere else to run

Locking up the wheels in a modern hot rod was difficult. Traction control did its magic, but even it had limits. By the time his speed was reduced, the tires were sliding and he was steering like an old movie stunt car driver.

Standing on the break with his left foot, he mashed the accelerator pedal with his right. He cranked the wheel just enough to whip the vehicle around in the most badass burnout he'd ever done. When he let off the break, he sent the Hellcat back the way he had come, looking for a turnoff.

The alien jump ship caught them almost immediately, and he repeated the maneuver.

"You can't just keep doing that!" Abigail shouted.

"Why not?" David asked, looking far enough ahead to see the road curved around a low hill barely worth the name. "Not a lot of options out here."

This time the alien jump ship was more careful, keeping enough following distance to minimize overshooting the Hellcat if David tried the maneuver again. They were almost to the curve when it fired a warning shot that blew dirt out of the ditch on his right.

Two motorcycles came around the corner in the opposite direction—one passing him on his left and the other on his right. Their closing speed had to be near to 300 miles per hour, because David had his speedometer pegged.

Dust and Abigail twisted in their seats to look out the back window.

"They're gone! Shit-balls, they were going fast," Abigail exclaimed.

The jump ship veered off, keeping pace with David for a

time, but then hesitating, apparently unsure of which target to go after.

The engine light came on. David stared at it for three solid seconds in complete shock. "This is a brand-new car."

Abigail laughed nervously. Dust stared toward the horizon, her entire body tense, one hand near the door handle like she might jump out and run the moment the car stopped.

That caught David's attention. "Stop squirming around so much, both of you."

He didn't wait for their arguments or shitty looks. The yellow hash marks dividing the road flashed underneath the Hellcat because he was straddling the center of the road. It still felt too narrow at these speeds.

The curve northward was long and gradual. He raced around through its apex like a NASCAR driver, then passed the small airport outside of Garden City. "We are about fifteen miles from town."

Despite his earlier demand, Abigail popped up in her seat, twisting around to look through one window after the next. "That ship is still gone. The stupid thing is probably still chasing the Rodriguez brothers. There's another curve about two miles ahead, in case you didn't know."

"I drive for living, remember?" David said. "You know those guys on the motorcycles?"

"I can't say for sure, but it could be. Not everyone out here is a pickup-driving redneck."

"Never said they were. What I don't get is how you recognized them in two-tenths of a second." David tensed before the long curve that would point him straight at Garden City.

"They're YouTubers." Abigail's exasperation with his ignorance was almost thick enough to touch.

"Stop!" Dust shouted, pointing at two pickups blocking the road.

David slammed the brakes. Neither of his passengers were wearing their seatbelts properly—because they just couldn't sit still. They were thrown forward and bounced around as the car skidded to a painful stop a hundred yards later. He winced at the damage he'd surely done to his expensive Yokohama tires.

For about two seconds after the Hellcat rocked to a stop, David stared at the people in the trucks—his hands gripping the wheel, his body tense, his gut telling him he needed to be driving hard for anyplace but here. They looked like a hunting party cosplaying as characters from a video game. "Someone has seen one too many action movies where everyone wears ghillie suits and carries sniper rifles."

Abigail snorted.

Each vehicle had a driver and two passengers in the cab, with three more in the bed.

"I assume they're on our side," David said. "Why the hell are they stopping us?"

Neither of his passengers had an answer.

"Go talk to them," Dust said from deep in her seat. She was scrunched down like a kid, eyes barely able to see over the dash.

He didn't move. The thought of getting out of the car seemed an awful lot like surrender, but his options were limited. There wasn't enough gas in the tank to go back and forth across Kansas, and the alien jump ship would either catch the motorcycles or abandon the chase soon. More would come.

"Why didn't that thing blast us?" David said.

"Don't ask me," Abigail replied.

"I wasn't asking you."

Dust refused to meet his gaze.

"I'll need an answer when I get back to the car." He stepped out, then strode forward, keeping his hands visible and his eyes searching for tricks.

A man in his late forties or early fifties swung down from the bed of one truck, then dropped his hood to reveal a face streaked with camo paint. He left his rifle behind but had a big revolver on his hip.

"This road is closed, friend," he said, planting his feet about ten feet in front of David. "But you seem to be in a big hurry, so I'm curious to learn what you're about."

"Just trying to get the hell out of Dodge," David said, wincing at the pun. He had barely slowed down for Dodge City on his flight westward.

"That's a fast car, but it won't be enough," the man said. "Trust me, I know several people who tried to escape that way. I'd say it's better to shelter in place, keep people around you trust."

"I was caught on the road and didn't have a lot of choices," David said.

"What about her?" the man asked as he thrust his chin toward the Hellcat.

Abigail, David realized without looking back, was moving up behind him.

"I think I know him, or my parents know him, maybe. I'm not sure," she said.

"Who's that?" the man asked. "Are you the Brighten girl?"

"Maybe. Who's asking?" Abigail demanded.

"We received notice from the North Central Kansas Chapter," the man said. "It said to be looking for Abigail Brighten."

David held her back. He suspected she was looking up at him questioningly, but he kept his eyes on the stranger. "Unless you know this guy, we should take this slow."

"He sounds familiar, but I can't be sure," Abigail said. "He stands like someone I should remember."

David took another step forward, casually putting himself more squarely between the camouflage crew and his passengers. The leader of the group seemed to understand what he was doing but didn't press the issue. A voice squawked over a radio, causing him to lift it to his ear to hear better.

Waiting had never been David's strong point, but in prison he'd learned the value of it even when his instincts demanded action. A breeze cut across the Kansas plains, moving wheat fields in rolling waves. An impressive silence dominated the moment. He heard a bird chirping in the distance and his engine cooling behind him with rhythmic clicks.

"A week ago the NCKC could have just sent me a picture on my phone," the man said. "Of course there was no such organization then, nor the need for it."

"What is that, the NCK whatever?" David asked.

"It's a resistance chapter," the man said. "If you don't want to live under the boot of these freaks, I suggest you find one and join. Prove you're not one of their lackeys and start doing your duty."

"I'll think about it," David said. "First, I need to find my family and check on them."

"I get that. Admirable. Probably not ever going to happen, but I don't hold it against you for trying."

David looked back at the car. For some reason he was glad Dust had stayed inside and stayed low. This man and his farmer commandos could have started shooting. They had the rifles for it. He wasn't sure why this worried him as much as it did.

"Are you Ed Henning?" Abigail asked. "You are! I remember you from that time you came to the feedlot."

"Abigail?" The man moved forward, his manner different now. "You remember that? How old were you then, eight or nine?"

Abigail didn't move from David's side. "Twelve, but thanks."

Henning stopped. "Your dad has sent requests to every chapter in the resistance. Something happened at Bob Jackson's feedlot. Fosk-ha goons came after them at the farm and they made a break for a safe house."

Abigail squeezed David's arm. This time, he looked down at her and recognized her expression as both hope and uncertainty. "I don't know what to do."

David thought it strange that this kid trusted him. What had he done other than drive fast and yell at her to get her feet off the leather? She knew these people, at least a little, and they appeared to have skills and resources to survive.

He met Ed's hard stare. "We're talking about it. Is there anyone else she might know?"

"Does it matter?" Ed asked.

"Yeah," David said. "I busted her out of the feedlot for Travis Brighten, not you or some other random end-prepper."

Ed laughed. "We're country out here. No need to prepare when you live right."

"Show us the message from her father," David said.

Ed waved at a younger man, probably a teenager but it was hard to tell under the camouflage hood. They consulted for several seconds, then Ed stepped forward with a new radio.

"How about we let her talk to her father, direct-like?"

Abigail ran forward, tears already streaming from her eyes. David tensed, sensing a trick and hating himself for his paranoia. The open highway felt exposed to the next Fosk-whatever ship that would probably appear at the worst possible moment.

He watched the complicated young woman snatch the radio from Ed and move back toward David, talking with her hands and crying unashamedly. She still looked like a pistol-toting badass wearing her brother's letter jacket and the Colt .357 Magnum holstered on her hip, but she also resembled a desperate teenager more than ever.

"He wants to talk to you." She thrust the heavy radio toward him.

David held the radio to his ear, still suspicious as someone who spent years in prison and was paying for a lifetime of bad decisions. "Yeah."

"Is this David Osage?" The man sounded like Travis Brighten as best he could remember.

"Yeah, that's me."

"Is Abigail safe? God bless you, sir, we thought all of you were dead," the voice said. "God bless you."

David listened to the man carry on, using the time to think the situation through. He'd been prepared to interrogate this person but it wasn't needed, not after the voice claiming to be Travis Brighten called him by name. These road-blocking strangers couldn't have known his name.

He tossed the radio to Abigail, then gave Ed his hardest, most intimidating look. "You don't know me, but there is nothing I hate more than a roadblock."

"Fair enough," Ed said, much more relaxed now. "I reckon they're not appreciated by someone with a fast car who knows how to drive it."

"Are you going to let us through?" David asked.

Ed waved at the trucks. The drivers immediately pulled onto the shoulder of the road.

"What if Abigail wants to stay with me?" David asked.

"Does she?" Ed asked, not looking at Abigail or anyone else.

"I have no idea." David looked at the young woman questioningly.

She hesitated, then threw her arms around him, hugging him like she might squeeze the air about of his lungs. When she stepped back, the crying had stopped.

"I'll stay with Ed and his people. My dad says he'll come get me as soon as he can."

"That's good enough for me," David said. "Tell him he owes me a tune-up. My engine light is on."

This made Abigail and Ed laugh.

"You can stay with us," Abigail said, then looked at Ed. "They can, can't they?"

"They?" Ed asked. "I thought someone else was in the car."

"We're not staying. I need to get to Seattle and find my little brother and his family. My sister should already be on her way there. You know how it is. Family." He trusted Ed enough to let Abigail make her own choice, but not enough to tell the man about the Osage cabin in Colorado and his firm belief that Charles and Laura would be headed there.

Two men joined Ed. "Who is in the car?" he asked, one hand on his pistol.

"No one you know," David said. "Get your hand off that gun and tell your boys to back away. You don't want to do this. I've been shot before. Not everyone dies as quick as they show in the movies. Before you pull that thing, you might want to think about how close we are."

Ed went pale. He was obviously a strong man ready to do what needed doing, but he wasn't David. He hadn't been through hell, yet.

"The Fosk came through here yesterday. Looking for a girl." His gruff voice caught on the next word and he started over. "They tortured people. Told us that if we hide her, they'd come back and do worse."

"Then it's a good thing neither of us have this girl," David said as his heart pounded in his chest.

"How do you know the kid in your car isn't the one they're looking for?" Ed asked, seeming to hate every word.

"There is no one in the car, is there, Abigail?" David said.

"Nope. Not one person. Wish there had been. Your music selection is shit," Abigail said.

The standoff didn't last long, but David knew it was real. Ed wasn't about to allow a fugitive from the Fosk-ha to endanger his people. The attack at the turnaround point forced its way into David's thoughts. Then he remembered alien ships searching with spotlights. At any point since this began, the aliens could have blasted David and his passenger into nothing.

So why hadn't they?

"The Rodriguez brothers just radioed in that the ship

isn't chasing them—which means it's on its way back." Ed signaled his crew, then faced David one last time. "You can pass through our territory but don't stop. If you find the Rocky Mountain Chapter, tell them we're not ready to go on the offensive and they need to establish new radio frequencies."

"I can do that. Keep your eyes on the sky," he said, not knowing why. Maybe he was still thinking about the day he picked up Dust and how the world hadn't ended yet. The sound of Gummy Bear's voice on the CB was strong in his memory. She'd seen Dust and told him to check on her. Now he was getting hunted by aliens who were probably going to keep trashing his car until there was nothing left of it.

Bullshit.

"Don't stop until you get to the Colorado line," Ed warned.

"I'll need gas," David said.

"There's a pump at the airport. Get it there. Don't stop in town." Ed back toward his truck but stopped when Abigail ran back to give David one more hug.

"Take care of her," she said.

"I will."

"See you around, Jackknife," she said, then ran to one of the pickups and jumped in the back.

―――

DUST DIDN'T SAY a word when he climbed behind the wheel and drove toward the little rural airport with only a handful of buildings. He watched the engine light, hoping it would go off. But it didn't. Because that's how his day was going.

Did he need an oil change? Was there a problem with his catalytic converter? Was the engine about to fuse into one solid block of metal? The entire situation infuriated him. *I worked my whole life for a car like this and what do I get?*

"They told me the Fosk-ha were here looking for you," David said. "Why would they be doing that, Dust?"

She didn't answer.

He steered down the access road, not pushing the issue, but not giving her an excuse to avoid answering. The covered gas pumps were between two-story sheet metal buildings. He didn't feel great about it as a hiding place, but thought his baby would be concealed from the jump ship if it came this way. The one runway airport was abandoned as far as he could tell.

"I wanted to tell you when they attacked us on the highway," Dust said. "But I didn't trust you and I didn't plan to stay near you."

David waited.

"They are after me. That's why I was placed with Agent Boyne. His teenage kids were actually young-looking agents assigned to watch me all the time. I still don't know if they were bodyguards or jailers."

"Or maybe he was supposed protect you from aliens?" David asked.

"Something like that. They interrogated me and did a lot of tests. You might've been to prison, but I was in a far worse place."

David checked his car inside and out, noticed the engine light had finally gone off, and they headed out, driving fast but not recklessly toward the Colorado line two hundred and some miles from Garden City.

"What now?" Dust asked.

"That depends on you." David didn't like anything about their situation, but maybe they were done keeping secrets. "Tell me the rest."

The sound of tires on the asphalt mesmerized him. He glanced at the girl from time to time. She looked like she was working up her courage to say something terrifying.

She rubbed her arm where she'd been bitten. "I'm not one of them, and never will be. It doesn't matter if they poison me."

"Why not? And pretend for the moment I even know what you're talking about."

Again, she shifted uncomfortably and didn't answer. "I think I can help them navigate. I have never been on one of their starships, never been abducted, and don't even speak their language."

"They speak ours," David said. "I don't think there will be a language barrier. Stop beating around the bush."

She flushed red, obviously embarrassed. "You're right. I'm going to tell you something I probably shouldn't. Part of the reason I ran away from Agent Boyne was an attack that put innocents in danger. I never liked him or his goons, but that didn't mean I wanted to see them get slaughtered. A week before you picked me up, they came and tried to take me."

"Who? The big alien freaks?"

She nodded. "According to Boyne, it wasn't the first time they tried—only the first time I found out about it. I decided I needed to be on my own and split the scene."

He leaned closer, still driving smoothly with his left hand. "The way you say that, it's off. How old are you? How old are you really?"

For a moment, the depth of her eyes terrified him. "I'm a

hundred and eight years old. You're the first person in a long time to notice anything. I'm good at hiding. Because the better I hide, the fewer people get hurt."

"You almost had me believing you are human, but you're not," David said. He'd almost accused her of being one of them.

"Believe whatever you want," she said. "All I can prove to you is that they want to capture or kill me, and it won't be long. I knew we were in trouble when the jump ship kept following us."

"So why wait to tell me?"

She waved her hand out the window, drawing his attention to flat, empty plains in every direction for as far as the eye could see. "I wanted to get far away from everyone. There's no one out here to see me die—or get hurt when that happens."

David's guts went cold. "What about me?"

"I don't think they'll kill you," she said. "Don't ask me why. It's complicated."

He was about to ask another question when motion in his rearview mirror pulled his eyes away from the road. Three jump ships popped into view, just specks in the distance, but moving faster than he'd yet seen.

"One more question," David said. "You said you couldn't or wouldn't help them navigate to wherever. What the hell does that mean and why are they still after you?"

"That's two questions." She chewed on her lip. "My compliance is irrelevant. They need to make sure I can't help anybody follow them when they leave Earth."

"What do you mean by navigate?"

"They came in translation starships," she said, looking him directly in the eyes.

"And you know how to fly one?"

"That's not what I said."

He had other questions, but the appearance of more ships demanded his attention. They were in three groups converging from the north, east, and south. Which made him think there was a trap waiting to the west.

CHAPTER TWENTY-NINE

OVER THE YEARS, David had passed many side roads and never taken them. He'd always wondered where they went, if they were dead ends, if there was some lonely farm back there, away from the rest of the world where nothing could touch whoever settled down there.

He selected the first dirt road that led away from the highway and took it because it cut through a hill, giving him some concealment. That was the way they did things in Kansas, dig the road through rather than use switchbacks.

The dust he was throwing was a dead giveaway, but at least they wouldn't know exactly who was heading this way.

No need to make it easy for them.

"How fast are you going?" Dust asked, her eyes wide with worry.

He felt the car wiggle beneath him, like it was hydroplaning. A friend of his who did Baja races had told him that sand or gravel could act like water if you were going fast enough. The feeling was terrible. He eased off the gas and immediately felt the front end of the Hellcat drift toward the ditch, which was very steep and deep.

"Easy. Eeeeasy," he said, playing a subtle game between the steering wheel, brake pedal, and gas pedal. The car slid sideways and then overcorrected by his gentle touch. Just when he thought they were going off the road to roll a half a dozen times, the decreasing speed found a happy medium with the physics of their environment.

He straightened out and kept driving, glancing down to see he was going seventy-three mph, still fast for a gravel road that was steeply graded for farm equipment.

"I didn't like that," Dust said. "Can we please not do that again?"

He ignored her, focusing his attention on the distance, searching for the drop ships. When he came to the section mile, he turned, found a service road probably only used by pickup trucks in the past, and rolled slowly down it, throwing almost no dust at all.

When nothing happened for several minutes, he smiled.

"Do you think we lost them?" Dust asked.

"I don't know, but I'll take it."

The words were barely out of his mouth when an alien jump jet popped into view. It had to have been flying low and fast to appear like this. He braked and swerved, barely avoiding a plasma blast that left a crater in the middle of the hardpan dirt. Two more ships came at him from different vectors. They fired and missed.

"Were those supposed to be warning shots?" he asked, not really expecting an answer.

Desperate now, he angled through the ditch and crossed into the field. Expensive wheels and tires flexed in unnatural ways; his touch with the entire vehicle told him stories of incredible damage to his beautiful Hellcat. Maybe it was his imagination, but he thought he could hear the support struts twisting out of place.

Hold on, baby. Daddy's sorry to drive you like this.

The field had appeared dry but was actually mud under the top layer. Every rock and the pebble that smacked the undercarriage made him cringe. Each stalk of wheat that slapped his once perfect paint job killed him a little inside.

"Those sons-of-bitches are getting a call from my insurance agent!"

Each energy bolt came closer than the one before it. "We're in trouble here, Dust."

"You shouldn't be helping me," she said. Right when it looked like she was retreating into one of her too familiar silent spells, she blurted a confession. "I'm not one of them, but I'm not one of you. All I ever wanted was to be reunited with my parents."

"Thanks for waiting until right now to tell me that," David said, then cranked the wheel, spun the car sideways in a long swath through the wheat field. The land sloped downward. For a moment, he could see for several miles. The highway was in view and looked inviting despite the complete lack of concealment in that direction.

If he couldn't find a place to hide the Hellcat, speed on the open road would have to be his best-worst chance to escape. Why not go out in a blaze of glory?

"Where are your parents?" he asked. An alien energy blast sizzled so near him that paint bubbled on hood of the car. "You motherfuckers!"

Dust gripped the 'oh shit' handle on the dash.

"Sorry. I just really like this car. Where are your parents?"

"I've always thought they were in the mountains. That's

why I got in the truck with you, because you were going that way," she said. "Look out!"

David swerved around a ship that all but landed directly in their path.

"We're not going to make it, are we? There isn't a place to hide and there's no one to help us," Dust said.

"There might be. This part of the state looks flat, but there are creek beds and even some trees if you can find a river or pond. At night, we could go slow with the lights off and be miles away. But I'm sure they have night vision in those ships. Feel free to offer a brilliant plan."

The alien airships tightened their circle. Night was hours away, and there weren't any creeks, farmhouses, or hidden Army bases to find. Nothing but miles and miles of open wheat fields—golden hills rolling like waves, sunlight streaming over the scene, storm clouds on the horizon.

"I'm glad you left Abigail with those people," Dust said.

"I should have left *us* with them. I bet they have places to hide seventy thousand dollars' worth of modern muscle car," David said, rounding the number up slightly. "I'll get you to your parents if I can."

A bolt of energy lanced out from an alien ship, striking the ground in front of David's car right before he drove over it. Down into a ragged hole the Hellcat went, striking the bottom so hard, the scorched hood bent like a stack of playing cards.

David's ears rang. Something hard shoved up against his face. He wrestled past the deployed airbag to tug on the door handle, but something kept the door from opening. "Change of plans," he growled, then shoved Dust out her side and followed her across the once-pristine leather seats.

They scrambled out of the crater and into the smoldering

wheat field. "Stay low and keep going. Crawl on your hands and knees, slide on your belly if you can."

"Okay." Her voice sounded scared.

Smoke filled the air. Sparks drifted close to his face. Heat grew from nothing to unbearable in less than a minute.

"The ground slopes downward. Follow the terrain. Don't stop." He rose to his hands and knees to look for the ships, not quite standing higher than the wheat but near enough that he could see whenever the breeze parted the veil of smoke.

Another blast struck near them. He pulled Dust back. Again and again the area was pounded by explosions.

"They won't stop!" Dust shouted above the noise.

David shook his head, pulling her along. "They can't see through the smoke."

"Don't be so sure of that."

He cursed. "Yeah, right. I forgot. Why wouldn't an advanced race of intergalactic murderers have infrared tech?"

"They use something different, I think," Dust said, tugging him in another direction. "They weren't always killers."

"Spare me the history lesson." He sensed her choice of direction was the right one and ran forward, still keeping hold of her hand to avoid being separated.

"I need to tell you everything."

"No shit, Sher—"

An explosion knocked David from his feet. He looked at his hand, wondering why he wasn't still holding onto her. His ears rang. He couldn't breathe and his lungs were on fire. He pushed himself up and swam through the thick smoke. "Dust! Where are you?"

She didn't answer.

Once, several years ago, he'd been in a prison riot and survived a brutal gas attack by staying calm and not moving until he had his bearings. Then he'd gone to the shower room and decontaminated himself while rioters and guards fought for control of the courtyard.

"Take it easy. Take it slow. Stay low." he muttered, then crawled in a circle feeling the ground for Dust's body. When he found her, she was alive but unresponsive.

"Wake up." He almost growled the words. Eyes burning, throat raw from coughing, he wanted out of the prairie fire. "I'm not carrying you, kid."

She groaned and moved one arm weakly.

Despite the ultimatum, David scooped her up, draped her over one shoulder, and headed down the field. He couldn't get his bearings but at least the jump ships had stopped firing.

Figures appeared in the gloom. He changed course to avoid them. The searchers shouted words he couldn't understand. At times, their shouts touched the edge of his auditory range like a badly used subwoofer.

Dust jerked her head up. "David?"

He squatted and let her roll off his shoulder, nearly dropping her flat on her back. "I'm here."

"Don't let them take me," she said. "I shouldn't have involved you. I knew it was wrong, but I can't let them use me. Can't go back in a cage."

"No cages for either of us. Now, try to walk." Holding her up, he found the creek he'd been hoping for. Their feet slipped in a slurry of sand and gooey clay. Erosion cut through the short prairie grass that bordered the wheat field, leading them to a pond surrounded by hoofprints. "Keep going, Dust."

When they reached the pond, he worked his way around the shore until he noticed the smoke was clearing. "We have to get wet. How long can you hold your breath?"

"Longer than you," she said.

"I'll bet you ten dollars you're wrong. Be ready." A ship roared toward them. "We're going under right before we see it. Three, two, one—now."

He pulled her down and prayed, not something he'd done for as long as he could remember. There were no words, just a desperate reaching out to whatever unfair power controlled the universe. It was instinct, but it made him think he needed to get his life together if he survived this.

Shapes moved above them, blurry through the water. He closed his eyes, felt even more trapped, and opened them again, holding onto Dust so she didn't float to the surface.

Seconds ticked by. Dust relaxed until she was limp in his arms.

When he couldn't take it a second longer and he thought the shapes in the sky were gone, he stood up, breathed deeply, then dragged Dust to the shore. "They're gone, Dust. Talk to me."

She coughed out water and babbled something in a strange language. Her hands pressed against the mud until it squished between her fingers and she slipped. Each attempt to get up was weaker than the one before and soon she lay exhausted and half-conscious on the bank. Her eyes fluttered shut and he feared the worst.

"Come on, kid. We need to find a way out of here."

"What?" she asked, sounding lost and afraid.

"I'm go you."

She leaned on him, talking but making no sense.

"I guess I win," he said, digging deep into his physical reserves to heft her and carry her in his arms rather than over his shoulder. "You're heavier than you look, kid."

"I heard that."

"Good, you can sass. Can you walk? Because lugging you through this crap sucks." Fire raced through his arms and shoulders. His back ached and his legs wobbled after a few hundred feet. Looking around, he saw the prairie fire far behind now—but with it, the smoke that had concealed them from the aliens.

"I can try," she said. "You carried me."

"Don't sound so surprised," David said, putting her on her feet. "I try not to leave women unconscious in a fire. Bad karma."

"Where did the ships go?" She took a step away, looking around as though the light hurt her eyes.

"No idea."

"It has to be a trap," she said.

"There were a bunch of them on foot, but we lost them in the smoke," David said, glancing back the way they had come. Now that the fire had shifted, he could see the outline of his car a half mile away, completely ruined.

"Look out," Dust hissed.

David turned to face a pair of the biggest assholes he'd ever seen marching toward him. Their armor seemed lighter than the ones who had attacked his truck on Interstate 70, but they looked meaner somehow. Their eyes focused on him like nothing else mattered but his death.

CHAPTER THIRTY

"CAN YOU SHANK THEM?" Dust asked, standing too near him.

He shook his head without taking his eyes from his opponents. "That's not how it's done. You need surprise to shank someone."

"Move away from girl," the first alien said, his voice echoing through a box under the chin of his helmet. A red stripe on his armor differentiated him from the other one. "Do now. Do! Do! Do!"

"Back away slowly, Dust," David whispered. "I'll buy you some time. Head for the road. Look for Abigail and her new friends." He stepped closer to the aliens. One chose that moment to flash a long, grotesque tongue. "Oh, damn. That's disgusting."

"What are you doing?" Red Stripe demanded. "Why is she move backward? No flee for her. No escape."

"Listen, jerk off, I don't do commands and you forgot to ask nicely," David said. When the alien opened his mouth and lashed the air with that horrible feeder tongue, David charged, tackling the first of his adversaries at the knees.

It wasn't a perfect takedown, but the big bastard landed on his back, head thunking the ground.

David rolled away as the other stabbed at him with a wicked bayonet. Once he was on his feet, he feinted forward but immediately retreated. "Come on, asshole. Come get some!"

Mr. Bayonet started after Dust. David sprinted past Red Stripe and was slashed across his back by a big knife. He caught the bayonet-wielding alien in the back, wrapped him up, and drove him facedown.

"Die, human!" Red Stripe hissed, moving in with his big knife.

David rolled off Mr. Bayonet, hoping Dust had escaped. When he got to his feet, both aliens rushed him with their edged weapons.

"At least you're not using those big guns," David said, clenching his fists low where they wouldn't see what he was doing. Here he was in the middle of nowhere facing two alien super soldiers with nothing but bare knuckles and bad jokes.

The aliens looked at each other and hissed.

This is better than dying in prison. David rushed forward the moment they weren't looking at him.

Red Stripe dropped his knife and pulled his long gun from where it was slung over his back. The other adjusted the bayonet on the rifle or energy gun or whatever it was.

When David struck, it was at a run, sort of a flying Superman punch with nothing held back. This was going to break something, probably all of his knuckles and his wrist. If he got really lucky, maybe he'd dislocate his shoulder too.

David and Red Stripe tumbled to the ground as the other started shooting. One of the bolts missed David and blew off Red Stripe's arm.

David grunted. "Why didn't you do that earlier? And could you shoot him in the head next time?"

Mr. Bayonet seemed confused by the question. "Why I shoot brother?"

David snaked his arm around his injured enemy and held him up as a shield.

"That is dishonor!" Mr. Bayonet shrieked.

David grunted and dragged his hostage back a step. "You gotta play for keeps, ugly."

"Play for…" The alien shook his head. "Does not matter. You give us Navigator. We will allow you to live among us."

Something moved in the gloom behind the rifle-toting alien.

"Release my brother. You cannot kill him. Or escape. Defeat is inevitable."

"For you, maybe," David said, cursing inwardly as he confirmed that it was Dust sneaking up behind the alien with the rifle.

Red Stripe struggled, so he tightened the rear-naked-choke forcefully enough to kill a man without the protection of armor. It was soft and flexible around the neck, but still provided more protection than David had anticipated.

"You are irrational. Give up. I won't shoot. Release brother."

Motes of light flashed beneath the surface of Dust's skin, and her eyes glowed from within as she came close enough to touch the Mr. Bayonet, which caused David's hostage to thrash violently. It took all of David's strength to continue dragging him backward and squeeze his throat hard enough to prevent him from shouting a warning.

Then Dust touched her victim. For a second, nothing happened, then it was like sound had been sucked out of the world right before something exploded.

"I'm sorry," Dust said, and her victim disappeared with a *boom* that hurled David and Red Stripe back ten yards. He struggled to his feet and staggered through the smoke. The ground shifted beneath him. For several seconds, there was nothing under his feet. Lights pressed into his vision. A blanket of cold misery wrapped him from head to foot.

"David," she said, and it was like a voice from a dream.

"What's happening?" he asked, feeling like he'd been punched out. *That was like football practice. I played football, didn't I? Wait, what's my fucking name?*

"You saved my life, so I saved yours," the young woman with the strange name said. "You won't thank me. Others will come."

"Ain't that the truth." David sat down, ass hitting the ground with authority. Dust, that was her name, leaned against him. His hands fell into his lap, limp and unresponsive—which was fine because he wasn't even sure they were his. "Why don't we get the hell out of here?"

"Which way?" she asked.

He wanted to think about it, but that made his head hurt. "Back to the road, and get down if you see more ships." While the smoke was gone, the shadows had deepened. Night wasn't here, but it was a good time to hide in the changing light.

They hobbled back through the parts of the wheat field that hadn't burned. Ships did come, and they lay motionless until they passed. Everything hurt. Sometimes he forgot where he was. Other times—well, he knew the questions he needed to ask.

"What did you do to that guy?" he mumbled when she helped him back to his feet for the fifth time. There was a sound coming that he knew was important but couldn't identify. Not a ship, not a car or truck, but something far more irritating.

"I made him a beacon," she said.

"That explains everything."

"Truly?"

"No, Dust. I think you're giving me this headache. We need to talk, seriously talk." He squinted toward the road. "I hear motorcycles, moving fast."

"I see them," she said, urging him to walk again.

Her impossible calm annoyed him. In his current state, it didn't take much to piss him off. Exhaustion, pain, and confusion turned him into an ogre. "Okay, if you say so."

"Why are you angry with me?" she asked.

He blew out a breath, cleared his head, and tried to focus. "What did you do to that alien soldier? What did you do to me?"

She stopped walking and faced him, looking up with her amazingly deep eyes. "They call me a Navigator. I can open ways to places, but it is dangerous. What I did to that Foskha warrior—who was about to kill you, in case you forgot—was like pushing him into a busy street. I don't know what happened to him. All I can say is that something hit him—maybe a particle of interstellar dust, maybe a gamma ray, or maybe even something I've never encountered before."

David weighed every word. He wanted to wake up from this nightmare, but he knew he wouldn't. "Are we on the same side?"

"We both want to be free. If we work together, we have a chance."

"That's not an answer, but it's close enough." He pointed to the motorcycles, which he hoped were the forward scouts for Ed Henning's group.

Leaning on each other, they reached the long, endless highway and stood on the shoulder. "I wish I knew someone with hitchhiking experience. Do I just stick my thumb out, or what?"

"Sure." She imitated his gesture and held it until the motorcycles passed.

"They're scouts," David said.

She nodded. "I guess that's smart."

The pickups approached and stopped. Abigail jumped out. "You look like hell. We heard the explosions and figured you were out here and needed help."

Ed Henning approached with less enthusiasm. "I didn't think you'd get far."

"But you came anyway. I thought you'd let them have us. Just to keep your own people safe," David said.

"Abigail convinced us you were worth having on the team," Henning said. "So my question is this. Are you ready to join the resistance?"

David looked to Dust. She nodded. "We are, actually."

CHAPTER THIRTY-ONE

LAURA DROVE past car after burned-out car. The Fosk had attacked civilian motorists during rush hour. Some vehicles were ripped apart and blackened by their energy weapons. Others were pushed into a gridlock of smashed fenders and busted glass. Bodies hung out of half-open doors, flies buzzing near the corpses.

The wound through her calf ached worse than ever. She couldn't seem to get warm. Shivering was her life now. All she thought about was Hahn-fosk-hon, the alien who'd bitten her. She wondered if he had bitten Brock Green. It didn't matter. In the end, Brock had tried to help the people of Chicago by following the rules. She'd killed him for it and gone on the run.

"Can I just catch a break?" Slowing to near walking speed, she wove through a particularly tangled group of cars. Not looking into the windows was hard but necessary. She'd seen enough, done enough, had enough. Maybe Brock had been right. Giving up seemed a lot more appealing now. Just go with the flow, bow to the alien overlords, eat rats.

But problems only multiplied—that's what David said when he didn't want to talk about his bullshit life.

The Fosk-ha had to be looking for her now, and their justice would rain down like a meteor shower. Her survival gear was in the first squad car she had stolen, but she was in Brock's cruiser now. No supplies, not much gas, and only her sidearm and a shotgun to fight with if she were caught.

Hunger and the need to go to the bathroom reminded her how unheroic she was. Neither David nor Charles answered her calls, and she was afraid to try too often.

A Fosk ship zipped toward her. She parked, turned off the car, and waited. This wasn't where she wanted to die. She opened the door, dropped to the ground, and crawled away. The ship hovered but she couldn't see it from her bug-like position.

Just keep moving. Give me a break, you viper-tongued alien son-of-a-bitch. Strangely, she thought of her parents. Good people, but safe and boring and spending most of their time bailing David out. Growing up, she'd mostly fended for herself. Just like Charles had when he went off to college on scholarships.

"All your fault, David," she muttered, finally catching a glimpse of the ship. It was looking in the wrong place, but it was doing so thoroughly. Like the crew had seen something.

She waited, thought about her family, her old job, and how she had made a mess of everything. What surprised her was that she didn't feel horrible about her choices. What the hell else could she have done?

"I resisted, I fought, and I refused to do their dirty work."
Yeah, good for you, Laura. You're a real hero. Ask Brock.

The ship came her way and began another search. She scooted under a car, pushing back images of a tire popping and a couple tons of steel crushing her head. Down the road, the alien craft was abominably patient, searching each section of the cluttered roadway like a supply clerk taking inventory.

She had no place to be. Was she uncomfortable? Oh, yeah. But she wasn't eating rats and working for the enemy.

"Come on, you stupid asshole. Don't you have an entire city to terrorize?" Her words did nothing to move the alien patrol craft. But it did move on, eventually.

"It's about time." She crawled out of her spot, brushed herself off, and found herself staring at a brand-new Ford F-150 pickup.

Gorgeous.

She laughed. David hated Fords—called them fucking old rebuilt Dodges and proclaimed he'd rather push a Dodge than drive another brand. "Perfect. He'll probably materialize out of thin air to give me hell over this beauty."

Gun out, approaching it like she would a felony car stop, she cleared it. All she found inside was a note that said *drive it like you stole it.*

"Nice. Thanks, mystery cool person." She turned the key, checked her mirrors, and headed south.

SHE PASSED THROUGH JOLIET, then went on to I-80 and headed west. No one was on the road. A month ago she would have loved having the highway to herself; now it made her uneasy. Her leg ached from the Fosk-ha wound. Her head throbbed from Brock slamming her on the pavement.

"He was trying to kill me!" she shouted at the interior of the truck.

The gas gauge flashed yellow. It was the last thing she wanted to deal with. There had been cops at the last two gas stations. Out here in the boondocks it wouldn't be any better. The local LEOs wouldn't have much to do besides look for a fugitive like her. The only good thing about her all-night drive—over five hours at eighty miles per hour—was the lack of Fosk patrols. She hadn't seen a single ship.

So maybe they weren't everywhere and all-powerful.

The first two farms she saw looked wrong. She couldn't say why, not being a rural girl. Chicago, and Denver before that, were the places she knew. She prayed the latter wasn't as bad as the former right now. There was no going back, and if she was being really freaking honest, there wasn't much use going forward.

The truck chugged and wanted to stop. If she didn't find a place soon, she'd be walking. And maybe that was just fine. How much worse could her situation become?

A mailbox at the entrance to a long gravel driveway announced it was the Thompson farm. "Shouldn't there be a timber arch with the letters branded in? What kind of second-rate place is this?" Her efforts to lighten the mood were wasted, as they often were when alone. She just sounded, and probably was, crazy.

Every door on the house was nailed shut from the inside. In her line of work, she'd smelled more than her share of dead bodies; check welfare calls often led to that sort of thing. After two or three minutes, she retreated, unsure of what her nose was telling her. Maybe the place was just stale. What was an old farmhouse supposed to smell like?

She knocked. No one answered.

There weren't flies in the windows, so maybe she was wrong, but why push her luck? Without much thought, she went to the barn and cleared it stall by stall. The loft was layered with hay and wasn't too damp. She climbed the ladder and pulled it up after her.

"Nowhere to retreat, Laura. You're a genius," she mumbled. Sleep was a long time coming, but when she closed her eyes, it was the best night she'd had in a long time.

Just before dawn, she awoke to the sound of an animal sniffing around near the corner of the loft. Three rats, none of them interested in her, searched the straw for whatever interested rats at zero dark thirty.

The cat came up the ladder just as she had but with deadly grace. She barely noticed it moving and certainly didn't hear it. The scrawny animal hunted like its life depended on it.

Could I eat a rat?

Wonder paralyzed her. Every time the rats moved, she tensed. Each time the cat advanced, she held her breath.

Who the hell am I and what am I doing here?

The undersized cat sprinted forward, catching two of the three rats. A ferocious struggle ensued, leaving the cat with one victim. When the victorious hunter noticed her, it leaped from the loft with its gruesome prize clamped in its jaws.

"That thing's almost as big as you are, you greedy little monster," she said.

Something very close to her face moved.

She turned as slowly as she could to face the first rat. Its nose wriggled harmlessly.

"You should have let the cat have you," she said.

A fierce need seized her. All those tame rats had escaped

her hunger. Now more than ever, she needed not just this thing's blood but its flesh as well.

Whoa, what the hell am I thinking?

Maybe there was food in the house—a box of cereal she could eat dry or some canned soup.

The rat's nose twitched and it crept forward, sniffing the air and the ground and her. Terribly small, it looked like the last thing she wanted to eat. She thought about the food and water she'd left behind after Brock tried to stop her.

Stop thinking about that.

She reached toward the rat, stopped, then grabbed it. "I wouldn't eat you even if I could." Running her tongue over the sharpest of her teeth, she put her mouth on the back of the rat's neck but didn't bite down. Tears ran down her face as her stomach cramped. The rat went still but didn't squeak. Images of Brock and the others flashed in her mind.

"This is stupid," she said. "You're too small. What difference can your blood make?"

Nose twitching, eyes staring, the rat said not a word.

Pain stabbed through her head each time her heart beat. Images swam in her vision. Standing caused her to stagger like a drunk. Resisting the call for blood was worse every time and it wouldn't be long before she became one of them.

Still gripping the rat, she walked to the edge of the loft and looked down for the cat or the other rodents.

Nothing.

Surprising herself more than the animal, she raised it quickly and bit down, piercing the flesh until blood flowed into her mouth. Horrible sounds—miserable, wordless moans—escaped from her and her victim. Or that was what she thought she heard. When it was done, she placed the creature gently on the ground.

It scrambled away.

She swallowed, realizing no blood went down her throat and she couldn't taste anything—not the hair, or the skin, or the blood of the rat. Her mouth grew numb. She lay down, closed her eyes, and went to sleep like she had died.

CHAPTER THIRTY-TWO

AFTER THE FIRST NIGHT, there were other barns. She scavenged food from a suburban home in Davenport while Fosk-ha patrolled the town in Iowa National Guard trucks. She didn't see a single cop or sheriff. There were almost no humans on the streets at all. Once she located the keys to a Nissan GT-R, she quietly drove out of town, timing each move to avoid the predictable pattern of the bloodsucking aliens patrolling the area in the jump ships.

They were the worst, way nastier than bloodsucking ex-cops like her. *Monsters.*

Something dashed across the street, a ragged-looking Fosk. Then two more. Then ten or twenty of the crazed freaks. She stomped on the accelerator, speeding out of town as fast as the car would go. In her rearview mirror, she saw two armored vehicles—one pursuing the wild Fosk-ha rampaging through the Iowa town, and the other following her.

"Not today, assholes," she said, and sped away. The armored truck dwindled into a speck in her rearview mirror.

Mile after mile she expected one of the ships to cut her off, but it never happened. Once, near what she thought smelled like a feedlot, she saw a dozen of their large, vertically landed ships parked on the horizon. There were a lot of lights and energetic figures moving near them—too far away for her to see.

She stole another car in Omaha and *befriended* two more rats before continuing west on Interstate 30, finally turning south on Highway 81 at York to head south toward Salina. Why? Because that was one of David's routes. He'd complained about traffic on I-80 versus I-70 even though she'd never seen a difference while on the way to her parents' cabin in Colorado.

Maybe I'll find David or Charles there, maybe I won't. Hours later she was heading west again and wondering if she needed a new car. She tried not to think, or listen to the radio, or remember how badly she needed to pee.

Near the Kansas-Colorado state line, she saw a Kansas State Patrol car—a white Dodge Charger *Enforcer*—parked haphazardly in the ditch. She parked a hundred yards from it, stalked through the tall grass near the ditch, and watched it for what seemed like forever. Farther up the road, hundreds of cars and trucks were scattered on both sides of the interstate like broken toys.

The sun touched the horizon as three big Fosk-ha ships streaked through the air, following the highway. She was really glad she'd parked the Nissan.

The trooper lay twenty feet from the car, AR-15 gripped in his hands, eyes staring at the sky as surprised as they were dead.

"I don't have a shovel—Trooper C. J. Morrison—or I would bury you." She sat beside him for a while instead, trying not to think about how he didn't smell that bad out here. His face wasn't pretty. Animals had nibbled away his nose and lips. She'd seen that before, unfortunately. When she was a rookie. Her field training officer had volunteered her for every dead body call on the dispatch board like he'd wanted her to quit.

"I'm going to search you, Morrison," she said. "Just in case you left a note or something. Do you have family somewhere? Someone I need to check on for you?"

There was no note, and he wasn't wearing a wedding ring—which meant nothing. A lot of cops didn't wear them on duty. What he did have was another Glock, an AR-15, and ammunition for both. The car had a shotgun in the rack and a full tank of gas. His lunch box, unfortunately, was full of something rotten so she pitched it and drove away, back toward Salina, back north to I-80, and west to where, perhaps, there wouldn't be a roadblock of destroyed vehicles and murdered civilians.

Every time she saw a wrecked semitruck, she slowed, hoping she'd recognize her brother's rig.

Or maybe I should hope not to see it.

She checked farms, but less frequently now. The farther west she went, the larger they were—something about the type of crops. The wheat that people grew in the Bible belt required hundreds if not thousands of acres to make a profit. That's what David told her one time. He learned a lot of useless crap in truck stops and always wanted to share it with her.

Some fuel tanks she located were dry. One had been set on fire, either on purpose or by accident, she wasn't sure. Several homesteads had been falling apart long before the aliens came and smelled like abandoned rentals to her. So when she found one, she started in the house then went to the barn, as was becoming her habit.

When she found a rat, she bit it just hard enough to break the skin, and took in some blood. It made her mouth numb. If she'd stayed with Brock, maybe she would have found out how much she needed or why she needed it. But he was dead, and she was free.

Laura left the shutters of the barn open this time, just feeling the breeze on her face as she tried to sleep and not think. Somewhere, a cat meowed. She wondered if it was hunting rats.

And then she was out like she'd fallen down a well.

SUNSHINE WARMED Laura's face long before she opened her eyes. Outside there were birds chirping, their songs muffled by the wooden walls. Light reached through two windows without glass and some cracks in the large main door.

Don't think. Don't move. Don't bother getting up. This is freedom, sleeping in a hayloft and starving to death with the dreams of rats crawling all over you while you slept.

She sat up and looked around. The world felt different.

Right when she was ready to stand, something banged near the door to the barn. A cat screeched and sprinted across the floor below. She froze for a second, then scrambled back into the early morning shadows.

The darkness wasn't enough to hide what she was or anything she had done. Someone was just outside, and she didn't want to be discovered. Not today, not ever again.

The door slid open. A man entered too slowly to know

anything about room clearing tactics but at least he was paying attention. He must have found her ride and now was looking for her.

"I'm up here," Laura said, her words sounding off.

"Why don't you come down?" the farmer said. "I'm not as young as I used to be."

"I'll climb up, Daddy," a blonde teenager wearing a letter jacket said. She had a Colt revolver on her hip that looked too big for either of them.

The man put a hand on her shoulder to stop her from approaching the ladder. "She'll come down." A second later he directed his voice up to Laura who still hadn't shown herself completely. "Won't you?"

"Yeah," Laura said. "Just give me a second."

Nobody spoke until she had her feet on the ground, expecting to be frisked but realizing neither of these two had probably thought of that.

"My name is Travis Brighten," he said, offering his hand to shake. "This is my daughter, Abigail."

"I'm just passing through. I don't want to hurt anyone. But I'll tell you up front, I have a bite," Laura said. She meant to explain much more than that but couldn't push the words out.

They didn't react like she thought they would.

"I knew a girl like that," Abigail said. "But I think she was different from the rest of us. Hard to say."

"What do you mean, different?" Laura didn't have time for myths and fantasies, but what was she going to do? She'd say anything to get the conversation over with and get back on the road so she could look for her brother.

"She didn't talk about it much, but some of the aliens are always after her," Abigail said.

Laura flinched. "I'd better not stay. If you have some food and water, some gas, I'll be on my way. I know what you're talking about. They've been chasing me for a while."

The teenager smirked. "It's hard to imagine the aliens hunting anyone as hard as they hunted Dust and that big jerk who picked her up."

"Can I get some gas?" Laura asked, talking to Travis now.

He nodded. "I reckon you can. You'll have to eat breakfast first or my wife will put me in the doghouse."

Abigail took her by the arm like they'd been friends forever. "I'll show you where to get cleaned up. Might be your last chance for a while if you stay on the run."

"Okay, Abigail."

"My friends call me Abs."

That made Laura laugh, and she relaxed. Maybe things would be all right.

CHAPTER THIRTY-THREE

"STAY CLOSE TO ME," Halloran said. "Once I get you back into WFG headquarters, I can keep you safe."

Charles nodded. What he had seen of the city, before and after their apprehension, distracted him from hearing the security specialist properly. "The Ravagers are a real thing."

Halloran clenched his jaw, obviously holding back some remark. After he checked to be sure no one was listening, he grabbed Charles by the arm and pulled him close as they walked. "Don't trust them. Sure, they have Ravagers. But try not to forget those blue fuckers brought them here. Let the corporate negotiators and political panderers kiss these guys' asses."

"I know, I know," Charles said. "But it's complicated."

"It's not complicated. They. Are. The. Enemy. We're biding our time to kill 'em all."

"Don't be a meathead. I was just starting to respect you."

"I could say the same about you but for different reasons," Halloran snapped back, almost as though he had anticipated the reaction.

One of the big Fosk-ha guards looked over a shoulder, then led them inside the compound, having to duck through the doorways. "Follow one at a time."

Charles slipped through first. *Boom*, the door slammed shut behind him. Panicked, Charles tried to rush back.

The guard stepped in his path. "He will go another way."

"That wasn't the deal!"

"What deal?" The guard glared down like he had all the time in the world.

The long, dim hallway was vacant. He didn't remember the compound being this cold. If there were still people, if the invaders hadn't slaughtered everyone, they must be in some other part of the facility. Which was troublesome, because he had studied the schematics more than once and didn't recognize this floor plan.

"You must talk to an interrogator," his guard said.

"If you insist, but I can better convey my findings in a report," Charles said. "That's how I was trained. You might get in trouble if I'm prevented from completing it."

"No trouble. Not for me."

With their conversation effectively ended, Charles cataloged details but found nothing to feed his analysis. It was as though the area had been stripped of the smallest clues. The floor looked like concrete but wasn't. He could tell by the sound it made when he stepped on it—like the material had sound dampening properties. This passage felt like one-piece construction, and he didn't remember that being part of any architectural modification.

"Where are we?"

The guard didn't answer.

"This isn't my level. WFG has strict rules about trespassing on unauthorized levels," Charles said. He hated improvisation almost as much as he hated fumbling around in the dark. Garbage in, garbage out—that was the programmer's mantra. How could he figure this out with no data?

Not that there was much to figure out. The world as he remembered it was over. Aliens were real. The strongest nations on Earth were defeated or near enough to make no difference.

"Are you listening to me?"

The guard continued to walk, reminding Charles of a lion or maybe a tiger, strong, graceful, and completely unconcerned with his prey.

What did the cat care if the mouse begged and pleaded?

"I'm cold," Charles finally admitted. "And the lighting is wrong."

"That is because we have arrived. Go through this door. Wait inside until someone comes for you."

"How long will that be?"

The guard steered him inside, shut the door on his face, and left—presumably. Since there was no window, and the door was several inches think, Charles didn't really know. For all he knew, the brute was dancing a jig and balancing plates on his head.

"What the hell am I doing here?" He needed to think, make rational decisions, face facts.

Face facts? Why was that phrase louder than the rest in his head?

He paced, and since no one was there to hear him lose his cool, he shouted until he lost his voice.

Emily is having an affair with Henry. How could it be more obvious?

CHARLES SAT against the far wall staring at the door without blinking. His inclination was to pace and worry, so he did neither. When in doubt, show defiance. It wasn't a rational response, but he wasn't feeling like himself.

Focusing his energy on the door took all of his attention. It made him feel strong, like he was doing something. Begging and pleading hadn't worked. Rationalizing the last several days did nothing to calm him. Shouting hurt his throat.

Sitting here, refusing to quit, that was the ticket.

"Why am I the one in prison?" He didn't like the sound of his voice, and the question was childish. The walls were closing in on him, something he'd always thought was bull.

The door opened and all he could do was stare. The alien who entered took his time, looked around the room, sniffed the air, then spread his hands in something very like a human greeting.

"I am Hahn-fosk-hon. You are Charles Osage. One of three."

Nothing the newcomer had said motivated him to stand, or move. "One of three? I run my own project; I don't have peers. Unless you're talking about our division, in which case I am a Vice President. But that is just a title with a small monetary incentive slapped on it."

"The Warfighter Games corporation has been dissolved as irrelevant," Hahn-fosk-hon said. "You should stand, perhaps walk with me. Or do you wish to stay here?"

"I could use a walk," Charles said.

The alien nodded as though this was expected, then escorted him through the door. He walked too close and stared too much.

"If you're trying to be polite, it's not working," Charles said.

"I was attempting to follow your customs," Hahn-fosk-hon said. "It is more difficult than my people realize. Not many of us care to try."

The hallway was strange. The lighting made him uneasy. He hesitated to respond, hoping to buy time and think. Escape was impossible; he understood that now. Going outside of the compound had only alerted them to his intentions. Now he was stuck here, separated from his family, and out of the loop with his company.

"There is something I want from you," Hahn-fosk-hon said.

"Direct and the point," Charles said. "Why wouldn't you be? It took your people about a week to conquer our planet."

"Maybe. But that is not why we came. The last thing we want is to stay. You can have your planet back the way it was, once we have left."

Charles laughed when he shouldn't have.

"Why is this funny?" Hahn-fosk-hon asked.

"Our world will never be the same. It's not funny, but sometimes we laugh when there's no other choice," Charles said. "I'll be honest with you, Hahn, I'm offended and more than a bit pissed off that you would think your invasion wouldn't scar the entire planet, possibly ruin the biosphere, and exterminate us."

Hahn-fosk-hon walked several strides in silence as if pondering Charles's comment. "We don't stay or leave anyone behind to study the effects of our refueling efforts. Perhaps this has been a mistake, but I don't see what good it would do to know that the worlds behind us perished."

"Maybe it would help you feel like the monster as you are," Charles said without thinking.

"I'm sure that it would, but I am equally certain it will change nothing. We can leave more quickly if we find a viable Navigator."

"Are you sure 'viable' is the right word? That makes your sought-after Navigator sound like an embryo or a theorem," Charles said, still looking for clues and finding little to go on.

"My language skills are inadequate. I will strive to improve. For now, let me tell you the purpose of my visit." The alien stopped, looked back the way they had come, then said, "Is your brother named David Osage?"

Charles hesitated. "I have a brother by that name."

"Can you contact him?"

This was the tricky part. What should he admit to and what should he deny? Why did this alien overlord want to know? Could he use the information to protect his immediate family?

"I can try. If you give me access to our phone system and our computer networks, it would be easier."

"That can be done," Hahn-fosk-hon said without hesitation.

"What do you want with my brother? He's just a truck driver."

This caused the alien's eyes to change. Charles wasn't sure, but he thought this information pleased him.

"Then he is the one we are looking for. More accurately, we seek the Navigator he has been protecting."

"And this Navigator will get you and your people off our planet sooner?" Charles asked.

"That is what is hoped."

"Give me a phone, and I will make the call."

PLEASE LEAVE A REVIEW!

I loved writing Invasion Day and hope you enjoyed it. The best way to find a story these days is by word of mouth. So please share this one with a friend and leave a review.

Thanks!

WHAT'S NEXT

Stay tuned for Resistance Day: They Came for Blood, Book 2.

It's about to get real for some trespassing intergalactic invaders.

ALSO BY SCOTT MOON

THEY CAME FOR BLOOD

Invasion Day

Resistance Day (coming soon)

Victory Day (coming soon)

Alien Apocalypse (coming soon)

A MECH WARRIOR'S TALE

(SHORTYVERSE)

Shorty

Kill Me Now

Ground Pounder

Shorty and the Brits

Fight for Doomsday (A Novel)… coming soon.

CHRONICLES OF KIN ROLAND

Enemy of Man: The Chronicles of Kin Roland: Book 1

Son of Orlan: The Chronicles of Kin Roland: Book 2

Weapons of Earth: The Chronicles of Kin Roland: Book 3

DARKLANDING

Assignment Darklanding Book 1

Ike Shot the Sheriff: Assignment Darklanding: Book 2

Outlaws: Assignment Darklanding Book 3

Runaway: Assignment Darklanding Book 4

An Unglok Murder: Assignment Darklanding Book 05

SAGCON: Assignment Darklanding Book 6

Race to the Finish: Assignment Darklanding Book 7

Boom Town: Assignment Darklanding Book 8

A Warrior's Home: Assignment Darklanding Book 9

Hunter: Assignment Darklanding Book 10

Diver Down: Assignment Darklanding Book 11

Empire: Assignment Darklanding Book 12

FALL OF PROMISEDALE

Death by Werewolf (The Fall of Promisedale Book 1)

GRENDEL UPRISING

Proof of Death: Grendel Uprising: Book 1

Blood Royal: Grendel Uprising: Book 2

Grendel: Grendel Uprising: Book 3

SMC MARAUDERS

Bayonet Dawn: SMC Marauders: Book 1

Burning Sun: SMC Marauders: Book 2

The Forever Siren: SMC Marauders: Book 3

SON OF A DRAGONSLAYER

Dragon Badge (Son of a Dragonslayer Book 1)

Dragon Attack (Son of a Dragonslayer Book 2)

Dragon Land (Son of a Dragonslayer Book 3)

TERRAN STRIKE MARINES

The Dotari Salvation: Terran Strike Marines: Book 1

Rage of Winter: Terran Strike Marines: Book 2

Valdar's Hammer: Terran Strike Marines: Book 3

The Beast of Eridu: Terran Strike Marines: Book 4

THE LAST REAPER

The Last Reaper

Fear the Reaper

Blade of the Reaper

Wings of the Reaper

Flight of the Reaper

Wrath of the Reaper

Will of the Reaper

Descent of the Reaper

Hunt of the Reaper

Bastion of the Reaper

SHORT STORIES

Boss

Fire Prince

Ice Field

Sgt. Orlan: Hero of Man

The Darklady

ASSASSIN PRIME

The Hand of Empyrean: Assassin Prime 1

Spiderfall: Assassin Prime 2

ABOUT THE AUTHOR

Scott Moon has been writing fantasy, science fiction, and urban fantasy since he was a kid. When not reading, writing, or spending time with his awesome family, he enjoys playing the guitar or learning Brazilian Jiu-Jitsu. He loves dogs and plans to have a ranch full of them when he makes it big. One will be a Rottweiler named Frodo. He is also a co-host of the popular Keystroke Medium show.

COOL STUFF FROM THE MOON

Want to know when the next story or book is published? Sign up for my newsletter at *https://www.subscribepage.com/Fromthemoon*

Thanks,
　Scott Moon

---

facebook.com/groups/ScottMoonGroup
twitter.com/scottmoonwriter
instagram.com/scottmoonwriter

Made in the USA
Columbia, SC
02 January 2025